UNDERCOVER

After a gang shooting involving an undercover police officer, Colin Harpur and his boss Assistant Chief Constable Desmond Iles are called to another Force's ground to investigate what the Home Office see as spectacular failings. Harpur can imagine the pressure the officer would have been under. If a gang decided to kill, a spy would have to go along with it. But with careers of fellow officers – who might be in secret, dangerous alliance with villains – at risk, Harpur knows that he and Iles have an exceptionally tough inquiry ahead.

UNDERCOVER

A Harpur & Iles Mystery

Bill James

Severn House Large Print
London & New York

This first large print edition published 2013
in Great Britain and the USA by
SEVERN HOUSE PUBLISHERS LTD of
19 Cedar Road, Sutton, Surrey, England, SM2 5DA.
First world regular print edition published 2012 by
Severn House Publishers Ltd., London and New York.

British Library Cataloguing in Publication Data

James, Bill, 1929- author.
    Undercover. -- Large print edition.
    1. Harpur, Colin (Fictitious character)--Fiction. 2. Iles,
    Desmond (Fictitious character)--Fiction. 3. Police--Great
    Britain--Fiction. 4. Gangs--Fiction. 5. Detective and
    mystery stories. 6. Large type books.
    I. Title
    823.9'14-dc23

    ISBN-13: 9780727896575

Severn House Publishers support the Forest Stewardship Council™
[FSC™], the leading international forest certification organisation. All
our titles that are printed on FSC certified paper carry the FSC logo.

Printed and bound in Great Britain by
T J International, Padstow, Cornwall.

ONE

There was, of course, a before and an after. In the setting down of events, they might have jostled each other and got a bit out of sequence. Never mind: some mucking about with the order of things, and with time itself, could occasionally bring extra understanding and a special clarity. So—

BEFORE

If they decided to kill, you had to go along with it. Pack law. Basic. Anyone who worked under-cover knew this. He had a nine mm Browning, not a weapon he would normally have picked. He liked Heckler and Koch products better, thank you very much, was trained on them. But the training had been police training. Police famously loved HK. Too famously. Therefore, Tom left his in the armoury and went for the Browning. This model gave no troublesome hints about its owner's possible past and true career.

There were four of them in the car, casual gear all round. Crook firms had their fashion rules, present and important, but nobody spelled them out. You intuited. It was a core undercover skill. For instance, people wouldn't put on a decent suit for today's type of mission, not because the smartness would seem freakish at a killing and a bit too Kray, but on account of the vulgar, showy bulge of shoulder holsters. That was plainly the thinking. When these lads bought their suits, reach-me-down or custom-made – but especially big-cost, custom-made – they wanted jackets to give a sweetly close and comely fit for normal social life; not tailoring that hung loose, shapeless, because occasionally, on crux outings like today's, it had to hide a full handgun bra and harness. Pick something less formal. For instance, a suede or leather or denim short coat with chinos didn't need to pass any strict, bandbox tests – in fact certainly *shouldn't* look too neat, sculpted and suave. Tom Parry – as he must think of himself now – had his Browning cradled under an absolutely adequate stretch of very dark blue, black-buttoned denim. Although it didn't feel like part of him, as an HK Parabellum automatic would have, this Browning nestled very nicely.

Jamie Meldon-Luce, the distinguished Wheels who drove now, esteemed the Browning, and so did many of the world's armies, including Britain's. No question, it had cracking credentials. Jamie was expert in many technical and other areas, not just handguns. He had expensive electronic gear that could neutralize the security

6

on any car, even the most modern, such as this stolen Volvo, and the stolen Ford waiting in Pallindon Lane as a switch vehicle. Jamie, early thirties, father of one, wore a heavy-looking, greenish cardigan. He reckoned cardigans were making a good comeback, and not just as necessary garb in poorly heated rest-homes. The ample wool betrayed no outlines. Tom sat driver's side back in the Volvo alongside Mart 'Empathy' Abidan, who had charge of this jaunt, despite what some regarded as the jittery abandonment of another intended attack not long ago when he had command.

Ivor Wolsey was in the front passenger spot. There'd been a stage, apparently, when Wolsey suffered from a deep dread of firearms: couldn't even handle a piece, loaded or not, without massive tremors setting in, a recognized sickness known in the game as *corditus allergius*. He'd fought it and fought it, and eventually turned himself into the company's finest handgun liegeman. Wolsey never boasted about his shooting, though. He seemed to fear that, if he crowed, the magic he'd achieved on his psyche could suddenly fall apart as punishment and drop him back where he used to be, paralytically weapon-shy. As Jamie Meldon-Luce had stated, there was no Samaritans counselling service for personnel who lost their trigger knack.

Naturally, Tom had his worries. When he said – obviously, said only and exclusively to himself – that if they decided to kill, you had to go along with it, that was as much as he meant. You 'went along'. You didn't try to stop it, but you didn't actually help, didn't assist in it. And this was where the big difficulties started. An officer who infiltrated a gang aiming to get enough inside stuff to convict its chief or chiefs could not be, must not be, a murderer, not even to preserve his cover. On some excursions, he would probably have to shoot, but he'd shoot only close; shoot to miss. No big purpose was big enough to excuse active responsibility for a killing; that is, none of the undercover officer's bullets should be found in the target, whether Browning or HK.

True, in some aspects of undercover, that dodgy doctrine 'the end justifies the means' did operate. If your spy penetrated an outfit, he, or she, had to behave like a member of the outfit – most probably behave criminally like a member of the outfit. But there had to be a stop point. No end could justify slaughterous behaviour as a disguise tactic. A police phrase had been concocted that tried to cope with and sweeten those episodes where an officer might for a while have to dispense with legality and morality. Its wording avoided the rough Stalinite bluntness of 'the end justifies the means'. Instead, it labelled such ploys as 'noble-cause corruption' – the purpose admirable and gloriously in the public interest, nobly in the public interest; the methods foul, though. And not even that clever jiggery-pokery with terms could allow the corruption to go as far as homicide.

This was one reason Tom felt glad Ivor Wolsey figured in their party. He would probably wrap up this execution before the others had even attempted a shot. And that's what counted – the execution. The objective. Tom's wayward blast on the Browning wouldn't be noticed, except as useless, frantic noise, he hoped. But he knew these were not dumbo people with him in the Volvo. They'd be alert to trickery, might spot it when someone was not aiming at the target, only at its safe surroundings. And possibly worse: they might be wondering about Tom already, and would be focused on watching how he behaved in a warm set-to. Yes, Tom had worries.

TWO

AFTER

Or so Detective Chief Superintendent Colin Harpur imagined months later.

Parts of it he *had* to imagine. He wasn't present at the shooting, of course. Court transcripts, witness statements, detectives' notes, and newspaper clippings gave him some undisputed and indisputable facts. But there were gaps. He tried to fill them. Detectives habitually did this – guessed at the thoughts and the likely talk and undisclosed behaviour of those involved in a case. It could show the various possible ways inquiries should go; and he and one of his bosses, Assistant Chief Constable Desmond Iles, had a special kind of exceptionally tough inquiry ahead.

They had been ordered on to another Force's ground, their task – yes, an exceptionally tough one – to investigate what had been going on there, or, more correctly, what had *not* been going on, when something *ought* to have been going on. Major people at the Home Office seemed to think there were spectacular failings in the way that Force had dealt with the shooting and its aftermath. And when major people at the Home Office felt such elite uneasiness, the procedure was to send senior officers from another outfit to look dispassionately, unsparingly, extremely unchummily at the way things had been done; or *not* done, when something *ought* to have been done. Iles and Harpur and their staff would be playing away from home, their task to examine and report on how their equivalents in this other communion had behaved. Already, Harpur sensed very dark areas ahead, and possibly very hazardous areas. He and Iles and the rest of the team would not be popular. Careers of some of their hosts might be torched. Jail would possibly loom for them. Perhaps dangerous, secret alliances existed between some officers and some villains. They'd try to look after one another, wouldn't they? On this kind of job you watched your back and your front and used the I-spy-with-my-little-eye machine under your car.

Case documents gave the exact timing, the exact street geography, the exact number of rounds fired, the specific type of gun used, the injuries, the death, the witnesses, the police resources involved, their tactics, the combatants. Maybe all this should have been enough. But Harpur added a slice of make-believe here and there – very reasonable make-believe, but make-believe all the same. He wanted a full impression of the run-up to the shooting and the shooting itself. In the search for this completeness he wondered how Tom would regard and get on with a Browning, having almost certainly been trained on Heckler and Koch. He still had the Browning in its holster, fully loaded, when his body was found on the building site.

Harpur considered, too, the chewy, hellishly deep and complicated dilemma of being under-cover when you and your supposed colleagues went on a killing spree. Tom must have had an intense fear of getting rumbled at the shooting and conceivably of having been half rumbled well before it. He'd see the need to participate – but without, in fact, participating. 'In fact', here, meant actually putting bullets into the target, the designated enemy, the intended victim.

Harpur tried to tune into Tom's thinking as he'd travelled in the Volvo, even trivial thinking. For instance, would Tom have chatted to him-self – silently, secretly – about his companions' fashion tastes and their relation to shoulder holsters and jackets' fit? Harpur needed to get to know these people thoroughly, and one way of doing it was to create some of their notions and actions, keeping these little embellishments as near to believable as he could.

Harpur's fantasizing always had a foundation in the real. Imagination wasn't his main flair. A green cardigan worn by the Wheels, Jamie Mel-don-Luce, had been described in a witness state-ment, its greenness pale, apparently, and edging towards turquoise. Did Meldon-Luce believe that cardigans had come back into fashion, and not just for the elderly? But Harpur realized that a heavy, generously cut cardigan of whatever colour or tint would be useful in hiding a holster and armament beneath its thick folds. And those thick folds would be easy to pull aside if the gun were required fast.

As to weaponry, papers studied by Harpur mentioned that Ivor Wolsey, one of the Volvo crew, was a gifted marksman who had emerged from a period when firearms turned him off completely. Harpur had come across people like that on previous cases. There was a jokey, mock-Latin description of the ailment: *corditus allergius*. Perhaps Wolsey mirrored some of those other converts to shoot-bang-fire and never trumpeted his pistol talent, in case this vanity got up Fate's nose and brought incapacity back.

Harpur longed to confer individuality and quirks on the main people featured in this post-event inquiry by Iles and him. Generally speaking, it was usually Iles who did the imagined and imaginary stuff. He would occasionally tell Harpur – no, oftener than that – he'd tell Harpur about 'my soaring mind, Col, disencumbering me from the banal and workaday'.

OK. But Harpur had grown fed up with being regarded as merely the nitty-gritty and plod element in the partnership. He might not be able to soar yet, and get himself disencumbered from the banal and workaday, but he could intelligently and constructively speculate.

THREE

AFTER

But some witness statements were so vivid and detailed that they made Harpur's attempts at intelligent and constructive speculation unnecessary. After all, intelligent and constructive speculation was only a puffed-up phrase for guesswork. Guesswork couldn't compete with the real and actual:

WITNESS ONE (Mrs Nora Clement):

On October twenty-fifth at about nine thirty in the evening I saw a red Volvo saloon drive into Monthermer Street and park on a double-yellow-lined bus stop where the pavement had been recessed, making a kind of lay-by. It was this blatant, possibly contemptuous disregard for road discipline that made me notice the Volvo and continue watching it for some minutes. There appeared to be four men in the car. Three of them left the vehicle. The driver remained, so some of my resentment about the parking shrank, since he could move the Volvo if the bus wanted to draw in. Nonetheless, a clearly designated bus stop should not be used for parking, no matter the circumstances, I believe. Disregard for such rules is symptomatic of a wider antisocial attitude, increasingly prevalent today, I fear.

At first I thought the driver to be a man between thirty and thirty-five. There was a street light above the bus stop which enabled me to see quite clearly the car and the four men at this stage. The driver had on a pale green, almost turquoise, cardigan. He was broad shouldered, wide-necked, with dark hair ridge-cut, which made me wonder whether he could, in fact, be as old as thirty-five, since this style of crude haircut is favoured by younger men. I cannot imagine why they should espouse this ugly style. But, then, so many of youth's tastes are incomprehensible to me, and to many of my generation. I consider the initial damage was done by a quite famous American singer-shouter, Elvis Presley, and things have got continuously worse since then.

The three men who had left the car walked away in a group together. They wore casual clothes. They seemed to me purposeful, as if they had some particular task ahead. Although they were fewer and not so well dressed, they reminded me of the group of robbers walking towards their next criminal operation at the beginning of that appallingly violent film, *Riverside Dogs*, which my son, Gregory, used to watch repeatedly on DVD.

{Correction: the witness probably means *Reservoir Dogs*.}

15

I think that when they reached the end of Monthermer Street the three separated from one another. That was my impression, though I could not be sure, owing to the distance and the evening darkness. I did not give the three very much attention because I had no idea they might be significant. But I'd say that two were somewhat older than the driver and one was around the same age. He and one of the other two had on denim blousons, I recall, with light-coloured trousers. The other man wore a dark leather jacket and jeans. The one I thought the youngest of the three who left the car was also the tallest – probably just over six feet – and thin. He had short fair hair. The other two were of middle height and strong build. One wore a baseball-style peaked cap. The other was dark-haired and possibly balding. The Volvo moved off the bus stop soon afterwards and drove slowly up towards Mitre Park. It went out of my sight.

WITNESS TWO (Mr Rex Marchant):

I was walking the dog near Mitre Park at about ten forty-five p.m. on October twenty-fifth – I habitually take the dog out for 'watering' at about this time before bed if the weather suits – when I became aware of a red Volvo parked in the shadows under some trees. We have problems with car-borne lovers in this area, and I assumed that the vehicle was here for that purpose. I would not want it thought that I stare in to such cars with a prying, voyeur intent –

termed, I believe, 'dogging', though I don't know why. It seems a slander on dogs, such as mine. But as I and the dog passed it, I could see that in fact there was only one person in the car, a square-built man wearing what appeared to be a green cardigan. He was in the driver's seat. He did not look towards me, though he must have been aware of my nearness to the car. I had the idea that he did not wish to show his face properly, or to offer any greeting, in case this caused me to stop and perhaps signal that he should open the window for a conversation. He might be expecting questions as to his intentions, or even a rebuke. I did not find his behaviour reassuring. It, of course, occurred to me that he might be what is called, I believe, 'casing' the district for future break-ins – or about to attempt a break-in there and then. I decided that on my return I must memorize the Volvo's registration number, which would be possible without having to pause and so alert the driver. I continued my walk.

Shortly afterwards, I thought I heard the running feet of more than one person. Then came angry shouting, all male, and maybe there was the sound of a struggle – shoes impacting heavily on the ground, and perhaps a degree of breathlessness in the shouting. I could make out some words. I think a man yelled, 'He's not coming I tell you. He's not coming. Never.' After a minute or so I heard a vehicle's engine start behind me, most probably the Volvo's, and then the slamming of two car doors. I deduced from this that two or three people had entered the Volvo, depending on whether two or one used the same rear door on the pavement side to get into the car, plus one into the passenger seat. I heard the car pull away in what seemed a rush. When I and the dog came back from our stroll, the Volvo had gone. I had therefore lost the chance to note the car's registration number. I can only say that it appeared to be a quite new model and not the anti-stylish, boxy type. It appeared that the car had waited at this agreed point to pick up the people I'd heard running, and then leave. But there appeared to have been some kind of dispute, which I cannot explain.

An odd factor – or in my view, at least, an odd factor – was that as I neared the site of where the Volvo had been I could see ahead of me the man I think had been in the driver's seat originally. I recognized – think I recognized – the green cardigan. The dog barked, having also spotted this figure in the dark and perhaps wanting to alert me. The noise caused the man to look back, and then he seemed to increase his walking speed and soon disappeared.

The Volvo turned out to have been lifted from a municipal car park earlier in October. The vehicle's registration number wouldn't have disclosed anything about the driver and his companions, even if Mr Marchant had managed to get, memorize and report it. Harpur wanted to believe him when Marchant said he wasn't interested in an ogle and objected to the night use of the area for car sex. People did get upset by lovers at it in parked cars close to their homes. Harpur couldn't altogether understand this, unless it was envy. The couples in the cars would be reasonably quiet and self-focused. Iles had a framed cartoon from an ancient copy of some American magazine, showing a man and woman leaving their car and carrying the back seat into the woods. The ACC would normally keep this in a drawer out of sight, but during that longish period when he was trying to drive the previous Chief Constable, Mark Lane, off his head, he'd take down the portrait of the Home Secretary in his suite and replace it with the cartoon, if he knew Lane was about to look in on him. Iles liked the multi-use of cars himself; would speak of it to Harpur sometimes. He'd said once, 'Col, think how this can bring humanity to what is otherwise nothing but a banal metal box with mirrors.'

'As you'll know, that's the exact wording of the Oxford Dictionary definition of a car, sir,' Harpur had replied. '"A banal metal box with mirrors." Or might it be *extremely* banal.'

FOUR

AFTER

Harpur went now to the police record of 'Interview One' with a member of the Volvo team that night: Ivor Wolsey, aged thirty-seven, one previous conviction, for theft. Wolsey had turned Queen's Evidence. That is, he would talk, would betray mates – tell everything he knew to the police. In exchange he'd expect kinder treatment by the court, suppose the case came to trial, plus special safeguarding as a snitch in jail, if he was sent down. Those who turned Queen's Evidence came in for a lot of hate in the crooked world.

INTERVIEW ONE
  Inspector David Hinds: 'I'd like to begin, Ivor, with you and the others setting out in the stolen Volvo.'
  Answer: 'Right.'
  D.H.: 'What was the purpose of your mission in the Volvo?'
  A: 'To locate and eliminate Justin Paul Scray.'
  D.H.: 'Eliminate?'

A: 'You know.'

D.H.: 'No.'

A: 'Kill.'

D.H.: 'This was the specific objective?'

A: 'The only objective.'

D.H.: 'Why?'

A: 'Leo had decided after a long time thinking about it that Scray was damaging the firm. I gathered he'd had warnings.'

D.H.: 'Leo being?'

A: 'Leo Percival Young.'

D.H.: 'Head of the firm?'

A: 'Right.'

D.H.: 'He considered Scray was damaging the firm in which way, ways?'

A: 'Oh, you know.'

D.H.: 'No.'

A: 'The usual.'

D.H.: 'That being?'

A: 'A firm within the firm.'

D.H.: 'I don't understand.'

A: 'Oh, come on. Of course you do. It happens.'

D.H.: 'What does, Ivor?'

A: 'Private dealing.'

D.H.: 'What kind of private dealing?'

A: 'As I said, a firm within the firm.'

D.H.: 'He looked for a clandestine profit?'

A: '"Clandestine" – that's it. That's the word.'

D.H.: 'How did he make this clandestine profit?'

A: 'Clandestinely.'

D.H.: 'Thanks, Ivor.'

A: 'He made that very-well-named clandestine profit by not telling Leo and the rest of us about a string of special punters he's selling to clandestinely. He clandestinely built his own little clandestine firm within Leo's firm and clandestinely siphoned off a lovely amount of clandestine gains.'

D.H.: 'But how did he finance that personal firm?'

A: 'Overmixing, mainly.'

D.H.: 'What does that mean?'

A: 'Oh, come on.'

D.H.: 'Overmixing what?'

A: 'Overmixing the commodities, of course.'

D.H.: 'Which commodities?'

A: 'Oh, come on. Charlie, mostly.'

D.H.: 'I have to get things clear, Ivor. We're talking about bulking out what was originally high-quality cocaine with cheapo additives like boric acid, procaine and so on, are we?'

A: 'I knew you couldn't be as dumb as you were making out.'

D.H.: 'So Scray drew a nice personal profit, did he?'

A: 'Of course. Purity low, low, low of some of the stuff he pushed – down to not much more than thirty per cent.'

D.H.: 'Thirty per cent charlie, the rest filler?'

A: 'So what he got from the firm – Leo's firm, the proper firm – went a good bit more than twice as far as it should have.'

D.H.: 'Scray and *his* self-created, parasite, discrete firm trousered the difference?'

A: 'Clandestinely discrete, that's right. Almost right. Not just trousering. He was looking for even bigger gains. He invested.'

D.H.: 'He was after growth potential?'

A: 'With the clandestinely discrete, parasite profits, Justin provided for growth potential, yes. You'll remember that parable of the bags of gold, called talents, in the New Testament. Some people hid their bags of gold away and although the gold stayed safe it didn't grow at all. But one guy went out and speculated with his in true risk-taking, entrepreneurial, capitalistic fashion, and he got Jesus's business award. And that's how Justin was. He used the surplus funds to buy stock from a wholesaler – not Leo's wholesaler, obviously – and then sold to his own special, very private list, offering them the top-grade substance he or an associate had been holding as custodians of quality, so establishing and developing a fine reputation for magnificent charlie and other products. What I meant by a firm within the firm. He looked as if he was working for us, and he *was*, partly, but also he's working for himself, taking care of a secret, select clientele, middle-class mostly, still OK for money, despite the recession. He could do the chat all right with that kind of punter. Justin had an education. Mortar board, gown, a rolled-up bit of paper signifying a degree – I've seen the photograph. Totally genuine, I'd bet on it.

Archaeology, mathematics, King Richard the third – he can talk about any of them without sounding at all like a bullshitter. Some of these professors and thinkers of that sort would say to him the trade should be made legal, and he'd have the sense to get on their side and reply, "True," but really he'd fucking hate it, of course, because there'd be no need for people like Justin if trading was out in the open. No need for people like Leo, either, of course.

'But the way Justin was going on would taint the firm's image – that's Leo's firm's image – by pushing poor gear to ordinary users. Some of the stuff was at kids' rave level. Plus, to up his takings more he was overclaiming bribe money paid to your Drug Squad friends and friend-esses. OK, that's commonplace, I know. Almost routine. There's no receipts for backhanders, so naturally people are ambitious and imaginative about what they'd like reimbursed from the company's coffer, please. Managements recognize this and are willing to do a bit of blind-eyeing. But with Scray, the difference between actual and claimed was enormous. Just one of a crateful of swindles. It had to be stopped.'

D.H.: 'All this had been established against him as fact?'

A: 'It had been established enough for management to decide he had to go.'

D.H.: 'You said he'd been warned.'

A: 'He'd lie low for a while, then drift back to it. A kind of pride. He considered himself worth

24

the extra. He considered himself brilliant to have set up his own private, loaded list. He considered himself a star salesman-pusher. A kind of arrogance. A type of greed. Yes, yes, greed is commonplace, too, I'll admit. As someone said, the economy is juiced by it. But Scray's was brazen, contemptuous, selfish greed.'

D.H.: 'And your selfish lad was already at the top of the main firm?'

A: 'The only firm, as far as we saw it. And, of course, it had a bossman.'

D.H.: 'Leo Percival Young?'

A: 'With Martin Abidan at number two, a trifle nervy now and then, but generally sweetly subservient, capable and obedient, not a bit selfish, in charge of this operation. A team guy, often referred to as "Empathy Mart" – no sarcasm. Someone like Scray challenged that kind of happy, ordered, effective set-up. He looked like future chaos, didn't he? So, get rid.'

D.H.: 'But it didn't work?'

A: 'No, it didn't.'

D.H.: 'He's still around.'

A: 'Obviously.'

D.H: 'Our witness says three of you leave the car and walk together up Monthermer Street in a "purposeful" way. That correct?'

A: 'Three leave the car and go up Monthermer Street, yes. I suppose you could say "purposeful". Yes, we had a purpose. We were on a hunt, weren't we?'

FIVE

AFTER

Iles looked in to Harpur's office and interrupted his reading. The Assistant Chief was in uniform for some local function he had to attend later in the morning. He looked especially insolent and impervious. Iles more or less always looked insolent and impervious, and many people who didn't know him probably thought his ordinary appearance of insolence and imperviousness was itself at the exceptional point. But he could up the insolence and imperviousness by at least two or three notches for some outstanding occasions. 'Royalty will be there, Col, as you'll have heard.'

'They'll know it's their good fortune, sir.'

'In what sense, Harpur?'

'To have you round and about there.'

'If they come trying to get familiar, I'll put in a word for you, Col.'

'Thank you, sir.'

'You won't be there in person, so you can't mess up any recommendation I make to them on your behalf by sight of your fucking clothes and

26

joke haircut.'

'I think it's called serendipity, sir.'

'What is?'

'The sort of accidental advantage that comes in a situation where you're doing your bit by being there and I'm doing mine by not.'

'I want something to distract them from embarrassing me with their overdone, obnoxious regard, Col. If there's one thing I can't tolerate it's being kowtowed to.'

'I've heard many say that.'

'What?'

'They'll remark, "That Mr Iles, if there's one thing he can't tolerate it's being kowtowed to." And some will add that they, in fact, have never come across anyone more hostile to being kowtowed to.'

'Which many? Which some?'

'Many. I'm glad to be useful in distracting the visitors from fawning on you in that way.'

'They, in their turn, can mention your name, perhaps, to some creep high in the Home Office. We have to go there soon, you and I, for a pre-task briefing. I'd like to think you'll get some respect from the bastards.'

'Thank you, sir.'

'This is how things operate, isn't it?'

'Which things?'

'A woman,' Iles replied.

'Which woman?'

'She'll give us the picture. Some Home Office blazing intellect. People like that won't have come across your kind of person previously, Col. I can sympathize with her. Preparation is needed.'

'Thank you, sir.'

'There'd be no benefit in shock.'

'Whose?'

'Hers. If someone influential has spoken your name she'll assume there's more to you than the distressing way you look.'

'Thank you, sir.'

'Maud,' Iles replied.

'What?'

'Her first name.' He sang in a persuasive, castrato voice: 'Come into the bear garden, Maud. I'll be there at the HO alone, but for Col Harpur.'

When Iles had gone, Harpur went back to the police interview of Wolsey.

D.H.: 'The three? You said three left the Volvo.'

A: 'Abidan, me, Tom Parry, as we knew him then. Tom Mallen, actually. Sergeant Tom Mallen. That soon comes out, after his death. Jamie Meldon-Luce stays with the car for our get-away.'

Harpur liked the switch to the present – the vividness, even though it was still only words on paper. So were books, but some could give you a lift.

D.H.: 'You walk together but then seem to break up.'

A: 'Like that, yes. Abidan directs. He would

28

go towards Guild Square. Tom had been allocated the Rinton shopping mall. I get the three arcades: Morton's, Victoria, New.'

D.H.: 'The thinking is that Scray will be out in one of these locations dealing, is it?'

A: 'We don't know exactly where. We do know he works at around this time – nine p.m. to eleven – and generally these are his stations. Whoever finds him is to mobile the others. He isn't somebody to take on one-to-one, because he wouldn't be just one.'

The tenses got mixed now, but still intelligible.

A: 'He'd have protection with him. Scray would know Leo was peeved. And he'd also know that when Leo was peeved, Leo was likely to do something to deal with whatever's peeving him: in this case, Justin P. Scray and his cherished, confidential list. Jamie would move the Volvo up towards Mitre Park. He couldn't stay at the bus stop. It would get him noticed.'

D.H.: 'It did.'

A: 'Cars parked in the dark around the Mitre are very usual. It's one of those intimacy venues – cheaper than a hotel room. Mostly hetero, but not entirely. More charming than a public Gents.'

D.H.: 'That's your exit point?'

A: 'Pre-agreed. Job done, we run to it.'

D.H.: 'But the job wasn't done, was it?'

A: 'You could say that. But we run to the Volvo, anyway. Job done or not done. There's a switch car at Pallindon Lane, a Ford, also stolen, of course. We have to get there and swap vehicles, leaving the Volvo. The front's in a mess after the incident, and noticeable.'

D.H.: 'But, Ivor, we've galloped ahead a bit. Go back to quitting the Volvo at the bus stop. The three of you walk up Monthermer and then split. Your personal duty to trawl the arcades.'

A: 'Well, you know the scene I expect. There's the Alfonso wine bar in Victoria. A deli and restaurant – *Au-Dessus*. And a coffee shop in the New. Half of Morton's is shut off after six p.m., but a One-Stop on the corner at the arcade entrance is open till eleven. Scray would meet people in any one of these berths – his personal-list people, mainly. Or that's what Empathy reckons, and he gets good intelligence. Scray liked, likes, *Au-Dessus* best of the lot, apparently. He can snack with a client, clients, in the restaurant. It makes things sort of civilized, but the French name gives a touch of raciness, too. That's an interesting combination for Justin Scray's quality snorters – it's chiefly snorters, but some H.

'Most of these places have big windows on to the arcade. Customers can look out on who's passing, on who's approaching. So, searching for someone is dodgy. The target might get a reception ready. I watched for one of Justin's toughs doing sentry outside the deli and the other locations. I'd be recognized, of course. All of them – Scray, plus his heavies – were still, in theory, part of our firm. But he'd been building his own little outfit – as I said, an outfit within the outfit. And Justin and his people could make a fair guess about why I was there. I reckoned the arcades assignment was the toughest of the three. I took that as a compliment from Empathy. He thought I could manage it.'

D.H.: 'You're a marksman.'

A: 'So are some other guys, though. But I saw no guards patrolling any of the nooks. I went into the deli and restaurant and did a quick eye-scan. He wasn't there, nor in the Alfonso. So, I was on my way to the One-Stop when my mobile rang and Empathy said he'd found Scray in Guild Square. Well, no, he didn't say that, but it's what he meant. He said only, "Where I am." Best not to blurt too much on a mobile phone. You don't know who might be listening. Remember the Prince of Wales and Camilla. Think of all that newspaper hacking into celebs' voicemails.

'Abidan hadn't moved against Scray yet. He wanted me and Tom – Tom Parry, as we thought of him then – to get over there, so we'd have enough firepower to take on Justin and his chums. I say as *we* thought of him, but I'm still not completely sure who knew by then he was not Tom Parry, not a member of the firm, but a planted cop. Obviously, Leo knew. That's why things had been organized like this. Who else? Anyway, Abidan's "where I am" was the coded order to join up with him. It sounded urgent, it sounded hairy, but it was in line with the original scheme. Empathy had foreseen this kind of climax. I felt almost relieved. I wouldn't have to work my way through the arcades.

'We'd all pre-decided the quickest routes from our search areas to anywhere Justin Scray might be found. I ran out of the town end of the Victoria, across Lavender Street, into Charlton Road, about fifty metres along, then left into the Square. I'd been a bit worried that when I reach-ed there I wouldn't be able to spot Empathy at once. I thought he'd be in a sort of ... well, in a sort of hunting, stalking position – watchful, but trying not to be watched. It didn't turn out like that, though, not at all. He'd got himself into full view, what seemed deliberately into full view, standing in front of the *Bonjour* caff big window and made very obvious by its lights behind him.

'When I arrived, he said we had to get out of there and back to the Volvo immediately. Scray had been in the Square with some of his people, trading, but had seen Empathy, although he'd tried to stay hidden at the end of a service lane. It was as though they'd been expecting an attack because of Scray's abuse of the firm. Abidan feared they would return with more of Scray's outfit – too many for us to take on, too many for us to protect ourselves against. Well, all this seemed to me panicky and woolly, but he was determined. There'd been another fiasco a bit like this, involving a lad called Norman Rice.

'So, now I asked, "What about Tom?" He hadn't turned up in the Square yet. Of course, I know now he would never show up, but in the Square then, as Empathy spoke, I thought Tom must have had a longer distance to come in response to Abidan's call. He said it would be madness to wait. He would get on the mobile to cancel his order, tell Tom not to come to the Square, but to return to Mitre Park and Jamie direct, for a quick exit. Empathy seemed to make that call, but I realize now he might have been speaking to voicemail. All this still seemed unhinged to me, but Empathy was the boss, so when he started moving towards the park, I followed.'

D.H.: 'The two of you ran to the Volvo rendezvous?'

A: 'Yes.'

D.H.: 'Jamie was there waiting?'

A: 'Yes.

D.H.: 'But he wasn't at the wheel for the accident or the rest of the getaway?'

A: 'He wouldn't leave because only two of us had arrived. Tom was missing. Jamie's a sort of professional Wheels. One of their trade rules is you don't pull away until everyone has returned. In fact, it's a major rule, basic, core. Empathy screamed at him to get clear, but he wouldn't. Empathy was shouting, "He's not coming. He's not coming. Never." He sounded so certain, as if he knew something about Tom. So, eventually, Jamie does the gentlemanly bit. That's how he could be. Someone who'd wear a cardigan like that – well, it's the kind of antique, noble behaviour natural for him, and he takes his daughter to Sunday School. That sort. He got out of the car, showed Empathy how to start it without keys, and announced he'd go back on foot and look for Tom between the mall and Guild Square. He said Abidan could take the Volvo if that seemed so important to him. This was calling him yellow without actually saying it. Like I mentioned, Jamie could be a gent. He has politeness built in. He said if he found Tom he'd mobile for a taxi and meet up with us at the firm.

'Empathy started the Volvo. I had only a second to make up my mind which one I'd go with. I think I made a half-guess that when Empathy said Tom would never come, he spoke from info only he possessed – only he of the four of us, that is. Not including Leo, naturally. I had an idea Jamie's decision was a mistake – as useless and gallant as that step out into the storm by Captain Oates. I wonder if Oates had a cardie on under his other gear. I jumped into the passenger seat. We left.'

D.H.: 'Abidan seemed to know Tom was not going to appear, did he?'

A: 'I didn't see how he could. Not logically. But I felt it, sort of sensed it somehow. You know how it can be.'

D.H.: 'Anyway, Abidan is not a Wheels, and so the disaster?'

A: 'No, he's not a Wheels, and we were doing big speed.'

D.H.: 'Leaving Jamie behind.'

A: 'He chose that.'

D.H.: 'Abidan didn't stop, but drove on to the change car you had parked ready at Pallindon Lane?'

A: 'He was driving like a loony. Up on to the pavement, knocks into those three girls from behind on their way to some clubbing, then we're down on to the street again. It seemed to me the kind of ... sort of, yes, contempt – not spoken, but real all the same from Jamie – this contempt had upset Empathy's balance. I was yelling at him to slow down. I wouldn't let him do the next leg, when we got to the replacement car.'

D.H.: 'You drove the Ford?'

A: 'I had to take over.'

D.H.: 'Which makes you an accessory to double manslaughter – woman slaughter – and failing to stop after an accident. Plus stolen vehicles and maybe a few other charges. Even a tie-in to the death of Tom Parry.'

A: 'Which is why I'm coughing the lot for you, isn't it? It wasn't me driving at the hit. And I don't want to be fixed up with the Parry death. I'm not involved, you know I'm not involved, but that might not stop you trying to magic a link. I want a note to let the judge know I've been helpful and can be rewarded by a cut sentence and some protection.'

D.H.: 'I'll see what can be done.'

And Harpur knew D.H. did manage something for Wolsey.

SIX

AFTER

Iles had spoken of a Home Office briefing he and Harpur would get before they started nosing into the conduct of those target police colleagues on their alien ground. It turned out to be grim and delicate: grim because the briefing presupposed harsh and intricate difficulties; and delicate because it suggested something totally evil and corrupt had most likely taken place, without actually saying what it was. Their job would be to find what it was and say what it was.

They went up to London by train for this pre-operation meeting. Naturally, Iles despised the Home Office. This was more than routine, simple, cliché hate for overlords. Although he knew comparatively few of the huge staff, he had a general suspicion of everyone who worked there. He reasoned they would *not* have worked there if they had taste, integrity and decent parentage. He especially mistrusted those in the top posts. Iles thought they had probably lurked and simpered around this department for years, and with time had come to consider as normal and even wholesome what he saw as its dirty, grossly and brazenly non-Ilesean, unforgivable ways.

Harpur himself didn't mind the Home Office. He'd been on several previous visits, some with Iles, some alone. Harpur found the whole Whitehall thing quite a comfort: civil servants and politicians in their well-ordered offices talked and behaved as if genuinely convinced they could bring at least some of that order to the population outside, quite possibly to the population's advantage now and then. This positive theme could be felt in the corridors and stairwells and was known among the super-clerks and Ministers as 'proactive commitment'. Harpur's spirits would almost always take a boost for a while from such confident optimism. He liked to feel that what often seemed to him the chaos and quandary of day-to-day, night-to-night policing were not really like this at all, but elements in a general scheme fully understood and subtly regulated by sharp administrators and government masterminds and mistressminds in the capital. Naturally, he recognized that this was probably bollocks, but it helped keep him going.

'Fucking Oxford *Literae Humaniores* fucking graduates with Firsts, the fucking lot of them,' Iles said as they passed through security into the building. 'But don't get scared, Col. I'll see they make allowances for you. I won't have them treating you as negligible, regardless.'

'Regardless of what, sir?'

'Well, yes, regardless, Harpur. You deserve quite a bit better than that. Yes, quite a bit.'

A screen. Harpur sat next to Iles halfway back in the little Home Office Projection Room to watch it. Maud, their hostess, had a front-row place. She wanted first-name conditions. Harpur thought she'd be late twenties or less. In another room, she'd introduced herself – Maud Logan Clatworthy, 'your permanent contact with the department during this project, my mobile ever-on if I'm not here'. She had a round, affable, rustic-sexy, swede-basher's sort of face, but Harpur realized there was no reason why someone with a round, affable, rustic-sexy swede-basher's face shouldn't have one of those fucking *Literae Humaniores* Firsts Iles had spoken of. Maud wore a dark-blue trouser suit with some kind of glinting gold thread in the silky looking material. It produced a sort of will-o'-the-wisp effect when she moved, which Harpur found deeply stimulating. Iles would be intrigued by it. He might love to create a will-o'-the-wisp impression himself. Harpur would watch to see over the next few weeks whether the Assistant Chief ordered the same kind of bright interlay for one of his custom-made blazers. On the other hand, Iles could probably decide he came over as sparkling enough, without help from fancy clobber.

Maud Logan Clatworthy had given them a

quick sketch of the case: 'This being your first official involvement with it, though you probably saw and heard reports in the media at the time, and I've sent you some of the transcripts and so on. OK, it's of this order: four men from the successful drug-dealing firm of Leo Percival Young are told to take out another member of the outfit, Justin Paul Scray, who has apparently been recruiting loaded punters for his own gain. Classic jiggery-pokery, establishing a secret, elite firm within the L.P. Young firm and diverting these gains to himself. Among the four is a camouflaged cop.'

Now, Maude operated a hand-held control able to put white rings around those elements in the film she wanted to call attention to and talk about, the way soccer analysis on television could encircle some players to illustrate sweet tactics in a game, or crap tactics. The film showed arcades, a building site, a square, a shopping mall, streets. Harpur didn't recognize any of it. This was a different police domain. 'Some are simply situation shots of the area done quite recently,' Maud said, the accent possibly refined Merseyside, out-of-town Merseyside, 'but we've spliced in CCTV material from the night of the shooting where this seems apropos. Some of it was shown to the trial jury, of course.'

She moved the film on to a new frame and held it. 'This is where things started, the recessed bus stop and Monthermer Street,' she said. 'No CCTV here, unfortunately. It's only a geography clip. But, as you'll have probably seen among the statements, a trial witness described three men moving off from a Volvo and into this thoroughfare, cocky like the crook team near the start of *Reservoir Dogs*. Remember them? That Keitel – so fit!'

Harpur thought he had this name – Monthermer – and a few others somewhere in his memory, either from official documentation he and Iles had been sent as introductory material, or from the media. Because of the big significance of the killing, the events of that night, and the accident trial when it took place eight months later, had earned major space in national newspapers and on television and radio. Harpur had followed some of this journalism, although he didn't know then, of course, that Iles and he would be sent to investigate the events and their aftermath. He imagined most police officers would have kept an eye on the Press and broadcast accounts, and especially those involved in any way with undercover work. They – he – might have absorbed some location details unaware.

The images changed again. Maud stopped the film and put one of her celebrity circles around a man walking past a charity shop, his face away from the camera. 'We think this is Martin Abidan, hunt-party leader and on the board of the L.P. Young outfit,' she said. 'The spot is the edge of Guild Square. Scray would sometimes appear in this area meeting clients, as he would, too, in the arcades and elsewhere locally.' She restarted the footage. The man walked on. 'Now watch this,' she said. He seemed to slow his pace suddenly and to stare at something over on his right. He halted and continued to gaze in that direction. 'It looks as if he's seen Scray, doesn't it?' she said.

'Yes,' Harpur said. 'Has he?'

'You'll remember that moment in *The Girl With The Dragon Tattoo*, by Stieg Larsson,' she replied.

'Oh?' Harpur said.

'Where the investigative reporter, searching for clues about a missing girl, finds a group photograph of her glancing off-picture at some-body or something that shocks and/or fascinates her,' Iles said. 'It's a kind of revelation. Actually, the reporter comes over as thick as shit, so he needs revelations.'

'Yes, a kind of revelation here, too,' she said.

They watched the man she'd called Abidan step into the shallow entrance porch of a com-puter store. For a moment he was lost to the street camera. But another one – presumably the store's own – picked him up in the porch, and Maud's technicians had tacked this new sighting on to the previous frames. He was talking into a mobile. Maud kept him and his phone in another bright noose.

Although she must have often seen this picture before, she gave it some special, priority mull now and, still seated, spoke over her left shoulder to Harpur and the Assistant Chief, not bothering to look their way because, at this moment, only the screen counted for her. Harpur knew the seeming casualness of this would infuriate Iles. During some city hall function, Harpur had once heard the ACC yell, at a police committee member who must have addressed him a bit aslant, 'Shoulders are undoubtedly fine and crucial to the skeleton and tailoring. I've no quarrel with shoulders whatsoever, but conversation flung at me over them – i. fucking e., the shoulders – is quite another commodity, twat.' He'd consider avoidance of face-to-face as insubordinate.

But Harpur had the feeling Maud wouldn't give a fish's tit *how* he considered it. That cheery, greenfield face hid ironclad wilfulness, as well as the kind of possible brainpower Iles had mentioned. When she told them her mobile phone would be always open, she didn't mean for chit-chat: it was to give updated advice, and Harpur felt the advice would actually be dogmatic orders. Perhaps it wasn't a hick face but a centurion's: 'I say do this and he/they doeth it.'

Maud told them now: 'Abidan made two calls. Each contained the same words – "Where I am" – a prearranged rendezvous signal. In theory, any of the three might have used it, depending on who found Scray first. A sort of "rally round the flag" summons.'

'Like in *The Red Badge of Courage,*' Iles said.

'True,' Harpur said.

'It looks a very credible, clever scheme, doesn't it?' Maud said.

'Looks?' Harpur replied.

'Supposedly, they knew the approximate area where Scray functions, but this is, in fact, quite a spread. They need to pinpoint. So they split up, and each focuses on an allegedly likely spot – the arcades, the square, the mall.'

'Allegedly?' Harpur asked.

'The lucky one summons the other two, and we're required to believe here that Abidan was the lucky one,' she said.

Harpur had another of his pernickety, echo queries ready – 'Required to believe?' Or, perhaps: *'Required* to believe?' – but he held back. He wondered why Iles hadn't picked up on any of these doubt-tinged words and phrases, the way the glitteringly well-read sod had responded to the tattooed dragon, or whatever it was, and flourished that red badge. Despite his possible annoyance at the way she delivered her observations, did the Assistant Chief sense what prompted the quibbles in Maud's commentary? Had he detected traces of some other narrative paralleling, running alongside, the obvious one and disputing its accuracy? Hell, what was happening here?

Seated next to Iles, Harpur saw only his profile as the ACC watched and listened to Maud. Harpur couldn't tell whether Iles full-phiz looked relaxed and understanding as Maud repeatedly inserted these strange riffs of scepti-

43

cism. Did he intuit what the fucking First in fucking *Literae* fucking *Humaniores*, whatever *they* might be, was fucking hinting at? Harpur felt his own plodding series of spoken carps and pleas for clarity might show him to be dull, naive, cumbersomely unsuave. Occasionally, he fancied becoming suave. He thought the children would like it. But he realized he had quite a way to go yet. Hazel had said one of his two suits looked as if he'd worn it when crawling through the Libyan drain pipe where they found Gaddafi.

'Here comes Ivor Wolsey, the reluctant marksman,' Maud said as the film showed a slight man of around thirty to thirty-five entering the Square from a side street. 'He coughed the whole project under interrogation, as far as he knew it.' Wolsey wore a denim blouson, light trousers and blue baseball cap. He moved quickly up towards the computer store, though was obviously all-round vigilant, an arm folded across his midriff, right hand probably closed ready on the butt of a waist-holstered pistol. The camera followed Wolsey for a while, but Maud didn't bother to install a loop around him.

He was still crossing the Square when the film left Wolsey and came up with a picture of the opening to another minor street. 'Tom Parry, as we must call him, should have arrived in the Square at this junction, short-cutting from the Rinton mall via a building site,' Maud said. 'Of course, he never did. It's why you're here and are going there. No CCTV at the building site, naturally. It's going to be an extension for one of the mall businesses, plus a lot of housing, but on pause then because of a money-trouble freeze on development.'

Harpur said: 'And talking of CCTV, is there any from that night showing Scray?'

'If you've read the transcripts, you'll know there isn't,' Maud said.

'But I haven't read all the transcripts. I don't know whether the ACC has,' Harpur said. 'We're at a fairly far-back start. Until now, we didn't know what the job was. Still don't fully know.' Harpur felt he had to show he wasn't just workmanlike and unsubtle. His mind could jump ahead, couldn't it. Couldn't it? 'Maud, are you telling us, without telling us, that our lad was set up?'

She stood facing them, her back to the screen for the moment. She blinked. 'You're quick,' she said.

'Col *is* quick,' Iles replied with a fond, admiring chuckle, as if praising his rescued greyhound which could still show some creaking pace if a tennis ball were thrown to play the course rabbit. 'Or quick*ish*. I wanted you to know that, Maud. His interpretation of your hints is a very obvious one, of course. But I stayed silent, so he could have his little say-so first. Good for his morale and general selfhood. It's sad, but this is the only self he has, and I'd like him to make the best of it. I've told Col I would take care he wasn't made to look moronic by you and your lot.'

Iles began to semi-scream. Acoustics in this little theatre were excellent and gave even only a semi-scream fine penetration and depth, plus a hint of considerable reserves and the possibility that Iles would move into a full, all-out, gloriously unmodulated scream before very long. 'You might well think, Maud, that this is foolishly kind of me after he had been banging my wife in fourth-rate rooming joints, under evergreen hedgerows, in marly fields, on river banks, in cars – including police vehicles – and, most probably, my own bed, despite the quiet distinction of the area where I live and the indisputable fact that properties standing in Rougemont Place include among their occupants a retired rear-admiral, from the days when the Royal Navy really was a navy, the proprietor of a workshop making vital shoe-wideners, a manufacturer of state-of-the-art double-glazed and centrally heated caravans, a lottery winner, and a paid-off football manager from somewhere up north. There would be occasions when work took me away, and Harpur did not demur. Harpur and demurring don't mix.

'So, Maud, let me tabulate the topics and subtopics, will you? One, you'll ask, and reasonably ask, why in this case do I wish to protect his unkempt, struggling ego? Two: why do I pick him to come on this assignment with me in another police region? I'll deal chronologically with these wholly justifiable queries. One: I am, I trust, a forgiving, large-minded man who, at the sight of mental frailty, wishes to do what I can, in the interests of humaneness, to help. Hence, kindness to Col. As a child, I was known by my mother as "Heartfelt Desmond" and, if brevity were not required, "Desmond-who-does-not-pass-by-on-the-other-side". That deals with Question One.

'But, then, we have to answer Question Two, don't we? Why select him as my baggage-man and toothpaste squeezer? And, so, here *is* the answer: am I going to leave this prick-driven laddie unmonitored while I'm away sorting out some distant police crew, my wife being there unchaperoned and vulnerable in Rougemont Place, and Harpur treacherously familiar with the environs?'

Harpur thought Maud looked appalled – altogether unlike the calm but commanding mandarin figure she had seemed a short time ago. She said: 'Mr Iles, Desmond, please: none of this has anything to do with—'

'Oh, I can tell you,' Iles replied, 'my wife, Sarah, and I have quite a joint giggle some evenings now when we talk of her goings-on with him in the past. We – neither of us, and I stress this, neither she nor I – neither of us is able to understand how she could possibly have opened up to someone of Col's grubby ilk. Notoriously, some women will go for what's termed "a bit of rough". Although people wrongly pronounce the initial A in Ava Gardner to rhyme with "day" or "say", I'm told she'd chosen it as her stage name because she liked to have a gardener occasionally, possibly *al fresco*.'

'Did he have something special for her?' Harpur said.

'Who?' Iles replied.

'Ava Gardner,' Harpur said, with the broad A.

'No, I meant did who have something special for her?' Iles said.

'The gardener, Al Fresco,' Harpur said, 'with the broad A.'

'So, yes, "a bit of rough" might be understandable, Maud. But Harpur?' Iles asked. 'To stick this label on him would disrespect the word "rough". There is, after all, rough, and then there's *rough*. However, I can sense your trained mind tackling this perhaps unexpected material. No doubt, Maud, you'll want to ask why, if my wife and I now regard their fling as absurd, should I fear that in my absence the two of them might reactivate their déclassé, nomadic intimacy, accompanied most probably by unbecoming, subversive jibes about me? I have to say, Maud, I do not know the answer to this. I am one who will unhesitatingly admit to gaps and even contradictions in my thinking.

'Possibly, you have not come across this kind of rampant honesty and frankness before. The fucking Home Office is hardly the place to encounter such limpid qualities. But, however one looks at this, Maud, I believe it would be a kind

48

of hubris to leave Harpur at large back there while there is also a fine, friendly woman to be exploited. Harpur won't, of course, know what "hubris" means. You, Maud, owing to a Classics background, will be familiar with the word and what it denotes – excessive, smug, foolish pride. But I'll say this for Col, he'll make a guess at it. OK, he'll get it wrong, but he will have tried. There's something admirable about such determination, although doomed. Many would find Col entirely acceptable, no question, but, also no question, they would *not* include those who've discovered that, in his abominable, un-holy way he has—'

'You're telling us, Maud, are you, that the whole supposed Scray hunt was a phoney? A device to get Tom so-called Parry into a spot – the non-CCTV'd building site – where he could be safely taken out?' Harpur said.

'This is what I would like you and Desmond to establish,' she said.

'If it can be established,' Harpur replied.

'I think we should come at things positively,' Maud said.

'But you won't be coming at them. We will,' Harpur said.

'Col can be sharp on phrasing,' Iles said. 'He has been shaped by what is referred to unapolo-getically as "the university of life". He had an Open Scholarship to that one.'

'It's among a hundred hazards of going un-dercover, isn't it?' Maud replied. 'The planted officer finds as part of his spying that some members of the infiltrated gang have a money arrangement with certain cops – probably Drugs Squad people. Perhaps he or she shows too much interest in this. His or her cover crumbles. Both sides – the villains and the corrupt detectives – decide he or she is a fink, and also decide he or she might expose their jolly arrangement. They want him or her dead, and soon – before he or she has enough evidence to convince a court. They scheme an operation where he or she can be seen off, as if by someone from a competing firm, in a company battle. So neat.'

'But *you* think he was killed by a police officer?' Harpur asked.

'Col can have flashes of insight. I did warn you,' Iles said. The ACC was calm again now, and rational. His fits never lasted long. He was aware afterwards that they'd taken place. No blackout. A couple of weeks ago he'd said to Harpur, following a bout, 'Debussy used to have mind-wobbles, too, but they didn't spoil his compositions, Col: in fact, they perhaps gave his music an extra, thrilling, other-worldly touch. Likewise, my work is enhanced.'

'I've often thought it should be *Clair de loon*, with double O not the "une",' Harpur had answered.

Maud said now: 'You'll have the full backing of the Home Office.'

'Oh, God,' Iles said.

'On the night, who knew what was going on,

Maud?' Harpur asked.

'Perhaps only Abidan,' she said. 'And the chief, L.P. Young, naturally. There was little drugs trading done at the mall. Very unlikely Scray would be there. It appears that Young wanted to fix a suitable route for Tom, so he gets that pitch.'

'But none of this came out in the trial, did it?' Harpur said.

'The trial was about something else entirely, wasn't it?' Maud said.

'And nobody charged for the death of Parry,' Harpur said.

'Quite,' Maud replied.

'Quite,' Iles said.

SEVEN

BEFORE

If they decided to kill, you had to go along with it. Pack law. Basic. Anyone who went under-cover knew this.

Yes, of course, Thomas Rodney Mallen did know this, but it was a while before he had to apply such obvious, tidy undercover wisdom to how he actually behaved. You didn't just stroll into the realm of secret duty and its special, non-stop moral puzzles. And into its special strains and perils – also non-stop. They'd come up with a new name for him, Thomas Derek Parry, and it would take a while to acclimatize. Undercover people often kept their first name, but *only* their first name; and only their first name if it was reasonably common: not Peregrine or Putsy-Pie or Sacheverell.

For years – decades – as children and young adults at home and in school, present-day un-dercover officers had responded automatically to that first name. So, to stick with it now in these hairy conditions reduced by a fraction the amount of play-acting needed, and therefore a fraction of the stress. Also, the name helped an undercover snoop hang on to a portion of his or her true identity, and in a protracted operation that could be useful: selfhood sometimes turned shaky then, like: *who the fuck am I?*

Iris and both the children said he shouldn't take on this change of duties. Naturally, Laura and Steve could have no real understanding of what it was about, but they'd been warned he might have to go away for long spells, and that disturbed them. Also, Tom sensed they'd noticed how his mention of the new duties badly upset their mother. Her agitation spread. Iris was very close to the kids, and they to Iris, so her feelings inevitably reached them; like osmosis, an absorbent process, but faster. Tom thought this was how a good family should be, but it did mean that on some issues he'd feel outgunned, three to one, which now and then pissed him off. Now.

Their objections wouldn't make him change, though. The brass had sent someone to ask Tom to do it, and he'd said he'd do it. You didn't get ordered into undercover. You volunteered. You accepted, if and when invited. Not many officers *were* invited. The role brought kudos. Tom wouldn't mind some of that. The role brought a kind of independence. Tom wouldn't mind some of that, either. Once you'd infiltrated a firm, you had to run things as you wanted them run. Interference from senior officers wasn't possible, because it might crack the spy's cover.

Tom's willingness – enthusiasm – would make it worse for Iris and the children to take, of course. He'd opted to go. He'd actually chosen to leave them, for who knew how long? He didn't really think it would be a dolly job and quickly over. There'd be more training, then the slow business of getting into the target crew, followed by the harvesting of information that made the slow business of getting into the target crew necessary and worthwhile.

Undercover people weren't supposed to tell even their spouse/partner about assignments. Tom considered this nuts. It would require someone superlatively dim not to guess what was happening. You couldn't brick wall all the inevitable queries. That would only magnify uneasiness and, maybe, resentment. Your replies to questions needn't be too detailed, though: they could be 'redacted', to borrow a modish term. 'I don't get it, Tom,' Iris said.

He reckoned this meant she *did* get it – or, at least the permitted outline of it – but wanted him to give her a full, clear description of what he was taking on. She'd be able to endorse it or counter it point by point then. Iris liked system. Obviously, life did need some system. Tom thought it shouldn't get to domineer, though. Iris had a brother, Jeremy, a Cambridge graduate, who often – it certainly *seemed* often – spoke about the intellectual 'rigour' instilled there. Iris hadn't been to Cambridge, but she could offer her own, home-made rigour. Tom didn't go much for Cambridge rigour, anyway. Hadn't that Lord who 'authenticated' the flagrantly phoney Hitler diaries become head of a Cambridge college? Dacre, his name? A faker fooled Dacre.

Tom realized that Iris might have been expecting the kind of announcement he'd made today – expecting, and possibly dreading. After all, he'd been away for a month on that course in undercover objectives and skills at Hilston Manor, the handsome country mansion, once home of a great nineteenth-century railways man. It was still handsome, but the industrialist and his heirs had gone, and the house and grounds now served as an assessment and training depot for all British police forces.

The course he'd attended had as its official, magnificently uninformative title, 'Actual Progressive Policing' (APP). Those selected were instructed to tell anyone outside who asked about it that the object was to improve police integration within the community. The last phrase – 'within the community' – should be used verbatim and with a pious tone, his tutor said, because the word 'community' had lately developed a kind of gorgeously holy tinge, and to be 'within' that blessed fold made things even holier: the curious would consider it crude to go on nosing if once blocked by this cosy, sanctified formula. He'd tried it on Iris, and she'd replied: 'Rubbish. You've been learning how to spy, haven't you, Tom? Active Progressive

Policing means getting disguised into a gang.'

Now, she said: 'It's a different police patch, and they want you to move there?'

'Not *move* there. Not a permanent thing, of course. A sort of secondment.'

'Which sort?'

'Strictly task related. When it's completed I'll be signed off. A very limited arrangement. Like a company calling in an IT expert to deal with some specific snarl-up.'

'What are you an expert at? What type of snarl-up?'

Iris had one hell of a down on jargon – assumed always that its purpose was concealment and evasiveness, not communication; anti-communication. OK, OK, she might be right. Often Iris got things right. He wouldn't want a wife who didn't. It could be a sodding pain, though.

'There'll be a full briefing before things get properly under way,' he said.

'Before what gets properly under way?'

'Some kinds of work can't be rushed,' he replied. 'It's not like answering a nine nine nine.'

'Which kinds?'

'Secondments of this sort.'

'Which sort?'

'Secondments are very various – and quite common. They allow a beneficial spread of resources.'

The gobbledegook shit made her grimace. 'How long do secondments of this particular sort last?' Iris asked.

'It depends.'

'On what?'

'On the degree of progress.'

'What kind of progress?'

'Progress towards bringing a properly documented case against the firm I'm placed with.' He had been going to say 'against the firm I'm embedded with' but corrected that in time. 'Bed', even buried in the middle of a bigger word, could suggest the wrong kind of intimacy.

'So, you aim to scupper them?' Iris asked.

'To bring them to trial.'

'You'll pretend friendship, and then betray them?'

'Not friendship. You're being deliberately naive.'

'You'll be workmates, apparently.'

'We're talking about mobsters, Iris. They kill people. I don't owe them loyalty. This might be the only way they can be neutralized.'

'"Neutralized" meaning destroyed.'

'Their organization destroyed, yes. If I'm lucky.'

'And will you be?' There had been a staccato harshness about her string of questions up till now: an interrogation. This one was not like that, but loving and anxious. 'They'll know the police are likely to try something of the sort, won't they? A new face in the crew – it's bound to make them wary, suspicious, isn't it?'

'The training showed us how to counter that.'

'Yes? How?' she said.

'Preparedness. Thoroughness.'

'Thoroughness at what?'

She'd returned to her attacking mode. He could feel possible trouble in this new area of cross-examination, but he had to respond. 'Thoroughness at sticking to the new identity. We prepare a full, convincing – and, of course, phoney – background for ourselves.'

'Which "we" is that?'

'Undercover candidates.'

'Are there plenty?'

'Plenty of what?' he said.

'Plenty wanting to do undercover.'

'They're never without volunteers.'

'Why?'

'It's stimulating. A lot of police work is deeply boring. This is a way out.'

'Stimulating because it's dangerous?' she asked.

'Because it requires non-stop skill and alertness. And the undercover officer will be solo, of course. So, it's one against a horde.'

'"Facing fearful odds", as old fashioned yarns used to say? More glory – if you win.'

'People will take on a challenge, yes.'

'If there are so many available, why can't they get someone from closer – geographically closer, I mean?'

'The distance is important,' he said.

'Important how?'

'There's a ... there's what could be called a confidential element.'

'Is that true of all secondments?'

'Not all.'

'You need to come from some way off so you won't be recognized by anyone – revealed, by an awkward fluke, as a cop?' Iris asked.

'And other factors.'

'Which?'

'Background – that kind of thing,' he said.

'The children and me?'

'It wouldn't be watertight if my home and family could be traced.'

'What wouldn't be watertight?' she replied.

'The confidential side of it all.'

'There's only one side of it all, isn't there, Tom – the confidential side? You have to construct a brand-new bloke, somebody with a make-believe past and no findable family or chums or career or education. Wasn't there a stink recently about undercover people with protest groups who actually gave their false name in court when prosecuted for their supposed protest activities?'

'Now and then police work is like that, whether it's here or there.'

'But this will be *there*, won't it? The distance factor – that *important* distance.'

'I'll be entitled to some travel allowances, if the work drags on. Home breaks are guaranteed.'

'Steve's birthday?' As well as her fondness for system, Iris knew how to play very dirty. She'd been at an expensive boarding school.

'Quite possibly I could get home for something like that,' Tom said. 'It would depend on how the project was going at the time. Clearly.'

'Clearly.'

'It's nearly two months away. Difficult to forecast.'

'An important anniversary. He goes into teens.'

'Anyway, I'd make sure there was a card and a pressie. I won't forget.'

'Long-distance daddy.'

'Work takes many dads – and mums – away for spells, doesn't it, Iris?'

'Which name would you put on the card?'

'What?'

'The new bloke's?'

'Please, Iris. "Dad" – as ever.'

'I heard that some people who go on undercover duties get sort of taken over by the new identity. It's as if they become somebody else. There's an all-purpose actor in a novel I picked up from the bookshop's bargain box who's described as "absolved for ever from being himself". And wasn't there a kind of doppelgänger for Field Marshall Montgomery in the war, who kept reverting to the role long after, although he wanted to escape it? Are we going to lose you that way, Tom?'

He disliked how she phrased this. It sounded as if he was sure to be lost: it could be a toss-up between (a) death by discovery, and (b) irreversible morph – transformation of himself into a stranger, a villain stranger: that *'Who the fuck am I?'* confusion. 'I'll still be me,' he said. 'Tests by shrinks on the course showed I have a strong, well-disciplined self-image, one I would always want to retain and return to after sojourns as someone else. I should be able to do imperson-ation all right, but that's all it would ever be – me pretending to be someone else, and all the time aware I'm trying to be someone else, maybe a bit like an actor, as you say, but nothing permanent.'

'This is an undercover operation, yes?' she replied.

'I spoke of a confidential side.'

'I don't remember the word "undercover", though.'

'So much police work is confidential. I thought it didn't need labelling.'

'I asked if it was undercover, not if it was confidential,' Iris said. 'What else *can* it be, for God's sake – the wipe-out of home and family, the absence of details, the woolly, go-nowhere replies, the daft optimism? How do I get in touch when you're at the other end of that important distance?'

Just ask for Thomas Derek Parry. But Thomas Rodney Mallen didn't say this, of course. Iris couldn't be given his alias name, nor any means to contact him, from the minute he moved into his new character. It would have to be one-way transmission, from him to her, when he could manage it, unobserved. He'd try to manage it

61

often.

'That damn country place,' she said.

'Which damn country place?'

'Where they trained and tested you.'

'They were very choosy. Only a few got picked for the course.'

'So, why couldn't you have fucking flunked it?'

'It's good for the career, Iris, good for the CV.'

'*Curriculum vitae,*' she replied. 'Translation, I believe: "Course of life." I hope so. Life. But your life's well on, Tom, isn't it? I'd have thought for this kind of work they'd go for younger volunteers and without a dependent family.'

'The opposite. They prefer someone mature, steady and in a good, solid relationship. It's like selection for space travel crews. Personal stability is crucial.' He wanted to get off this topic. 'The tests also showed I had most of the other basic qualities needed, some not sounding too pleasant. I'm manipulative, opportunistic, plausible, temperate, resourceful,' he said.

They were having a late breakfast. Iris had taken the children to school. She shifted to a chair nearer him and put her arm around his shoulders. 'As to that damn country place, when they trained and tested you, I hope they did it well, especially the training. The testing? Well, I know you'd be good at anything you put your mind to. You couldn't, in fact, flunk.'

He kissed her on the cheek.

'You smell of Marmite,' she said.

'They seemed very competent. All the tutors had been undercover themselves. It wasn't just seminar-room old rope. Some were going back to the same kind of work after their stint at Hilston. They'd got hooked on it.'

'That I don't like,' Iris said.

'No.' But Tom could understand the pull. It must be quite a treat to shed your usual self for a while – get 'absolved' from it, to pick up Iris's word – and become somebody else, all one's customary worries, vanities, doubts temporarily ditched; subordinated because so much energy and skill would be required to fool your new mates, and to keep fooling them. Despite what he'd said to Iris, this wasn't really like being an actor, a game where you tried to mock-up your cast character until the final curtain, then went home on the tube, not, say, as the warrior loud-mouth, Coriolanus, but as your real you, with a break on Sundays. Undercover, you took on the alternative identity for every minute, every day, including Sundays.

Tom remembered from school that, in fact, Coriolanus in the Shakespeare play compared himself at one remorseful point to a 'dull actor' who had forgotten his part. The actor playing this dull actor had better not forget *his* part, though. For the show's three hours or so he mustn't forget to forget. But the undercover officer was concerned with much more than regular spells of a few hours. He or she must not forget their part for days, weeks, maybe even months or years.

It must be a great tonic to know you'd successfully penetrated a firm and made monkeys of a clutch of clever, vigilant, distrustful crooks. And, yes, you might get a taste for those kinds of sneaky victories. At Hilston, one of the undercover people giving a talk said only volunteers who survived the intrusive, gruelling psychometric examinations at the Manor could be considered for what he called 'Out-located' work: cut adrift from family and colleagues and canteen. He argued that the toughness of these selection methods couldn't actually guarantee success, but almost. Tom had thought that perhaps it shouldn't be 'almost' but 'maybe'. He considered 'maybe' an acceptable gamble just about, though he knew Iris certainly wouldn't. She probably did not understand how monotonous and soul-clamping so much policing could be, nor sympathize with the search for excitement, even if that excitement came almost entirely from risk and its abiding partner, fear.

And, of course, there was the great unspoken between Iris and him: sex – the reason he'd baulked at 'embedded'. To preserve their credibility as true crooks, undercover people had to create a complete alternative life for themselves, and a complete alternative life might include relationships. Besides that 'stink' Iris had mentioned about the officer giving a false identity even in court, there'd been a lot in the Press lately to do with undercover officers who infiltrated those civil disobedience movements and scored with one or more of the protesters. It could be to maintain cover, or get extra information via pillow talk – or, possibly, just because they fancied it. When all this was revealed, women had marched on Scotland Yard to condemn the false cockery, stating they'd never knowingly have shagged the fuzz.

They claimed promiscuity became part of the police job, blind-eyed, or even openly tolerated, by senior officers. One of the march banners Tom saw on television news read: 'Why detectives are called dicks.' Former undercover officers quoted by a tabloid said if you didn't have it away here and there you'd be a freak – and therefore noticed and suspected. The reporter commented that this sounded like 'noble-cause concupiscence' and gave 'penetration' a second meaning. A headline boomed: 'Undercover leg-over.'

Iris had probably read some of these articles, but he knew she wouldn't bring up that category of worry. She'd see it as an insult to suggest he might have to multi-fuck his way to full fellowship and acceptance by the tribe. Perhaps she'd like *him* unprompted to mention these newspaper stories and dismiss such behaviour as gross and sleazy. He didn't though. Silence might be wiser, he decided. In any case, he wasn't concerned with a *pro bono publico* protest group, where there'd most likely be an equal number of youngish men and women made hot and horny by enthusiasm for the cause, and therefore very much up for it: a kind of solidarity. Tom had to find a place in a professional, crooked firm. There wouldn't be many women, perhaps none. Sex shouldn't figure, surely.

EIGHT

AFTER

Maud stopped the film for a while and turned in her front-row seat to talk to Iles and Harpur behind. Maybe she'd decided, after all, to show some politeness and avoid pissing Iles off. She didn't put the Projection Room overhead light on, and they remained in three-quarters darkness. Harpur found this soothing. He recalled happy popcorn sessions in the stalls while watching movies as a youngster, though these shouldn't have happened because his Plymouth Brethren Sunday School condemned cinema as worldly. He'd strayed now and then. Popcorn would probably have been all right, but not in a cinema. The trouble was, *people* went to the cinema and St Paul had told the Corinthians to come out from among people and be 'separate'.

Maud said: 'It's simpler if we continue using Mallen's cover name, Parry, in our discourse here. I think it would be apropos for me to give you some notion of his character and personality. Very limited parts of this you'll find in the trial transcript, but, regrettably, the trial was not about Parry or his murder. There's been no trial about Parry's murder yet, has there? Which is why I want this investigation, re-investigation, by you two eminently thorough, impartial and committed detectives.'

Iles gave a bit of a groan. He did not usually mind flattery, and, in fact, would generally fail to find flattery flattery at all, simply a justifiably awed stocktaking of his assets. But he'd suspect praise now because they were in Home Office precincts, listening to someone doing well here, and who must, consequently, be a conspiring, egomaniac two-timer: conspiring very specifically against *him*. In any case, the Assistant Chief would hate having his abilities referred to as equal to Harpur's, or even comparable to. The ACC could just about swallow blandishments, but not if he knew Harpur was getting them, too. Suckholing to Iles had to be carried out with discrimination, a discrimination which should naturally exclude Harpur, or it would be suckholing with no special distinction for the hole being sucked.

'I meant it – about your famed doggedness, your dedication to a task,' Maud stated with a very genuine-seeming smile.

'Thanks,' Iles said. 'It *is* a big help if you tell us when we can rely on what you're saying because you mean it, as against all your other chit-chat when you don't.'

'Selection methods for undercover people utilize research done here in GB and in the

USA,' Maud replied. 'On the face of it – yes, on the face of it – Parry looked ideally suited. Most police chiefs prefer their undercover officers to have had at least four or five years of ordinary detective experience. And ideally they should be in settled domestic relationships: this is taken as proof of a balanced, businesslike, well-rooted nature.'

Iles said in a quibbling, fussy, unnaturally quiet tone, sort of decorous seminar mode: 'Harpur tended to get himself well-rooted *outside* the home environment. Very well rooted. That is, of course, outside his *own* home environment. Other people's home environments were quite another consideration, and could be shame-lessly—'

'Parry had done six years as a general duties detective,' Maud explained, 'and was in what appeared to be a classic, two-child family situation. He fitted the approved age range – early thirties to early forties.'

'Fucking lunacy,' Iles said.

'Now, clearly, there can be, and are, objections to this pattern of recruitment,' she said. 'Should officers with dependants be favoured for what is undoubtedly exceptionally risky work? If something goes wrong it isn't only the officer who suffers.'

'I don't allow undercover on my ground,' Iles said. 'Not married or single or civil partnership. Not young, not not-so young. We had a death there, too, you see.'

Iles had never completely recovered from his distress at the murder of Ray Street, an undercover man put into terminal danger with the ACC's agreement. Now and again, Harpur would see him slide back into almost disabling grief and self-condemnation. This sensitivity seemed to clash with his usual bland flintiness and snarling poise; though, yes, quite often he could fall into the screaming abdabs, lip-froth included, about his wife, Sarah, and Harpur, a liaison long over. Iles had become obsessed about the safety of his people. Maybe the indecisiveness and hesitance that resulted had killed his chance of a Chiefdom somewhere. He did believe there was a conspiracy against him, Home Office-based, but conceivably wider than that, taking in the European Parliament, the Church of England, St Andrew's golf club and the BBC. Perhaps his paranoia had some cause. Perhaps it didn't: he might be a natural second-in-command; eternally second.

'Both GB and the US recommend mature, father or mother figures for undercover,' Maud replied. Obviously, she had very quickly worked out a procedure for coping with Iles: ignore him, or use waffly generalities to swamp his bleats. Perhaps this speed and ruthlessness was natural to graduates with fucking Firsts from fucking Oxford in Latin, Greek and the side dishes.

Maud said: 'Occasionally, it's true, the police brass opts for a comparatively new recruit to infiltrate a villain outfit: they pick someone who

70

hasn't had time to develop a standard police mindset and attitudes which might automatically take over suddenly in a crisis undercover and betray him or her. Also, the officer will be unknown to local criminals. He or she might have gone straight into plain clothes and be free from any lawman, law-woman, history. A possible boon. However, as we know, an alternative way to guard against recognition exists: choose a mature officer but from a different Force. This brings us to Parry.'

'But it doesn't, of course, bring Parry back to his family,' Iles said.

'Naturally, neither safeguard can be totally efficient, and we certainly have to wonder whether the distance tactic worked for him,' Maud said. 'Members of crooked firms move about the country looking for better business, or to be near a girlfriend or boy friend, or to escape a spell of police heat on their usual ground, or to look at second homes to invest their smart gains in. And one of them could have run across Parry before he took on his undercover role, and remembered him.'

'You said, "On the face of it," Maud,' Harpur replied. 'Said it twice. "On the face of it" Parry looked OK for the undercover operation. Why only "on the face of it"?'

'Harpur will fix on a phrase,' Iles said. 'It's a valid flair.' He had quit the sombre tone, for now. 'Don't write Col off as just my sweeper-up.'

'Parry got killed,' Maud said. '"On the face of it", he shouldn't have got killed because he was near-perfect for undercover, according to US experts and our own. His entry to the firm seems to have been brilliantly carried out – patient and in slow stages. He did some buying, as if for personal use, with officially provided funds. Then he increased the purchase, said he had friends who'd enjoyed some of his stuff and wanted their own supply. He became a sort of courier and could graduate from there. Classic. It's an expensive way of working because, obviously, he had to be supplied with repeat money, and more repeat money. That can't be avoided. The outfit was alert to attempted penetration, of course, but very gradually they apparently got to trust him – as much as any of them trust any of them, which is never totally, but say fifty-eight point seven three per cent. So, he's in and seemingly secure, yet then gets wiped out.'

'He was ambushed,' Harpur said. 'No blame on him for that, surely. Who could have dodged it?'

Maud said: 'Well, who? Yes. And who could have laid it on?'

'The Home Office loves blame – blaming, that is, not *getting* blamed,' Iles said.

'Parry was a solid, four-square officer. Those are considerable assets. But perhaps they preclude some other essentials which a different officer might possess,' Maud said.

'Which different officer?' Harpur said.

'Notional,' Iles said. 'It's a concept, Col, not an actual person. We're in the realm of the theoretical.'

'Which essentials?' Harpur said.

'You see what I mean about the way he'll pounce on a word and get at its innards?' Iles said. 'Like a lioness with a zebra.'

'Instincts,' Maud replied.

'Instincts?' Harpur said.

'The undefinable, but essential,' Maud replied. 'Shouldn't he have sensed, smelled, intuited there was something suspect about the route selected for him to take when Abidan's call came? He would have learned the local geography by then. We're referring to a blacked-out construction site where he'd have to walk slowly and gingerly to avoid tripping over foundations and discarded hods. Slowly and gingerly and therefore very hitably. Uncompleted buildings offered fine cover and useful firing points for a sniper, especially if the sniper had night-vision equipment.'

'So, you *do* think the whole sortie was pre-shaped for the execution of Parry?' Harpur said.

'We have no CCTV sightings of Justin Scray that night, but we do know that Abidan put the rallying signal out, which would bring Parry from his search at the shopping mall along the agreed route, including the building site,' Maud said. 'Crucially including the building site.'

'You regard the hunt for Scray as a charade, a fiction, to fool Parry and get him into an easy target area?' Harpur asked. 'The real hunt was for *him*? No likelihood of finding Scray at the mall existed?'

'Or anywhere?' Iles said.

'My function is to suggest such questions,' Maud replied. 'Only that. But I'd hope they're questions that have not been adequately dealt with so far, and which, perhaps, you will prioritize.'

'You believe Parry was reliable and competent but naive?' Harpur asked.

'There *are* people like that, believe me, Col,' Iles said.

'Perhaps he *was* naive,' Maud said.

'But you told us he'd been chosen for his maturity,' Harpur said.

'Maturity in certain basics,' Maud said. 'Important basics, though lacking that vital something else. The experts' formula for the ideal undercover candidate might need amending.'

'So, selecting him was a terrible error?' Harpur asked.

'*Any* selection for undercover is a terrible error,' Iles said.

'But that's rather negative, isn't it?' Maud said.

'No. Not "rather". It's *totally* fucking negative,' Iles replied.

'I think undercover has been known to work,' Maud said.

'We can't ask Parry to confirm that,' Iles said.

'We *can* get his assassin, assassins, though,'

Maud replied.

'And you believe the assassin, assassins, could be a police officer, police officers, scared of exposure as payrolled protectors of the firm?' Harpur asked. 'The cop killer – or killers – is – or are – cops?'

'As I've said, my job is to suggest questions,' Maud told them.

NINE

BEFORE

Tom drove alone to a would-be welcoming place, brilliant for confidential meetings and basic grub – a motorway service station, this one on the M4. Neither party got the advantage of home ground, and anonymity was easy in the changing crowd. They had his registration number and car colour and make. He didn't have theirs, but the instructions said to wait in his Megane and they'd locate him and tap his driver-side window in gentle, friendly style. Cash for petrol used and a day's subsistence would be provided, without need of a signed receipt from Tom. The petrol and subsistence claim should be rounded up to the nearest £5 multiple, so there'd be no awkward fiddling about with coins.

They'd take a table in the service station eatery and organize snacks, or just tea or coffee. The car park would have CCTV, and to conduct their little conference inside the building like this was considered less noticeable than three men in a Megane evidently talking something important, notably not using any of the on-hand facilities, and passing money, even without coin complications.

'So, Tom, you'll ask: why are we here? What's the objective? Important to have an objective. Army orders always name an objective, and we can learn from them. In my opinion, that is. Well, it's like this, isn't it? You've been picked out as suitable for undercover – oh, but more than just suitable, outstandingly suitable ... yes, outstandingly. Terrific results from Hilston, and Hilston isn't known for its generosity in assessment. That's all taken care of, then – the general potential aptitude, the overall flair. No question it is there and ready for use. But for use how, where? This is what I mean by the objective. It's time for us to focus your talent – seek to apply it to a specific situation, namely the piss-awful situation that I and others have been confronted by on our patch for upwards of a year, an impregnable drugs firm.'

He introduced himself, while they walked from the Megane to the services restaurant, as Detective Inspector Howard Lambert. The smaller, physically slighter man with him he said was Mr Andrew Rockmain, a psychologist working mainly with the London Metropolitan police, but available to other forces if needed. He had the rank in the Met of Commander, more or less equivalent to Assistant Chief Constable in a provincial outfit. He'd be around thirty-five to forty. He had longish fair hair and wore a blue denim top with khaki cargo trousers and sandals, no socks.

Lambert said: 'Mr Rockmain is not like that Cracker character on TV, using psychology to solve mysteries. Mr Rockmain looks at situations and applies his special skills to say who'd be best to deal with them. Personnel selection of a very crucial kind.'

'I'm here mainly re the women, Tom,' Rockmain replied. He spoke almost apologetically, as if he thought Tom must have already cottoned on that Rockmain was here mainly re the women and didn't need to have it blatantly spelled out.

'Which women?' Tom said, though, naturally, he could make a guess.

'Yes, the women,' Rockmain replied. 'This can be a troublesome area. No point in denying. Rather, face up to it. Cater for it. That's happening now, thank God.'

They queued for food and drink. Lambert settled the whole bill. He said: 'Tom, your subsistence allowance is related to the time you spend on a duty, not on your actual expenditure, so the fact that I'm seeing to the tab now doesn't interfere with your right to claim. And, while we're talking about such arrangements, let me say a bank account with five grand cash available in your operational name will be set up, with cheques and a debit card. Likewise a credit card, limit nine thousand pounds.'

'Howard will look after you, Tom.' Now,

Rockmain's tone suggested Howard Lambert would be OK, possibly very OK, on the rudiments, such as canteen nose-bagging, general finance, and manipulation of an expenses sheet, but that he, Rockmain, would presently disclose the core purpose of this meeting.

Tom took sausages, mash and peas, with a large milk coffee. Lambert had shepherd's pie and a pot of tea. Rockmain went for the super-mixed-grill and a bottle of fizz-enhanced spring water from a burn in the Scottish highlands, which was pictured on the label. Rockmain led them to a table in the middle of the big room. He had short legs and took short steps, but they were vigorous and confident. Perhaps he thought skulking out on the edge would have been more conspicuous. He must have decided they should blend in. There were occupied tables all round them. He would know more about camouflage than Tom. It was part of his trade. The certainty and swiftness of Rockmain's choice seemed to confirm he dominated: what should be expected from a Commander.

Tom felt estranged and deeply different from the customers around them. Their imperative was to enjoy a bite and a swig, then point themselves and their vehicle again at a destination. But for Tom and the other two this was a policy-making centre, a tactics venue, the roads to and from, and the meals, secondary, if that. Now and then tonight Tom wished himself part of one of those groups: eat, drink and get motorwayed. He wasn't sure he saw himself as a policy maker, nor as a tactics expert.

Rockmain said: 'They'll have told you, Tom, how undercover is organized. You'll work to a handler and a controller. Howard here is your handler. Above him is the controller. You don't need to know who that is.'

'But he knows who *I* am,' Tom replied.

'He or she, yes.'

'I like the wariness in you, Tom,' Lambert said.

'Wariness is on the whole an attribute, Howie, an asset,' Rockmain said. 'It can become tiresome, though. It can drift into indecisiveness, or sluggishness.'

'Well, yes, I suppose,' Lambert said.

Rockmain carved one of two chops and lifted the chunk to his mouth. Tom wondered how he stayed so skinny, if he always ate like this. Perhaps he didn't: only when the job was paying. 'You'll ask how I come into the proceedings, Tom,' Rockmain said. 'Why more fucking psychology? You thought you'd done with all that at Hilston.' He spoke with terrific clarity, at the same time managing the meat in his mouth with a skill that might be inherited, congenital. 'And, to some extent, you *have* finished with psychology.'

'Which means I haven't, does it?' Tom said.

'This is more wariness,' Lambert stated, with a happy chuckle. 'A refusal to accept the superficial. I love it, Mr Rockmain. I'm sorry – I know there's a downside to wariness, which we should, as it were, be aware and wary of, but in Tom I see it as creative caution, if that's not a contradiction.'

'Some contradictions are extremely fruitful,' Rockmain replied. 'Paradox has been defined as "truth standing on its head to attract attention" – apparently contradictory, yet true. I'll admit that Tom's wariness does have a positive, encouraging side.'

'My view, certainly,' Lambert said. He poked at the shepherd's pie with his fork, seemed to find something he'd been prospecting for and ate it.

'What Hilston couldn't measure or investigate, Tom, was how well, or otherwise, you and your handler would suit each other,' Rockmain said. 'I'll be assessing that. They wouldn't know the handler, only the general role of handlers. It's quite a bond, you see, officer – handler, a bond nearly as strong as marriage; in fact, stronger than many marriages. Someone's life depends on this working bond: in the present case, yours, Tom.'

'I think I can say I feel such a bond between us forming already,' Lambert said. 'But, of course, I realize that Tom will view this unilateral statement from me so soon with a certain wariness, wariness being such a major element in Tom's make-up. I do not object to having this wariness directed towards me. It's a natural reaction by Tom, given his plain and bold leaning towards wariness, a leaning which I admire, and which is vital in the kind of work he will undertake. What, I ask, after all, is the opposite of wariness? Casualness? Naivety? Gullibility? These are hardly desirable qualities in an undercover officer.'

'There must always be full and constructive communication between the two, officer and handler,' Rockmain said. 'You must bring him your findings, obviously. They want to know about the structure of the Leo Percival Young firm, its money resources, its part in any deaths or injuries during turf wars. A complete profile as substantial aid to exposure and prosecution.

'On top of the bank accounts, Howard will be the one who supplies you with ready cash funds to buy drugs on a scale, Tom, that helps you at the start to get your entrance into the firm. He will also be the one who takes the purchased materials from you – mainly, I'd expect, coke, hash, crack, conceivably some H, skunk. Howard will collect such commodities and see to their due disposal. Now, these will not be nicely documented and detailed, account-book matters. There can be no record of monies or drugs that pass between the two of you. Hardly! Therefore, top in these transactions is trust.'

Tom always felt uneasy when offered too much alliteration. It might show the speaker was more interested in impact than meaning. Rockmain obviously liked a bit of pairing and tripling. Maybe psychology taught this helped direct a listener's mind. It didn't work on Tom, though. 'Your job is to judge whether we trust each other and can work together?' he asked.

Lambert said: 'I will know that if I can, as it were, survive Tom's initial wariness – a wariness I entirely sympathize with root and branch – if I can get past what we might call first base with him, then the trust will establish itself and must be the more valuable for not having been arrived at facilely. Facilely is not the way to achieve trust. As for trust in the other direction – my trust of Tom – this already burgeons *because* of that very wariness he exercises. It gives him stature, solidity, practical wisdom.'

'Yes, *part* of my job is to assess how you two will function – fuse,' Rockmain replied.

'You think you can foresee that?' Tom asked.

'It's tricky, perhaps, and vague, and packed with variables, but necessary,' Rockmain said. 'As is the sex aspect.'

'Which sex aspect?' But, yes, he could guess.

'This is going to put massive responsibilities on handlers like Howard,' Rockmain answered. 'Closure responsibilities.'

'Closure of what?' Tom said.

'Severance responsibilities. I mentioned the women earlier,' Rockmain replied.

'Which women?' Tom said.

'Rather late in the course of things, I fear, we have acknowledged – accepted – they have a genuine grievance which we should not ignore but try to deal considerately with.'

'Who have a genuine grievance?' Tom said.

'This is a decision that comes from at least the Association of Chief Police Officers, and possibly from higher still – the Ministry of Justice? It will settle new, subtle duties on handlers. In these extra, demanding tasks, Howard can call on me for advice and support. So, you'll see how the psychology element resurfaces.'

'What are we talking about, Mr Rockmain?' Tom asked.

'I expect you know,' Rockmain said, with a sudden, stop-pissing-around tone that seemed alien for someone in sandals.

'This will be another demonstration of Tom's wariness,' Lambert said. 'He demands definitions, transparency.'

'Above all we want you to feel assured, Tom, that any untidiness involving a woman or women connected to your time undercover will be managed in a careful, humane, understanding fashion,' Rockmain said. 'We do not want you to be burdened – badgered – during that time with anxieties about relations with a woman, women, who believe you to be other than you are. Obviously, you will have read of complaints by young protest-group females who consider themselves deceived in that way: giving it willingly to men they thought fellow members of the group, but discovering later that they'd been sleeping with the enemy – sleeping with undercover cops, some of them married and with children.

'A woman has a right to feel piqued if she's been putting out night after night deluded. The publicity from that kind of mix-up is not at all helpful, Tom. It makes undercover policing look unscrupulous and amoral, which, viewed from some angles, it is, of course. We don't wish to emphasize this, though. There have consequently been some important undercover procedures added to those already in force. You'll ask, which? A categorical ban on all undercover sex is patently impossible. The undercover officer has to establish a full and credible life in the firm, and this is almost certain to mean attachment, attachments, usually hetero.'

'You're telling me to shag around?' Tom said.

'I'm telling you that nothing should stop you behaving in character – in your assumed character, that is. I'm telling you, Tom, that when difficulties arise afterwards – *if* they do – they will be efficiently considered and coped with. We accept now that these women have a compensatable case. Financial grants may be made to them from a new, dedicated slush fund, referred to slangily, I'm afraid, as the "conned cunt caddy", conditional upon their agreement not to broadcast – broadcast in the widest sense – details of the affair, affairs.' He took a few mouthfuls of burn water. Then he said: 'I notice you frown, and all credit to you for it.'

'I would have expected frowning from Tom at this point,' Lambert said. 'He would argue, I think, that emotional damage cannot be adequately repaired by money – *mere* money, as it is sometimes dubbed. This is, yes, an admirable reaction. We all know that Beatles number that states "money can't buy me love", I'm sure. However, it will be my mission – and the mission, no doubt, of other handlers around the country, with the aid of inner soul experts like you, Mr Rockmain – to convince these women that the romancing was not a heartless or flippant act, acts, by the officer, but a necessary and valued part of his facade; and to convince them also that acceptance of an honorarium, running into four figures most likely, for this service and their buttoned lip in no way reflects disparagingly on the women and is not in any degree to be confused with payment to a whore *post hoc.*'

Rockmain said: 'Naturally, we are aware that the proposed doling out of currency to excuse what these women regard as fleshly exploitation might seem cold and mercenary. Perhaps an insult, even. Handlers such as Howie will have to shape their healing approach very subtly, very delicately. It will not be a rushed matter, and I'll be ready with specialist support for him at every stage of the challenging negotiations. I should be able to judge the state of the woman's, women's, mind, minds, from what Howard tells me, and suggest detailed techniques, distinct and custom-made, individually fashioned, for each and every dupee concerned, thus assuring progress. So, you see, Tom, the potential situation, situations has, have, been very thoroughly reviewed and measures made ready. You may – must – use every means to protect your substitute identity. You can do this certain that all possible subsequent problems will be properly, generously, humanely resolved.'

Tom dealt with the remains of his meal. 'We'll be away,' Lambert said. 'Best not leave together.'

'But we came in together,' Tom said.

'There's that fine argumentativeness again – refusal to take any statement or proposal glibly!' Lambert said. He offered a congratulatory chuckle. '"Glibly" is not a word to be associated with Tom. I believe much has been accomplished this evening. Accord? In-depth mutual understanding?' With a gentle movement of his arm, as though about to stroke a kitten, he put three fifties flat on the table near Tom's empty coffee beaker. 'This OK for fuel and, so to speak, grub?' he said. 'You'll see that, as per guidance, it's been rounded up to multiples of five.'

The details of this procedure baffled Tom. He had not seen Lambert take the fifties from his pocket or a wallet. It was almost like a conjuror suddenly producing something out of nowhere: next, a rabbit? And the notes lay uncreased on the Formica surface, not crumpled as they would surely have been if concealed for a while in Lambert's fist, waiting for the moment. Tom admired Lambert's deftness. Perhaps he had done the same sort of handover often before and perfected a method. It would have appeared blatant and clumsy to fish the notes from inside his jacket or from a bill-holder. Ungraceful. Vulgar. No wonder they called these officers 'handlers'.

Rockmain and Lambert stood. Rockmain leaned over the table to talk reasonably quietly to Tom. Rockmain said: 'These women, protesting about false provenance pricks trapezing up and down their skiters, were probably bullied into making a fucks-fuss by some libertarian pressure cell. Such groups proliferate. It's an industry, Tom. But clearly, we have to take very serious and authentically respectful notice, ho-ho, while also ensuring as far as we can that the safety of undercover lads like you, Tom, and – even more vital – the future of undercover itself, are suitably preserved. To that end the women may be offered a silencer sum, a gagging *douceur*, by wad not traceable cheque, obviously, the fee quite possibly deserved and inevitable, given the flagrantly enlightened and sodding fair-play notions that dog us non-stop these days.'

He and Lambert left, Rockmain ahead again, frail looking and boyish from behind, his sandals probably making a fast, flip-flap clacking on the caff carpet as he headed for the exit stairs. Tom finished eating and picked up the money. And, harvesting those three fifties from among the used crockery, Tom felt real satisfaction. Of course, he examined the notes separately and carefully. Each was new and looked brilliant, untrammelled and full of hearty promise, in splendid contrast to all this low-caste fodder debris. He could see the silver strip running through all, and the darker areas, a bit like piano keys. Near the Queen's face glinted a rose and a medallion. These notes could not be more genuine. They were exemplary. The Queen would be proud to get her picture on such notes. Shops would take them OK. Pubs maybe not, especially if they'd been caught out by fakes earlier. No matter.

But it wasn't so much the money itself that pleased Tom. His attitude to it – this was what delighted him. The amount hugely and plainly exceeded his petrol costs getting here. Evidently, it came from an account subject to only the vaguest kind of auditing, if that. Although he'd bought none of the food and drink, Lambert told him to claim just the same. These fifties, and the unquestioning way Tom accepted them, showed he was seamlessly moving into a new kind of life. This thrilled him. It was on a par with his appreciation of Lambert's graceful finger-magic with the fifties.

At Hilston Manor there'd been psychology seminars aimed at helping future undercover people get used to grey-area thinking, authorized criminality, furtiveness, corner-cutting, consciencelessness, in the interests of the greater eventual good. Wasn't it lovely to be freed from tedious regard for regulations and exactitudes? Collecting the fifties as a routine entitlement proved, didn't it, that he had sound and slinky undercover potential? Hilston had said the same, but it was heartening to see himself, in an actual situation, automatically applying what he'd learned there. He even began wondering for a couple of seconds why Lambert couldn't have rounded up the sum by fifties not fives and made it £200. Tom recalled a film, *Wall Street*, and the professional principles of its villain-hero, Gordon Gekko: 'Greed, for lack of a better word, is good.' But maybe the lack of a better word could be remedied. How about: 'Greed is natural?' 'Greed is a career-builder?' 'Greed is necessary?'

On the drive home, he decided he'd give the fifties to Iris as a fall-back fund to pay for Steve's birthday present and celebration, in case Tom were unable to get time off to come home. Maybe the three of them, Steve, Laura and Iris, could go out for a Chinese meal. Putting the money towards a happy family occasion would prove – prove to himself – that nothing smelly and off-colour soiled the hundred and fifty, nothing to taint Steve's special day. Money was money, nuff said. Tom might have drawn it from the bank. In fact, he wouldn't have drawn the cash in fifties but in twenties and tens, because they could be more easily managed and didn't get hassle in shops. But that was a quibble. Tom needed to demonstrate – demonstrate to himself, as before – yes, demonstrate the basic ordinariness of these notes, the normality of piping them positively aboard.

But as he turned into their road and saw the house, some of its lights shining out from the sitting room bay window, saw also the clipped, boxy outline in the darkness of the front garden privet hedge, the radiantly correct recycle bin for tomorrow's collection on the pavement, the shallow, cubbyhole porch, he dropped those previous ideas about use of the Howie windfall. This domestic vignette was what ordinary, normal items really looked like, surely. Perhaps something dubious about the cash threesome did exist, something he didn't want his son linked to, even in the most roundabout, oblique way.

Also, he thought Iris would be puzzled by the arrangement and wonder where the fifties came from. She knew Tom didn't usually get his cash in forgery-prone, half-ton chunks, and she'd regard them as symbolic in some fashion of the changes taking place, unhealthily symbolic. *He* regarded them as symbolic himself, didn't he, though not altogether unhealthily symbolic? Iris would think he already planned not to be home for Steve's birthday.

It turned out that while he'd been at the meeting with Rockmain and Lambert, she'd Googled 'Undercover Policing' and downloaded some material, mostly American. 'A remarkable amount of it is about looking after the safety of the undercover officer,' she said.

'That's good, isn't it?' he said.

'In a way it's good, yes. But the fact it's treated as so important must mean there are big risks,' she said. 'Pages of precautions. And justification of close relationships.'

He could tell she'd struggled to speak about that last item. He preferred to ignore it. 'Yes, they're risks that have been recognized, faced up to, and can therefore be countered,' he replied.

'"Therefore." That sounds very neat and optimistic, Tom,' she said. 'QED, like those geometry problems we used to do at school.'

'The people who actually control and run undercover are learning, adapting, improving all the time.'

'Because the risks are always there and getting worse?' she said.

Tom couldn't work out whether she worried more about his safety than she did about the women an undercover officer might feel compelled to familiarize himself with as part of his cover; or the reverse.

'Listen to this, Tom,' she replied and read from a piece of A4: '"There are officers who have an unexplainable flair for picking out villains, and, likewise, some villains have an unexplainable flair for picking out undercover spies."'

'We're trained to defeat that type of flair,' he said.

She looked at the sheet of paper again. 'It says undercover officers can give themselves away by too much liveliness in their eyes. Druggies' eyes look blank. How could they train you not to have lively eyes? Think dull? Think desperate? Think cold turkey?'

TEN

AFTER

At around midday following the first film-show Maud said they should have a break and gave Harpur and Iles further documents, statements and Press cuttings, then led them to a small conference room. It had several easy chairs and a long oak table. A buffet lunch with a bottle of claret, a bottle of Sauvignon, a jug of tap water, cutlery, glasses, plates and a corkscrew were laid out there. 'Please read the material, help yourselves to a meal, veggie, meat or fish, yogurt desserts, and perhaps we could reassemble at half three in the cinema,' she said. 'Early afternoon I'm spoken for – have to interview a Chief Constable and kick him in the scrote for lassitude bordering on torpor.'

'It could be any one of ten,' Iles said. 'Torpor would be brilliant progress in at least three of them.'

'Won't take me more than an hour,' Maud replied.

And it obviously didn't. The new, three-thirty session opened with a picture on the screen of what Harpur assumed to be the edge of Mitre Park, where the Volvo and career Wheels, Jamie Meldon-Luce, would have waited. As well as actual driving talent, and the skills and electronic tool-kit to crack any car's security, a Wheels should know how to hang on and hang on for a latecomer; know how to make sure loyalty, solidarity and patience blocked out panic. This was a situationer photograph only, taken in the daytime and with no parked Volvo or any other vehicle present. The houses in the background looked markedly unshabby. Harpur came quite close to sympathizing with the residents' rattiness at having their otherwise dandy road routinely picked for back-seat affirmations at night, with condom litter. Harpur liked suburbia – its general spruceness, customary peace and absence of starving dog packs – but he did understand that it cost a lot to run a car, and some folk thought it should earn its keep by more than only motoring. And, yes, Iles himself did like multi-purpose cars.

Maud, in the front row again, turned to address Harpur and Iles squarely. She'd quickly learned some manners and knew now it was unwise to treat Iles like a caddy, throwing words back at him and Harpur and not bothering to look their way. She said: 'So what we have, according to Wolsey, is Martin Abidan and Ivor scampering to the Volvo because Abidan fears massive retaliation from Scray's gang within the gang and wants to hop it while hopping it is an option.

The hunter might get hunted. Classic upending. Or that's what Abidan tells Wolsey. Although Ivor considers this a pretty feeble and confused analysis, he believes it's how Abidan genuinely feels. Since Abidan's in charge of the operation, Wolsey must go with him, although he knows Empathy is liable to nerviness now and then.

'They reach the Volvo and Abidan orders Jamie to exit pronto, according to the agreed drill. But, it's *not* according to the agreed drill, is it? Tom Parry hasn't shown yet. Wheels also has heard of Abidan's occasional frailty. Jamie seems to believe fear of Scray's troop within a troop has poisoned Abidan's guts and judgement. Meldon-Luce decides he can't accept a command based on funk. Maybe he's seen a rerun of *The Caine Mutiny* lately on the movie channel, or even read the book, where jittery orders by the captain are ignored. To obey Empathy would run against Jamie's deepest instincts and on-the-job training. He's determined that Tom Parry, as they know him, is not left behind to be savaged and destroyed on his own by Scray and Scray stalwarts. I gather Jamie has a thug neck and upper body. Despite this, he is nobly gallant and old-style honourable, the cardie man.'

'I can see Abidan's thinking,' Harpur said.

'I told you Col has flairs, Maud,' Iles said.

'Adiban considers that if they get away fast there's nothing to link him or anyone in the firm with the building-site trap for Tom,' Harpur said. 'He realizes the area will buzz with police as soon as the killing's discovered, especially as Tom's handler and controller know the victim was an embedded cop and may disclose that now. So, Abidan reasons, do a swift bunk.'

'But he doesn't have to reason, does he, Col?' Iles said, in a mild, greasy tone, as if explaining something to a slow-witted child. 'That would be the set plan from the outset: mock up the targeting of Scray to get Tom to a suitably terminal spot, then scarper. Job done. Reasoning's redundant. Scray's irrelevant. Scray's a pretext, to be dealt with, sure, and possibly eliminated, but at some other time. Only Mart Abidan of the Volvo party knows this, though. The other two believe they're in a sudden, unexpected crisis, because Empathy was spotted on Scray's trail; and Scray might return with big, backup defensive-offensive firepower. Jamie considers Tom could have been delayed somehow, and those imperishable Wheels ethics say you don't ditch a mate, leave him wheel-less, while there's still a chance he or she might show, as scenarioed. There was no chance, but that's hindsight, and although a Wheels on the job has a rear-view mirror he hasn't any hindsight.'

'Abidan sails near to telling them they're wrong – wrong, that is, because he's never given them enough truth to be right,' Maud replied. 'Wolsey says Abidan shouted, "He's not coming, I tell you," meaning Tom. "He's not coming. Never." The witness, Marchant, also heard these words, though too far away to see who spoke them. Ivor reports that Abidan sounded totally certain Tom would not appear, even though Empathy had supposedly mobiled him to abandon the Scray search and go straight to the Volvo for strategic withdrawal.

'And, of course, Abidan *was* totally certain Tom would not appear, supposing the building-site murder went OK: we think he had a "Done" text from the site. But Jamie couldn't swallow this display of certainty from Abidan. He gets out of the Volvo and says he'll go to find Tom on foot, like, "Oh, where is my wandering boy tonight?" He's no longer Wheels within wheels. If it's a success they'll call a taxi: Wheels hires wheels, instead. He urges Abidan to replace him in the Volvo and drive away, meaning, without saying it, because Jamie's such a thorough gent, "Vamoose, Emp. Save your precious fucking poltroon skin. Oh, and, incidentally, Ivor's skin as well."'

'It *is* a kind of mutiny,' Harpur said. 'The chauffeur's giving commands.'

'And the commands add up to, "Get lost, you shit-faced wreck,"' Maud said.

'Harpur doesn't mind foul language from middle-class, educated women,' Iles said. 'He sees it as part of emancipation. They – you, Maud – should be allowed to talk like gutter-snipes. Think how feeble that statement would be if you had to say "faecesed-faced wreck", despite the alliteration.'

98

'It looks as though Abidan could smell the contempt in Jamie's words, and they push him towards a kind of assertive frenzy,' Maud replied. 'But he's still set on getting out. Maybe he'd been cast-iron briefed by bossman Leo Young to quit the area fast, dodging any connection with the murder. So, anyway, Abidan does what Jamie suggested. He takes the wheel. Wolsey's with him in the passenger seat.'

'And the assertive frenzy reaches the driving?' Harpur asked.

'It's as if what Jamie Meldon-Luce said to him makes Empathy loathe his own behaviour – abandoning a mate. There's still a touch of loyalty and courage in Abidan.'

'*Apparently* abandoning a mate,' Harpur said. 'The mate's dead.'

'Apparently abandoning, yes,' she said. 'But Jamie's scorn hurts, just the same. So Empathy drives in a flashy, risk-taking, derring-do, foolhardy style to prove he's no craven creep. He's proving it only to Wolsey, because Jamie's been left behind doing the on-hoof, selfless bit, and Empathy doesn't really need to prove it to himself because he knows, of course, that this seeming withdrawal from the Scray chase is preschemed tactics, not cowardice. I think he prized Wolsey's good opinion, longed to maintain it. Ivor is someone who by will and determination changed himself from a firearms failure into a wonderful marksman. This was outstanding mental robustness. And paragon

Ivor mustn't be allowed to think he's present at an entire collapse of will and determination in Martin Abidan, a top man in the firm and supposed to offer leadership.

'You'll have seen from the additional, over-lunch papers that Wolsey says he was yelling at Empathy to cut speed. This would most likely gratify Mart, given his state of mind. He'd imagine he appeared dauntless, indomitable. Ivor Wolsey's shouting was probably before the accident. Maybe after that he wants to speed an exit as much as Abidan does. Conceivably, Wolsey would have been shocked into silence.'

'The car wholly out of control for those minutes?' Harpur said.

'As you'll have read, some witnesses thought a driver's heart attack. You'll have read, too, that the Volvo mounted the pavement at what might be over sixty miles per hour and smashed into the three girls from behind – three young women, out on the town and walking towards the *Panach*é club: two killed instantly, the other wheel-chaired and near blind for life. One bystander thought the hit deliberate, didn't he – the Volvo aimed specifically at the three, as if a vengeance attack? That was obviously not so, but it shows how horrific the bump looked. Abidan doesn't stop – daren't stop – but gets back on to the road and makes for the switch vehicle. They reach there without more trouble and do the change.'

Maud brought another situationer picture on to

the screen, Pallindone Lane, the swap location, though now without the Volvo and Ford Focus. 'There are witnesses to this car shuffle, also, as you'll know. The front of the Volvo is damaged and marked, headlights bloodied. It's conspicuous – has obviously been involved in something bad. People watching the move from one car to the other would be on to the police at once. Wolsey doesn't say so, but there may have been a tussle about who'll drive the Ford. That would get added attention from people in the street. Alternatively, Abidan might have been played out, exhausted by then, and so did what Wolsey told him to do: quit the driving seat. Anyway, the nine nine nine calls would have gone out, and a couple of squad cars stop the Ford only a few miles away. Abidan and Wolsey are arrested, Wolsey driving.'

Harpur said: 'The trial transcript, as I read it, doesn't make any connection with the building-site murder.'

'There *is* no connection, Col,' Iles said, in that same sickeningly helpful voice. 'Not that that's known to anyone but Abidan and, presumably, his master, and they don't talk.'

'Wolsey's statement figures in the trial and so does he, of course, as one of the accused,' Maud replied. 'But the statement only says they in- tended to kill Scray. They didn't kill him or make an attempt to, so the statement counts for not much. It might sound like big talk bullshit. The trial is about other deaths and injuries, isn't it, *actual* death and injuries – the three clubbing girls? It's about criminally mad driving and manslaughter, two stolen vehicles, unlicensed firearms carried by the occupants, failure to stop after an accident. There's a note to the judge, most probably, mentioning Wolsey's cooperation. But he gets only a year less than Abidan, and that's not on account of his cooperation, but because he wasn't driving when the girls were struck. Some of the media pointed out the apparent coincidence that this clash happened on the same evening as the building-site murder, but they can't go beyond that – nothing explicit. They don't know any more, not in a usable form.'

'Who does?' Harpur said.

'That's why you're here, isn't it?' Maud said. 'And will soon be there – to find the links.'

'This Chief you were hammering earlier – does he run the patch we're due to visit?' Iles said.

'I thought you might ask that,' Maud said.

'And?' Iles replied.

'As you pointed out, it could have been any one of ten,' Maud said. 'Civil Service rules prohibit me from disclosing the names of those warned or disciplined about their work.'

'God, Col, we're being entertained by a fucking jobsworth,' Iles said. 'Didn't I tell you what the Home Office was like?'

'That Wolsey,' Harpur replied. 'He seemed to have transformed himself into something he wasn't by nature, but when the stress gets too much it's he whose personality and morale crumble. He loses his strength and confidence and turns blabbing fink. The real, primitive, unalloyed self is always there, dormant, maybe, but ever ready to make a comeback.'

'You mean the id?' Maud asked.

'That kind of thing,' Harpur said.

'The ego makes us try to shape the id so it can cope with the world outside. Wolsey wills himself to love guns, or seem to, wills himself to get good with them, because that's the kind of milieu he lives in – the reality he has to cope with,' Maud said. 'But ultimately the id will always win against the ego. What's bred in the bone won't come out in the wash.'

'Along those lines,' Harpur replied.

'When he's not leching, Harpur often does a bit on the psychiatry side,' Iles said. 'Don't imagine he'd be a complete dick at that, merely because of the yokel appearance.'

Maud gave a bemused sort of smile. 'Naturally, I looked into Colin's circumstances as soon as I heard you were taking him on this job,' she replied. 'I hadn't had your explanation then, of course, Desmond. You're a one-parent family, Colin, aren't you? Megan, your wife, victim of a terrible murder? I believe Hazel, your elder daughter, is only fifteen. Is it proper – indeed, is it legal? – for you to leave her and the younger girl alone in the Arthur Street house for what might be quite lengthy spells during this operation?'

'My sister – divorced, no kids – will move in while I'm away,' Harpur said. 'We've had this arrangement several times before because of the job. Hazel and Jill get on well with her, luckily.'

'Plus Harpur has something substantial and deeply non-Platonic going with an undergraduate at the university up the road from where he lives,' Iles said. 'Modules: lit, langs and engineering drawing. An all-rounder. I expect she'll call on the girls now and then.'

'This would be Denise Prior?' Maud asked. 'College lacrosse and swimming teams.'

'She's not much more than a child herself, but, of course, that wouldn't stop Col,' Iles said. 'Stop him? Hardly. The opposite.'

'She doesn't live at Arthur Street permanently, though, does she?' Maud said. 'She has a student room in Jonson Court. Sleeps at Arthur Street only off and on.'

'Much more on than off,' Iles said. '"Cohabitation" is her second name.'

'And it would be only when Colin was there, wouldn't it?' Maud said.

Iles said: 'That's Jonson without an h – Ben, the plays and poems, not Dr Sam, the dictionary. Ben's often commemorated. I'm reading a novel set late nineteenth century where one of the boys is in Jonson House at his boarding school.'

'And getting buggered in standard fashion,' Maud said. *The Children's Book*, by Byatt.'

'I adore scholarly talk,' Harpur said. 'Have

you and Mr Iles rehearsed this?'

'Yes, Harpur can turn envious of an education and grow sarcastic and bitter, poor sod. I don't know what her parents think of their daughter running a relationship with someone like him,' the ACC said. 'As I understand it, they're quite decent people now, though students themselves in the 1960s, that freed-up, pill-gifted, wild time.'

'You made a play at one stage for Hazel, I'm told, under-age or not, Desmond,' Maud said. 'Didn't you flourish a glamorous crimson scarf?'

'Mr and Mrs Prior are from the Midlands area,' Iles replied. 'I expect they have grand hopes for their daughter. Does that mean Harpur will show some compunction and restraint? I don't think so. "Unbridled." Is that the word for him and his tendencies? If you can think of a better one, Maud, text me with it, would you? The classics have a grand range of nicely graded terms for degeneracy. How I'd hate to be unjust to Col!'

'You're afraid of him, Desmond, aren't you?' Maud replied. 'Scared of his good sense and solidity, plus an ability to pull women. Why you keep trying to put him down. It's become an obsession with you, a kind of mental palsy.'

Iles took a couple of seconds to mull this. Then he said, 'There might be something in that.' Astonishingly, the Assistant Chief would occasionally listen to criticism, accept it, without a brain-storm or lip foam. She must have impressed him. 'Do you feel pulled, Maud? Am I in the way?' he asked.

'Who am I to tell an ACC he's in the way?' she replied.

'You're Maud,' Iles said. 'You're the Home Office. That's your job – to treat me like an obstruction.'

'No. We've selected you for a very tricky assignment because we think you can do it – with Colin, of course.'

'Oh, of course,' Iles said. 'But you didn't know I'd pick him.'

'I hoped you would,' she said.

'You *do* feel pulled,' Iles replied.

'I'm in a relationship already,' she said. 'And so is Colin, as you've just explained,' she said.

'That kind of thing doesn't worry, Col, as I've also explained. He could fit you in,' Iles said.

She looked hard at Harpur for a moment but then seemed deliberately to get the conversation back to work topics.

ELEVEN

AFTER

Maud said: 'From the documents, you'll have noted two motoring sequences. Ultimately, of course, we have the Volvo. It ferries the supposed assassination group. It waits at the park. There's a dispute about stay or go. It goes, though without the designated driver; a panic-merchant, instead. Then on the pavement it runs down the three roistering girls, killing two, gets back on to the road and speeds to a vehicle switch.

'But there's also an earlier car trip: a disciplinary excursion aimed at a comparatively low-caste member of the firm, Claud Norman Rice, address, twenty-seven Delbert Avenue. Not the Volvo. We're pretty sure Tom was present for this prior bit of motoring. He might actually have driven the punishment party to and from this pre-Volvo assignment. Jamie Meldon-Luce, the usual Wheels, couldn't make it. Tom took them to Delbert Avenue and brought them back. The point about Wheels was, he had to be present when his daughter, Carol Jane Letitia

Meldon-Luce, aged eight, played Mary Magdalene in a church mini-drama for kids and parents. Jamie's strong on family, and, I understand, feels fairly OK about churches.

'It's true, Tom never mentioned this Rice episode in advance to Howard Lambert, his handler. You'd think something potentially so major would figure in one of their chats. We're talking about projected severe injuries, at least. But, no, Tom doesn't make mention. You won't find any account from Lambert of such a meeting. Or at least Lambert *says* Tom didn't speak of it. That might be Lambert looking after himself. If he knew of the intended sortie, perhaps he thought he should have done something to prevent it. It's one of those customary horrible dilemmas in undercover work – pounce now, make one or two arrests, prevent a crime, or wait for the bigger moment, and bigger prey, the recognized objective. Have a glance at a book called *Black Mass*, about the way the FBI in America allegedly let South Boston gang chief James "Whitey" Bulger commit all kinds of deep villainy because he gave them information about other gangs. Incidentally, he's been located in California lately and charged.

'A Rice beating up would never get officially reported to the police. He'd rely on paracetamol, first aid and nursing from friends. Perhaps there'd even be a tame, gorgeously-well-paid doctor around. Rice wouldn't want the police brought into things. That's not how matters are handled in the gangs, is it? They deal with the situation privately.'

Iles crooned with feeling and unsoftly, in fact, little short of a bellow, an updated version of the 1930s' song 'Marta': 'Omertà, rambling rose of the wildwood; Omertà, with your shtum code malign.'

Maud said: 'Yep. So we're guessing a bit, presuming a bit. Tom had been back to Hilston to get kitted out with a car. I've seen their records for that. He could hardly use his own vehicle when working his way into the firm. They'd be routinely suspicious of him, wouldn't they? All right, he's from another police outfit, not local and not recognized, but they'd be routinely suspicious of *anyone* new, and on guard non-stop against possible infiltration. There's been so much publicity about under-cover that all criminal outfits are *qui viving*. Most likely the firm has a paid voice inside the Licensing Authority who could do a check on his registration and come up with a name and address – Tom's real name and address. Not good. That's only one step away from a visit to neighbours and discovery he's a cop; confirma-tion he's a cop. "Oh, yes, Sergeant Tom Mallen and his family live there. Why do you ask?" They'd ask because they wanted to expose a snoop, but they wouldn't say that.

'For the Hilston BMW, though, we could arrange for a number plate tied to Thomas Derek Parry, born twenty-seventh of April 1974, and living at the time of registration in West Ham, London. The actual address was a big, old multi-flatted house where there'd be continual occupant changes, making a trace of some ex-resident more or less impossible. Hilston gave him a familiarizing pack on the district, including, of course, popular drug-pushing spots, to help Tom manufacture a recent background scene in case of questions. It would be reasonably credible that he'd forgotten to, or neglected to, inform the Authority of a new address.

'We think Tom chauffeured the people who'd been instructed to clobber Rice. Hilston did consider a location bug for the BMW so its whereabouts would be always known and logged and fast-aided in case of trouble. But this idea was ditched because in any vetting of Tom by the firm they'd search the vehicle as a basic ploy and find his seven/twenty-four little telltale. From your points of view, Desmond, Colin, what you might wish to establish is whether Tom's behaviour on the Rice operation produced doubts of his genuineness. You've heard of that call in some US jails – "Dead man walking" – when a prisoner's on his early morning, manacled way to the topping parlour. Was this Rice episode "dead man driving" for Tom – the start of progress towards wipeout on the building site, though it wouldn't actually come for months ahead? This could have been the first test of his genuineness. Would he seem sufficiently eager as they neared Delbert Avenue?

The driving would be a comparatively un-demanding job, at a remove from the actual hammering: no blood or screams for pity, no deep involvement. It might be as far as Tom wanted to go. Was the Rice jaunt a giveaway for him?'

'But even if that's so, what makes you believe the subsequent wipeout was done by a police officer, officers?' Harpur asked.

'I'm suggesting a direction your inquiries might take,' Maud said.

'Why do you choose that direction, though?' Harpur said. 'What's the evidence?'

'There are several directions you'll want to follow. I'm nominating one, that's all,' Maud said.

'Why though?' Harpur asked. He knew he sounded like the third degree, maybe on account of the cinema setting: old films on TV some-times showed US detectives bullying a suspect like this. Also, he realized some vanity came into it. She'd shown interest in him. He wanted to demonstrate he was worth taking an interest in. He'd like to appear wise and dogged.

Iles half-helped in that unique half-helping, half-savage style he sometimes assumed. 'Col sticks at things,' the ACC said. 'He'd hate to hear police officers bad-mouthed, especially by someone in this particular governmental sty, the Home Office. He's police through and through himself, though, of course, that doesn't mean he'd hesitate about debauching the wife of a superior in the force, often using disgracefully untoward places, including the shrub section of a garden centre on a busy Saturday afternoon.' The ACC's voice climbed with ease to, say, three times the already loud volume of his adjusted Arthur Tracy theme number, 'Marta', just now. Harpur remembered hearing the song when a child, performed emotionally by one of his uncles, but with the proper words, concerning love and loss.

Maud turned very quickly and changed the screen picture. 'This is Rice's place,' she replied. It's a semi in what looks like a quiet, ordinary, petit-bourgeois street.

Iles leaned forward to get a closer view. He smiled with true, gratified warmth. 'I love Victorian-style coloured glass patterns in a front door, don't you, Maud: the dark, slumbering reds, the pale green tendrils, the turquoises and ochres?' he said at normal pitch; at droolingly affectionate pitch. Harpur reckoned that if mood swings hadn't existed before Iles he would have invented them. 'Thank heaven the door pane wasn't damaged on their visit,' he said.

'The beating wasn't scheduled to take place here, of course. They'd meant to motor him into the country. He lived alone at present while his partner, Cornelius, finished a jail sentence at Long Lartin, so there'd be no nuisance third-party present. But his next doors might have heard the sudden evening boisterousness and yelps through a shared wall. We think this foray wasn't just about Rice himself, a ranker only. He worked to Justin Scray, his appointed line manager, and became, also, part of the firm within a firm. This would be a warning to Justin Scray, sort of: "You're next for something even rougher, Justin, dear, unless you stop pissing about with an elite private customer list." Scray was still an eminence in the firm, not much below Leo Percival Young himself, we believe. Leo might not have wanted to get extreme with Scray at that stage and make him an all-out enemy. In contrast, Rice didn't matter much. He could be used as a frightener, his wounds red badges of punishment, and very visible and pithy, as badges always are. But, of course, as you'll have read, nothing about this operation went as it should have.'

Harpur said: 'I've been hearing a lot about red badges lately.'

TWELVE

BEFORE

If they decided to kill, you had to go along with it.

And even more so when it was only a beating up, definitely not quite a murder despite the possible thoroughness and force of the hammering. Tom saw that from the law aspect this must be a fair bit less serious than an outright death, and involvement in it – either actually helping, or as passive spectator – not so morally disturbing for him, surely.

Willingness to take part in some hefty crime could be used as a test by gang members if they suspected they had a spy in their outfit. The ethics of this type of situation had been talked about and talked about and talked about at Hilston, without producing much clarity, though. Impossible. The underlying, immovable problem remained: much undercover work required a law officer – a disguised law officer – to behave as though he/she operated *above* the law and could ignore and flout it. Identities were split. Years of behaving one way, and of being intensively trained one way, must be chucked, forgotten. Villain values took over. They had to be applied with full commitment and obvious – very obvious, very concocted, very convincing – enthusiasm.

No wonder undercover gave some officers long-lasting psychological trouble, took them down the road that might even lead ultimately to schizophrenia. Tom felt a bit dodgy himself, occasionally. There had been cases where ex-undercover detectives sued their police author-ity for not warning them about the permanent personality damage that might come from this work. Some officers with bad reactions were pensioned off as sick – 'hurt on duty'. This didn't mean physically injured in some gang war. It meant mind stress. It meant deep con-fusion at a switch to career crookedness. Yes, Tom did feel a bit dodgy himself occasionally, or oftener.

Yet this episode had begun almost comically – quaintly, at any rate...

THIRTEEN

BEFORE

'I'll be wanting you to use a van for this, Tom – a special van, a van with unnatural talents, you could say. This *seems* a very ordinary van but it's got brilliant observation items in the rear. Oh, yes. In red paint on each side is ACME LAWN AND GARDEN SERVICES, and at the top joining point of each pair of open legs of them eight capital As is a very useful hole. Pardon me, Tom, if that sounds fucking crude and anatomical, and altogether too much of a good thing. It's a trick to make them little windows not noticeable because they're at what is referred to as the apex of the As – just lurking there, for observing through without being observed. You heard of a judas hole in a door so you can see who's out there before you open? Like that, only there's eight of them.

'There being four As on each side of the van, you can move about for your squints and watch a truly wide stretch. A panorama? Would that be the term? You're in there casting an eye through them capital A facilities, left, right, distant,

116

close, up, down, and nobody knows. Think of one of them German U-boat submarines in the last war, concealed under the ocean, its periscope up but part hidden by waves and the captain watching a convoy and deciding which ship to hit. Same for us. To people outside it's just a van with a name starting with one of them As so as to be high in the phone book list and get noticed due to the alphabet. They think the driver and maybe passengers are at work in one of the backyards nearby tidying up a rockery or spreading beneficial mulch.

'Leave your BMW with us, Tom, and we'll give it a top-class service while you're absent on this important jaunt. When the spy job in the van is finished I might want you for something else, but then using your own car, so it got to be just right and prime. Ariadne, our motors lady, will get it up to super-perfect, plugs, points, suspension, the lot! She lives under bonnets, hair bunned tight at the back so it don't dangle into brake fluid etcetera, which would be of no advantage to anyone.

'The thing is, Tom, Jamie and the Volvo might not be available for this future trundle. He got some churchy thing on. He's like that, not all the time but intermittent,' Leo Percival Young said. 'If it was one of the others in the firm I'd tell him, "The church can go stuff itself. Your stipend here is bigger than the archbishop's so I want you on call, not idling in some holy pew trying to look mild and godly." But this is Jamie, and Jamie I got to offer max respect to, haven't I, Tom?'

Leo gave a shrug, but not a shrug meaning casualness, a shrug and slight hunching up and lip bite that meant he blamed himself for being stupid and shouldn't have said what he'd just said. 'But you wouldn't know about Jamie's role, would you? You're new. You haven't caught up on the firm's history yet. I'll explain: Jamie and me – well we've seen off a lot of trouble together. It could be described as "a mutuality" if you're familiar with that word. It's like support both ways – me to him and him to me. That's mutuality – taking, giving. Very much so. I mean years. I mean the long, hard march towards present comfiness via good profitability. Things like that don't happen without a lot of work, Tom – it's not just luck. Difficult bastards have to be smashed and walked over and on, the bastards. They got to learn they're fucking blockages and have to be cleared. Jamie was always there as reinforcement. He seems quiet and a piety fan sometimes, but just put a Browning in his hand and you'll note a difference. This sort of completes his wardrobe.

'All right, he buys them sodding rest-home cardigans and sometimes – you got to believe this – sometimes he'll wear moccasin style brown shoes, bold as you like, as if it was normal. Well, moccasins *was* normal – for Red Indians. But he don't come to work on a mustang. We got to put up with kinks of Jamie's sort for the sake of what he can do, though – the driving mainly, yes, but other aspects such as laundering our cash intake with no filthy, nosy, intelligent awkwardnesses from the law or the Revenue, and steaming his way around an accounts book. Jiggery-pokery – he can spot it in just a glance at a cash column. Instant, like a holy revelation. Figures talk to him. They got their own lingo and Jamie knows it fluent.

'You can see him have a little smile or a pout at what they're telling him – saying that things are going super-great, or that someone's not playing right, someone's doing a shameless percentage of rotten skimming and personal pocketing. Me and you, if we looked at them figures, they'd be just figures. We can count OK, yes, and do the multiplication tables up to sevens or eights, but we don't hear the tune them figures are playing – their deep message, that holiness of communication I just referred to. They might tell us a tale eventual, but it would be very eventual, maybe too late eventual, the damage having been done. We'd have to ponder, maybe spend an hour with the calculator. Jamie? It's like what's known as an "instinct" with him. Precious, Tom. Consider a hare in a field and he sees a greyhound coming. That hare knows from instincts he better get sprinting off. This is built in with the hare. It's an instinct. Jamie's like that with numbers. All right, he can get a bit independent at times, which might be a fucking full-scale pain, but that's another of them factors we got to accept on account of his knacks.

'Of course, it was Jamie who gave me the pointer that leads to this – leads to you in the ACME van doing a peep session on our behalf. The van's got a commode for extended duty. This is important. Didn't that wrong shooting of the Brazilian boy up in London happen because one of the surveillance went for at least a piss? When God planned the human body and its ways, he didn't give all that much thought to excretory problems during a big stretch of surveillance. You won't get any of that in the book of Genesis. People in them early days was mostly in the desert where such difficulties never cropped up owing to plenty of sand dunes where it was possible at all times to have a crouch or just a stand-up.

'This commode is bolted to the side of the van, so it won't go sliding about and tipping over, slopping over, when you're cornering, say, creating unpleasantness. Ariadne, plus a power hose, would clean it up, yes, but fortunately that won't ever be necessary. Also, Thermos flasks in a little rack. You should fill them with tea or coffee or soup before you start in case it's a long stretch watching. This has got to be run like military. The flasks are super-flasks and will keep stuff warm, or cold, for at least twenty hours.'

'Detailed planning is always important,' Tom

said.

'Detailed planning *is*,' Leo replied. He sounded joyful. 'It's because I knew you would share the thought that I picked you for this task.'

'Thanks.'

'You're new, as I've said, but I got that impression of you. Instant. This ability is referred to as "man management flair". Many would say I possess it, so I'm not just being boastful. I get a sort of *feeling* when someone seems so right – and when someone seems so wrong, naturally. The *flair* is the valuable bit of the feeling, but it's the *management* bit that tells me how to make the difference between yes and no, isn't it, between right and wrong? Think of a great piano player, Tom. It's his or her flair that provides all the emotion when he or she's into an Albert Hall gig, but it's the management side of him or her that makes sure he or she don't keep banging the wrong notes and fucking it all up, with booing and fruit from the audience. I get this feeling re you Tom – the *right* feeling, but not just feeling, management judgement, too.'

'Thanks.' Tom wondered whether it all meant he was accepted now as one of the firm. Parts of what Leo said delighted him. It sounded as if Tom would land a mission to handle solo – the ACME project. This was trust. This was integration. And then another assignment later because Jamie might not be around, but bunking off to church. Equality with Jamie in Leo's opinion – definitely a plus. So, Leo and the rest of the leadership had faith in him to cope OK with whatever these operations were, did they? So – to go more basic than that – they believed in him altogether now, as the latest entrant to the firm, did they? 'You're new,' Leo had said. That meant Tom was in, didn't it – all right, newly in, but in. "New" suggested a context for him to be new in, a setting, and this context and the setting was the firm, wasn't it? That programme of buy, buy more, then buy more still, had worked, had convinced all round.

However, 'Leave your BMW, Tom.' This piece of the briefing he didn't care for so much. It was spoken by Leo as offhand, routine, of no great significance. But that could be a ploy. Was Tom being sent off somewhere in this commodious van so they could give the BMW a total frisk, hunting a trace bug and/or eavesdropping bug, and anything else that might hint where Tom came from, who he was, besides Tom Parry?

'Yes, you're new, Tom, so I got to explain the structure of the firm, its sinews and ligaments, we might say, comparing it to the human frame. We've just been discussing the body as to excretion, but now I'm using it as what's known as a metaphor – but probably I don't have to tell you that. A metaphor for comparing the way the body's put together with the way a firm is, or this firm, anyway. Such as we speak of the "head" of a firm, being myself, but it's also got other resemblances.'

L.P. Young lived in a converted and extended Victorian farmhouse, Midhurst, on a hillside overlooking the city and beyond to the sea. He had invited Tom there. They sat in brown leather easy chairs facing each other drinking tea in what Young referred to as the drawing room. It looked out on to a gravelled yard in front of the house and, to its right, several outbuildings in stone. Young had made the tea himself. He said his wife had gone into town for a meeting of the museum committee, which she was chair of for a two-year stint. 'Really ancient things, she loves them, Tom, understands them.'

'Known as heritage,' Tom said.

'She's familiar with all aspects of it. Mention the word "time" to her or "centuries" and she'll immediately see ramifications and can discuss them straight off.'

'Museums can tell us much about ourselves.' Tom felt it vital to go along with the half-baked nature of this conversation. It suggested geniality and friendship, beyond mere business concerns.

'Cavemen, for instance, and their early drawings of behemoths on the stone,' Leo said. 'They needed something sharp and strong to do that with, otherwise they would have had to give up and we'd have no idea of behemoths. A museum can show us them hard tools that made the behemoth pictures possible.'

'It's a mark of high civilization in a society that it's interested in its distant past,' Tom said.

'This is a trading firm, Tom,' Leo replied, 'the trade being in what are known as "recreational commodities", or to put it simpler, gear. Well, that's obvious.' He crossed to a fine rosewood antique bureau. He took a rolled ordnance survey map of the city from one of the drawers and spread it on the flap of the bureau. Tom stood and went to join him looking down at it. Leo put a hand vertical, resting on the length of his little finger, at the centre, marking a division. 'Think of my hand as like the late Berlin Wall. To the left of this, the west of the city, is our territory, Tom, our sphere, if you know that term.' He turned his hand flat and rested his palm on the left half to show possession, to show command, to show achievement in the spots where he and Jamie had smashed difficult bastards and walked over and on them, the bastards, teaching them what blockages they really were and the need to clear them.

'Things are not so clear to the right, the east – there are battles between outfits there all the time as slices of ground are claimed by this one or that one or that one, how things used to be about Czechoslovakia in Hitler times. It's messy. It's primitive and wasteful. AK 47s, machetes, torchings, a disgusting fucking absence of what is known as decorum, Tom, meaning in good order. Some of that might be necessary at the start when building a firm and getting rid of the bastards who might be a fucking blockage, I admit, but this goes on and goes on. However, what we got on the west is nice and settled and brilliantly civic now. Look around the west and you won't see one site where a property has been arsonized.' He let the map roll itself up and returned it to the drawer. They went to sit in their chairs again.

'This area – the west of the city – is a lot of ground, Tom, with a selection of all sorts. I mean different classes of people, different *grades* of people – that kind of thing. I don't want to be snobby, but it's got to be admitted the population of these isles, the GB isles, can be very mixed. There are men and women out there who don't have no idea what "decorum" even means. That wouldn't include you, Tom, I'm sure.

'So, I've tried to divide our parish up into, like, sections. Three sections. I give them names. There's Section Arabella, called after my dear mother, God rest her soul, a woman worthy of remembrance, which all who knew her would admit without even minor hesitation. It's the north of our ground, an area gracing her: streets broad and tree-lined, very clean, Sealyhams on leads, detached properties, that kind of thing. The centre I think of as Montgomery Section, reminding of that great soldier in the Second World War, taking the Jerry surrender in a tent on a heath, very crisp and victorious. The south is Millennium Section, to mark how time moves on constant and demanding, bringing change, which Emily will confirm. For instance, it can't be BC no longer but is very AD, because, of course, you couldn't refer to a time as BC until you was into AD. BC people didn't know they was BC, because there wasn't no C.'

'All these area names have quite a ring to them, a resonance,' Tom replied.

'What I aimed for. You've hit it – resonance. That's what I mean, you see, Tom.'

'What, Leo?'

'This feeling I get of rightness – when someone *is* right, that is. That word "resonance", it's not a word I would come up with spontaneous, although I know about it, and when I hear it from you I realize it's the exact word for it. This is two minds in a kind of harmony.' Then he spoke slowly, weightily, intoning like an awards ceremony, or the runner's names announced at a greyhound track: 'Arabella, Montgomery, Millennium: yes, resonance.'

'These three words take strength from each other and, spoken together, become a sort of impressive chant, or a bold drum roll,' Tom declared. It was necessary.

'Here, again, metaphors. This is more mutuality,' Leo said. 'The three helping each other towards a grand effect.'

'Certainly.'

'Now, each of these sections has its own staff and its own local chieftain. This is what's known in the commercial scene's terminology as "delegation". That's to say, I give them the power to look after their particular district and make sure that region of the business hits target or even better.'

'Many companies function like that. They have their headquarters where the chairman and chief executive work, and then branches maybe all over the country or even the world, each with its own head man or woman,' Tom stated.

'The same with the police,' Leo replied.

'Well, yes.'

'In London, the Commissioner – top man. And then in all the boroughs, as the sections are called there, other top men or women in charge of their area. They are the top man or woman in that particular region but not as much a top man or woman as the Commissioner.'

'Or Rupert Murdoch and his empire.' Tom could have done without this mention of the police, but thought he kept his face reasonably blank, reasonably non-panicked. He'd wanted to get off that topic, though.

'Murdoch, yes. He's the boss of bosses, but sometimes things can go wrong with one of them lower level execs. Think of the *News of the World*, Tom, or, more vulgar, *News of the Screws* – its collapse. Now, the thing is, you see, I've got trouble with a local manager, too. This is in Arabella.'

'North section?'

'It's always a danger with delegation. You can get let down. They are supposed to work on behalf of you, but, of course, they are not you yourself as such, and they might drift off in a foully selfish mode. As my dad used to tell us, "If you want a job done right, do it yourself."'

'Murdoch himself had to come to Britain to try to sort it all out.'

'This is not to do with phone hacking but serious matters for the business. Action's got to be took, Tom. A priority.'

'I'd trust your judgement on that.'

'There's a lad called Scray, Justin Paul Scray, controlling things in Arabella for me,' Leo Young replied. 'We done a lot of research on him, and Scray seems to be his real name, although I never heard of any Scrays before. Martin Abidan said the family might of been immigrants way back – that's centuries, not now – from some country where Scray was quite a usual name, such as Germany or Mongolia. Scray could mean a carpenter or a blacksmith in one of them places, the way we have names such as Carpenter and Smith. People can't be blamed for their names.' Leo paused. Then he snarled: 'I mentioned he's controlling things for me in Arabella. I want to pull that statement back. I think he's controlling things, but controlling *some* of the things, and most likely the juiciest things, for himself, the bastard, not for the firm.

'Or not the firm as you and me think of the firm, Tom. No, his own sort of splinter firm. Basically, that's what your trip in the van is all about. And if you're in the back, Tom, scanning, and a local who's seen the ACME LAWN AND

GARDEN SERVICES words comes, like, inquiring to the driver's cabin because he wants help with wisteria on a pergola, that kind of thing, you just got to stay quiet and not seen until he goes away. We don't need no complications. This is a delicate campaign.'

'You want me to take the van to Arabella?'

'This is a district recalling memories of my mother, so my anger at Scray's behaviour is greater than if it was in Montgomery or Millennium. It's an insult to her, a considerable disrespect. But, no. Though Arabella is where the problem starts – to Justin Scray's mighty shame, he knows it's named after my mother – yes, it's where the problem starts but not where we deal with it at this junction.'

'Too head-on?'

'Too hasty, Tom. Not enough info, not enough research.'

'You're very careful, Leo. Scrupulous.'

'That's another of them perfect words that shows you grasp a situation although new to the firm.'

'Scrupulous. Measured.'

'In this kind of vocation we got to be. This is not like, say, being a doctor or a colonel where there are rules of the game such as the oath where doctors promise to do what they can in surgery hours to keep people alive. We don't have an oath like that. How could we? People in this type of career got to work out for theirselves how to stay alive, perhaps with help from bodyguards if the expense is not too much: someone to get between you and the bullets for a good fee. We have to supply our own rules for the profession, and one of these says we should have proper, thorough info before turning against a member of the firm, especially if that member had enough going for him previous to get him to number three. I mentioned doctors. If a doctor's going to get struck off, as they call it, because he been dicking patients as part of the treatment, there has to be proper info from the women before he can get kicked out. Them patients must prove penetration on a consulting room couch with unnecessary removal of under-garments – unnecessary from the medical aspect, that is. It's got some other purpose, i.e., the penetration while people out in the waiting room have to hang about. The details are different but we must prove absolutely re Scray and his carry-on in the firm – that is, *in* the firm and *not* in the firm.'

'I hadn't thought of it like that, the medical side of it.'

'Scray's got two kinds of customers, we think. One kind, the ordinary punters. We know about them and the sort of money to the nearest K they spend with the firm through Scray. They're in the accounts and all obvious and normal. The stuff they get is OK, but only just OK because it's not much quality to start with, and then it gets a load of makeweight mix.

'But – and this is the but of fucking buts, Tom

– but we think Scray's also got another kind of punter. This other is for his private use. This other is most probably your richer, smarter set. Way back they probably used to think nostrils was for breathing through, but now they've found this extra, snorting use. They can afford to spend big and therefore get the very best stuff, and gladly cough up tidy money for it.'

'Which Jamie can't find in the accounts?'

Leo gasped then chuckled. 'You got it, Tom. You got it right away. But why am I surprised? I should of known you would. Didn't I say I had that feeling about you? Didn't I mention this mysterious flair for man management? I don't expect no special praise for that. It's just there, inside me, that's all, the way some are born with music seeping out of theirselves even at a very young age, such as a composer called Wolfgang Amadeus Mozart. The way you ask about the accounts is another bit of evidence that I picked correct in your case, Tom. You can see where this story is going. Good! But I want you to think about what it means if Jamie can't find no sign of these on-the-side deals in the Arabella accounts.'

'But how do you know the extra, personal deals are being done if they're not in the accounts?'

'That's a wise question, Tom. One I would expect from you. Although you didn't realize we have to make our own professional rules, you're quick on other aspects.'

'You and Jamie think Scray's doing secret transactions?' Tom asked.

'But *how* does he do them, Tom?'

'On the quiet somewhere.'

'I'm not talking about location,' Leo replied. 'I'm talking about the wherewithal, if you know *that* word, too.' A sort of schoolroom atmosphere had taken over, Leo the gentle, patient, gobby teacher, but a clued-up teacher.

'Which wherewithal?' Tom said.

'How does he get this extra, elite-quality stuff?' Leo replied.

'He diverts a proportion of what he's supplied with by you, by the firm – that is, the firm proper – and diverts it to his own racket.'

Leo smiled tolerantly at the blazing stupidity of this, never mind Tom's other smart aptitudes. 'But that would be obvious in the accounts, wouldn't it, Tom? We know how much stuff he's been issued with, and we know how much it ought to produce in takings. There has to be a nice relationship.'

'And the accounts don't show a shortfall?'

'The Arabella accounts are absolutely OK,' Leo said. 'On the face of it they're a grand and wholesome tribute to my mother, as she well deserves.'

'But Jamie sees something wrong?'

'Jamie does.' Leo Young waited. He smiled with extreme kindness, giving Tom a chance to suggest an answer unaided, as a good teacher would.

Tom shook his head. 'This is almost super-natural. I'm stymied.'

'What he sees as wrong, Tom, is that the Arabella accounts are *too* absolutely fucking OK. They're what's known as immaculate. That's a word with quite an impact in the religious area, but it's got other meanings, too, like kosher. Scray's accounts don't show no dips or surges, they're just steady.'

'Is that bad?'

'And why are they so steady?' Leo replied. 'Because Scray don't want no special attention aimed at his trading. He'd hate an investigation of Arabella. He wouldn't know where it might go, such as more than one direction. He'd like to tell us through Arabella's accounts that every-thing is normal and regular and worthy, as a memorial to my mother, who he's aware is eternally precious to me. But in this business, Tom, things are hardly ever normal and regular. This is not like being a greengrocer or a baker. There's ups and downs, very big ups and downs. That's what's normal in this trade. That's what's regular – not being regular is regular. Our busi-ness has what's known as "variables". These variables can come from all directions, some-times lapping into one another like waves on a beach, sometimes staying separate. Perhaps you could tell me what some of them variables might be.' Again that lovely, encouraging smile from Leo.

'Well, economic conditions,' Tom said. 'These

could affect what punters have to spend. If someone's out of work, there'll be less disposable income. Now. The recession. Why burglaries are increasing, it said on TV.' He hastily stuck the television reference on in case he sounded like a cop well-up on burglary stats.

'Right.' Leo lifted both hands and did a moment of imitation clapping. 'And another variable?'

'The cost of the original commodity, depending on plentifulness or scarcity.'

'Right. Another?' He didn't persist with the silent applause.

'Some drugs can go in and out of fashion, such as coke. No explanation for it. You mentioned nostrils. They've sort of come into their own during the last decade. Many in the professional world consider a line and a sniff one of life's major enhancements currently.'

'Right. Another?'

'Trouble in the source country, Colombia? Politics. War. Weather. Cargo intercepts at sea.'

'Right. Another?'

'I can't think of any more.'

'Here's one: the amount of police activity around selling points,' Leo said. 'Or other kinds of police attacks on the profession. Dealers and punters might have to lie low if there's a purity campaign, which can happen now and then, sort of: "Clean up the world and start here!!" This could last anything up to a fortnight. Some think purity's got a lot going for it.'

'Right,' Tom said.

'The point of all this is accounts will show signs of these changes in the situation, these variables, won't they, Tom? Or *should* show signs.'

'Right.'

'So, then, we ask: why is Justin Scray trying to lull us with his absolutely constant Arabella accounts, although them variables are always going to be part of the business and bound to show theirselves in accounts?'

'Tactics, you think?'

'Tactics I fucking *know*, Tom. The answer's got to be, he's trading on the side and confidential. What we got with him is a bad case of a firm within the firm, as it's described. The figures for that secret corner of his commerce would give the dips and surges – such being how a real list is. It don't just flatline for ever. But, of course, we don't see them accounts, because that trade is not supposed to exist. Jamie thinks there might be so much profit from the hidden list that Scray can top up any slippage in the ordinary business – the business we *do* see the accounts of – so everything looks sweet and there won't be no questions about how things are going in Arabella, no questions at all aimed at Justin.'

'But if he's running an extra list, a special list, he'd have to get a supply of more stuff, wouldn't he? You say he can't use some of the gear that comes to him routinely from the firm.'

Leo laughed full out this time. 'You've got it again, Tom. There'll be certain snags and gaps to your understanding, which is only natural, you being new. But the main matter you can see. You realize the factors straight off. Yes, he's got to get a supply from someone else, or the accounts here would scupper him. This is why the trip in the van is important, the ACME project.'

'Oh? The van?'

'Justin Scray – as I said, he's not a nobody in this organization, Tom. Number three, after self and Mart Abidan. It means I can't move against him without some decent proof he's playing things dirty. There's sort of honour involved. If I don't give respect to his rank it means I should never of let him get to number three – a bad mistake by me. He's got many a good aspect that I can't ignore, don't *want* to ignore because it would be a sort of denial of leadership judgement. Therefore, the van.'

'In which respect, Leo?'

'Where d'you think I got the idea for this van, Tom?' Leo replied.

'There's a film called *The Conversation*. Gene Hackman. Harrison Ford. It comes up on the movie channel. It has an important van at the beginning.'

Leo struck the arm of his chair a right whack with his fist. 'You're there ahead of me yet again, Tom.'

'It's a van full of equipment for trying to

record a target couple speaking in the park outside. One-way windows.'

'Surveillance. It's a surveillance van. Our van is not so hi-tech as that, but the same aim – to ascertain info without it being known that the info is getting ascertained. This is necessary in case surprise action will be the result of ascertaining this info, without that being known by the people it's ascertained from.'

'What kind of info are we trying to ascertain?' Tom replied.

'We're looking for a link.'

'What kind of link?'

'The link between Justin and another wholesale supplier, different from ours. If we get that, we know he's into private trading, don't we? He'll have far more of the commodities in store than he'll have taken from me, from us. Then we can act. It won't matter he've been number three. That has become only a sentimental thought now. He's trying to fool and rip off the firm, and the firm says, "Right, we got to smash the bastard." The firm's got a moral duty to look after itself and smash the bastard because he is a blockage in the way of company progress and got to be cleared out of the way. Consider my responsibilities, Tom – people in the firm with mortgages, and/or paying alimony, and/or financing their women's fashion, and/or coping with their kids' fees at Oxford or in seminaries. I must keep this firm efficient. You heard the saying *"noblesse oblige"* at all, meaning the top dog got responsibilities not only privileges? Me – I'm the top dog.'

'We watch some bulk supplier's place through the A-holes?' Tom asked. 'But how do we know *which* supplier?'

'Jamie's got an idea re that. This is another thing with Jamie, besides the driving and the accounts. He got considerable knowledge of the scene. He can focus on what's likely.'

'It's a guess?'

'It's a Jamie guess, which is not really only a guess at all, it's inspiration, it's knowledge. He's like them people with a twig who can tell from the way the twig jumps where there's water below.'

'A diviner? A dowser?'

'Obviously, Jamie don't do it with a jumping twig, but the same sort of very mysterious power, weird power. A sort of sensing. Either Scray himself or one of his Arabella staff, such as Claud Norman Rice, might turn up to collect the extras. I got photos of both for you. They was taken unknown by the two of them so they're not like posed portraits, but they'll do. You can identify from them.'

'But won't Scray and Rice recognize the van?' Tom said.

'It's kept here, in the stables block. We don't bring it out except for a particular role, such as this. It's a long time since I had it used, most probably before them two joined. Scray and Rice have never seen it, to my knowledge, or heard of it. In any case, the ACME name is new. Previous, it used to be A1 CARPETS AND CURTAINS done in black not red. Same number of As for the holes. Every so often I get it changed. It's easy. I don't believe everyone realizes how many words got A in them, Tom, such as SPECIAL CLEANING AND LAUNDRY SERVICES, or PAUL'S PIZZAS AND SAVOURY PIES.'

'I heard of someone who wrote a book with no Es in it, but never with no As. We might not have a word like "abundant" if As weren't abundant and able to provide two.'

'Very true. It's not just the *number* of As that got to be right, but they should be spaced out, giving a wide vision, which is why A1 CARPETS AND CURTAINS was great, with the As there from the start and nearly at the end in CURTAINS. But it's not a clever idea to keep the same name too long. Things get noticed. We put a phone number with the name, but, of course, that don't lead nowhere.' Leo went into a sing-song, bitchy voice: '"The number you have dialled has not been recognized. Please check and try again." Of course it hasn't been recognized because it don't fucking exist. So, anyway, they do try again, and get the same rigmarole. But, look, Tom, we don't have to make do with talking about the van. We'll go and see it, shall we?' He stood. 'I'll give you a little tour.'

Tom got up, too, and they went outside, the

gravel rasping and crackling under their shoes.

Leo smiled again. He seemed very fulfilled. He gazed down at the ground and spoke a kind of fond congratulations: 'That's the way decent gravel *ought* to sound, Tom. Hasn't it been silent under the sea for quite a while, such as the kind of aeons Emily deals with? If you know that term, aeons, Tom – meaning ages – lying there quiet in storms and doldrums-calms, slowly getting turned into gravel from rocks, most probably. But now it has a chance to sound off and let people know it's there, dredged and spread on a driveway, dealing very businesslike with feet, so mud won't get walked into the house, and having also a fine look and sound to it.'

FOURTEEN

The outbuildings seemed to have been re-roofed in genuine slate and generally restored. Leo pointed at the heavy double-doors of what was obviously once a large barn. 'Emily's swimming pool,' Leo said. 'We had filtration problems, but Ariadne fixed that. Her swimming is very dear to Emily – crawl, butterfly, backstroke, you name it. Talking of nostrils, water up her nose? She don't care. And she can duck-dive for a coin on the bottom in the deep end. It's not easy to pick up a ten-p piece like that, because of the flatness of the pool bottom and another flatness, the ten-p's flatness, being there flat, lying on the pool's flatness. She'll get a fingernail under it, though, while non-breathing, and bring it to the surface without hardly a gasp at all. This is quality. It's not that we need the ten-p, but salvaging it is a skill. Consider that together with the important museum post and you'll see she's an all-round person.'

He opened the door to the next building. Horses occupied two stalls. A Mini, a large, this-year's registration, black Mercedes, an Audi coupé, and the van were parked alongside them. Young unlocked the van's rear doors and they climbed in. 'You can get familiar with them A-holes now,' Leo said. He spoke with pride and true affection. Tom tried both sides, pressing his face hard against the metal of all the apertures to get intimacy and prove enthusiasm. This man, Leo Percival Young, believed in him – didn't he? didn't he? – and Tom felt that, in return, he should act appreciative – more than appreciative – thrilled, yes act *thrilled* by Leo's workaday toy. Tom was in the firm – he *was* in – wasn't he? wasn't he? – to collect facts fit for a prose-cution about the scale, shape, methods, accounts of Leo's business. That didn't mean, though, that Tom must never show a little politeness and supposed mateyness along the way, especially as the politeness and supposed mateyness might help with Tom's only real purpose: to get Leo and a handful of Leo's people crushed by the law, he, Tom, being an emblem of the law; the only emblem of the law at present nosing about inside Leo's company.

'Good?' Leo asked as Tom stood enjoying the narrow view through the ACME A, up towards one of the horses.

'Excellent.'

'Multi-angled outlook?'

'Panopticon.'

Leo flipped a lid back. It gave a grand, re-assuring sound of real wood against real wood.

'The commode,' he said. 'Quite a large bowl, which can be removed and emptied when an operation ends. Vigil duration no problem in view of this bowl.'

Tom had to agree it brought dignity to spying. 'Right,' he said.

Leo pointed to another fitting on a van wall. 'Here are the Thermos flasks. An array, so you can get variety.' He pointed down. 'Beneath them, folded away for now, are several plastic-on-metal-frame beach chairs roped to a side strut to stop them moving about when you're driving.'

'What does Emily think about the van with this made-up name and bogus phone number on it?' Tom replied. 'Would she ever ring and get that "has not been recognized" formula you mentioned? Doesn't she find it strange that you accommodate in your stables a vehicle apparently belonging to a company she knows nothing about and which suddenly and frequently changes its name? Has she ever noticed the glut of As and the holes at the top of them?'

'These are more fine questions, all of them, and there is quite a grouping, Tom, and so much in tune with your character, as I judge it. But Emily's very sensible. Practical. She knows money don't drop from heaven like them bread rolls in the Bible.'

'Manna.'

'God looked after the Israelites, and good on Him for this, although some would ask why

He'd let starvation nearly finish them before that. In any case, *we* got to look after ourselves. This is an undodgable duty. We all got this responsibility. That's my thinking.'

'Existentialism.'

'That sort of thing. I'd ask you to consider bin Laden's wife, one of them.'

'Does she come into this van side of things?'

'She said his business was not her business, so she didn't ask any questions. Emily realizes this van is here for a purpose.'

'Well, yes, Leo, but...'

'You don't get to head a museum committee if your thinking's dim and flimsy,' Leo replied. 'They're handling a big budget, buying in ancient jewellery, paintings and sculptures, tools, old chinaware from many a country, valuable artefacts, if you know that term, meaning items from history. This is capability, Tom. This is someone who's learned fast what life is re, and who knows how to blank off certain aspects and how to stay silent when that's best. Plus, she looks after them two mounts more or less solo in term time when the boys are away at their prep school. We're thinking of Charterhouse for them next, though Emily's also keen on Winchester. She says the town of Winchester used to be the capital of old England when London hadn't really got going at all. This is the sort of thing museum people know. Toss a coin to see which school? Or would that seem flippant for such a major matter as education?'

'Do you all ride?'

'Definitely. We love it – for instance, the weather in your face on a canter, and the power of the animal under you, directed, controlled by only a couple of thin strips of leather. Have you ever thought of that, Tom? It's a picture of human power over beasts, fragile looking, yet effective. We discuss such topics, Emily and me, when we're out together in the saddle, the horses taking a breather, walking after the canter.'

'This is interesting,' Tom said. It was the best he could come up with. He felt almost smothered by guff. He said it pretty matter-of-fact, no heavy, fascinated trill laid on, otherwise it would sound like sarcasm – apparently admiration, but really piss-taking words that stood in for the true meaning, which amounted, approximately, to, 'Fuck off, Leo, you verbose, anti-grammatical cunt.' Their whole conversation was possibly as it seemed – or its total opposite. All that shit about his instant sense of Tom's total, organic OKness could be genuinely what Leo felt: another case of his brilliance at personnel selection. Alleged brilliance.

Alternatively, this endless, go-nowhere waffle might be a lulling exercise, a screen, a trap, a frightening, malevolent game; and Tom's delight at being handed a couple of jobs just naivety, perhaps lunacy. But, of course, he must get into the lulling game himself. He had to react as though relations between him and Leo

145

were developing happily and at a pace – at a canter, maybe – and as though Tom's only aim was gloriously to justify Leo's immediate and deep trust in him. Alleged, again. This was how undercover worked. The officer had to create trustworthiness out of falsity, and to keep an eternal watch in case the people around him gave little, accidental signs that they didn't trust his trustworthiness and had glimpsed glints of his bogusness.

Leo always dressed formally and was in a dark grey single breasted suit, including waistcoat, white shirt with buttoned down collar, and unvivid striped tie, light blue on a dark blue background. He wore nicely polished black lace-up shoes. Tom felt certain that when Leo went riding he would also have all the right accessories, fine quality jodhpurs, no question and a possible cravat. He was short, about five foot five, his head and face too small even for that kind of frame.

It was an unscarred face which could have been genial. But his features lacked sufficient room and looked cluttered, crammed into a paltry space and competing with one another for position, like too many survivors in a lifeboat. Possibly Leo's cheeks were economized on in the womb – his mother might have smoked when pregnant – and although, of course, they'd extended as he went into adulthood, they had not extended enough to catch up with normal cheeks for someone of forty-two, according to the dossier. It didn't seem the sort of appearance you should have if discussing humanity's clear superiority to animals while out riding one with Emily.

Although Leo's face missed coherence, Tom could imagine it as frightening enough if he decided you were a bastard menacing his firm and the mortgages, alimony, fashion costs and/or Oxford and seminary fees of his people. It was a face that could probably do cold condemnation, and, when it did, the close, uneasy bunching of features might make things worse, as if they'd grouped together to give a combined insult, like a mob. Leo had fair, wavy hair worn longish and a tiny, Hitler-style moustache, but also fair. Possibly, he realized that a big moustache on such a limited surface would look as if it was taking him over and had already started eating his cheeks, the way ivy could dig in and spread on a house frontage.

'Tom, I don't want nothing but a sighting – Scray or one of his team, most likely Rice, calling at the wholesaler's place and coming away with stuff. Describe it. Name. Clothing. Time. Date. Method of collection. Vehicle used. Registration. That's enough. It's an evidential matter. Yes, evidential. I don't know if you've met that term before. I need the evidence so I can move justly, fairly, unavoidably against them. The procedure has to be correct. You carry a Browning, don't you?'

'It's a reliable piece. The army use it. And

Jamie.'

'No argument. Take it with you, if you like – I'm not going to come between a man and his armament. Your morale might be tied up with that gun, and morale is vital.'

'There's inspector Harry Callahan in *Dirty Harry* and his love of the Magnum.'

'Some people don't operate properly unless they can feel a recognized, comforting metal shape against their skin,' Leo replied. 'But this will not be a shooting trip, not at this junction, even though you might get angry seeing Scray, or a sub for Scray, betray the firm in such sickening fashion. What you do, Tom, is observe and report all you see to myself or Mart. Then we'll decide on the required response, possibly a cleansing response. Oh, yes, almost for certain, that.'

They climbed out of the van, and Leo locked it. Then they walked back to the house. Leo spoke some more about riding and mentioned how upset he, also, would have been to wake up in the morning and find the chopped-off head of one of his horses in bed with him, like the film producer in *The Godfather*. Tom said it would come as a definite shock, though he realized this was a dud sort of comment.

FIFTEEN

When he got the van in place for his surveillance job he found it was the A-hole in the AND of ACME LAWN AND GARDEN SERVICES on the passenger side that gave him the best view of the entrance to the target building. He had the ACME LAWN AND GARDEN SERVICES lettering clear in his memory and could there-fore work out inside that it was the AND A by counting along until he came to the fourth hole. In addition, the LAWN A – the third – was quite useful for the approach road. Tom could see why Leo felt pride in the van and its tactically punc-tured As. Obviously, As on the driver's side couldn't be applied here, but would have been if he'd arrived in the parking spot from the oppo-site direction. Quite a bit of thinking and skill had gone into this van. It was equipped for many possibilities. It recognized that life, vision fields and street geography were complex but could be managed given skill and plenty of As.

He had been in position for only half an hour when through the LAWN A he saw Claud

Norman Rice arrive in a red Lexus and pull in. Tom spoke its number into his pocket recorder. Rice took a lightweight suitcase on castors from the boot and pulled it behind him by the telescopic handle as he entered the building. Tom had to move now from the LAWN A to the AND A. There was a decisiveness about Rice, as if he knew he'd get a happy welcome. The suitcase was almost certainly empty. Rice would pay in cash and he'd probably have it in his pockets and/or a bumbag on his waist belt, bundles of twenties mainly. The case would be for the purchases and return journey. Its covering was done in a tartan design, which Tom thought suggested unexceptional, innocent travel, to tourist spots like Crete or Florida. Clever.

As Leo had promised, identification of Rice now was simple. There'd been four pictures of him to look at when Tom and he came back to the drawing room after their stables visit at Leo's home yesterday. No, the photos were not perfect but clear enough. There were also five of Scray and a couple of this apartment block where the wholesaler and his family lived. Jamie's information and/or intuition had turned out accurate again, as Leo had forecast. The pictures showed Rice as slight with cropped dark hair. He looked about twenty-seven. He might have been a jockey or a featherweight boxer, though an unmarked one. His face was slightly gaunt, bordering on anorexic. 'Here's the best,' Leo had said, holding up a more or less full length photograph of Rice, a profile shot but still closer to a head-on likeness than any of the others. He seemed to be laughing at something, his thin lips pulled well back. Good small teeth.

Viewed now through the AND A, not as a picture, Rice looked cheerful enough, but not dozey-cheerful, not on-a-trip-cheerful. He was obviously alert, and his eyes did a street inventory while he took the case from the boot. That survey included quite a stare at the van. The intensity of this inspection made Tom automatically step back, as if his eye might be spotted in the AND A aperture. Leo claimed that neither Rice nor Scray had ever seen the van. They might have heard of it, though. Leo didn't control gossip in the firm. Possibly Rice had a suspicion of all parked vans. He might have seen *The Conversation.*

Tom set up one of the chairs alongside the AND A hole and waited and watched. He realized, of course, that he was a spy twice over. He apparently worked for Leo and had been ordered to get the dirt on Scray or Rice. He actually worked for his masters and mistresses in the police, his chief mission to get the dirt on Leo. This address, and the procedure here, would figure in one of Tom's undercover reports. While showing Tom the photographs yesterday, Leo had said that Jamie gave the apartment number as sixteen, on the first floor, rented in the name of Robert H. Cochrane. In one of the photographs, a couple of windows had been circled by a highlighting yellow pen. 'That's it,' Leo had said, pointing. He seemed to consider explaining more about the apartment, but just then his wife returned from duties in the museum committee. Tom had heard the rich splutter of her tyres over the excellent, formerly low-profile gravel. Leo must have picked up the sound a moment earlier and at once put the building photograph back with the others, placed them all in the bureau, and rolled down the lid. 'I don't ever rub her nose in it,' he said.

'In what?'

'The intricacies.'

'Of?'

'The trade. Do you have that trouble, Tom?'

'Which?'

'Making our kind of profession acceptable to a wife, a partner.'

'Well, yes it can be tricky,' Tom had said. And how.

'They know about it, live on it, *Vogue*-clothe themselves on it, smart-shoe themselves on it, status themselves on it, but there needn't be too much definition of what it actually is. That would disturb and even upset them. The detail – they don't want to be bothered with it. Too ... well ... too detailed, too itemized. No reason to show Emily that we might have to do something robust about Scray or Rice, or more likely both the bastards, on account of non-stop treachery. That word "robust" is around quite a bit lately. I don't know if you've run into it at all, Tom. It's one of them words that can sound strong and all right, but might also cover something else. Well, in fact, "robust" means fucking severe and thorough, maybe final. Ah, here's Emily. How did it go, darling? Meet a new member of the team, Tom Parry.'

He stood up from his easy chair. They shook hands. She gave a little frown of concentration. 'Don't I know that name? *Sir* Thomas Parry. Founder-head of the National Library of Wales.'

'Oh, you museum people and similar!' Leo had said with a good laugh. Anyone could see he felt proud of her knowing not just about Wales but a fucking *library* in Wales.

'Not me,' Tom said. And he could have said: 'Not *that* Tom Parry, and not *any* Tom Parry.' He felt himself disappearing up his own aliases. It was like one of those mirror on mirror shots, but in his case mirror shots of nobody.

'Sort of introducing Tom to the ways of the company,' Leo had said.

'I hope you'll be very happy with us, Tom.' She was tall, smart in an above the knee blue dress, not a power-suit, dark-haired, full of go, possibly a year or two older than Leo. Yes, she probably needed Leo's loot to keep up this classy presence. 'You asked about the meeting, love. Tolerable, just. We managed to achieve a couple of decisions – to do with halberds and stuffed wolves for the "Europe Once Upon A Time" exhibition. I'll make some fresh tea, shall I?' she asked and went out to the kitchen.

'When I say "robust", Tom, I don't mean I want you to do anything in that line on this excursion. I'm repeating the instruction because I must have it properly understood.'

'Yes, I do understand.'

'People can cut loose, become manic when presented with a situation. You'll be in a situation there, outside number sixteen. Stay outside. No reason to enter the building. Ours is a properly run firm, Tom, with good business standards – for the kind of business it is. I hope that's the main idea you take away from here today. It's *because* it's a properly run firm that we might have to neutralize people like Justin Scray and Norman Rice.'

'Neutralize?'

'It's another interesting word around, in the sense of, take the fuckers apart. That kind of thing. Their activities are not in line with behaviour expected in a firm of this quality.'

'Right.'

'Reputation, Tom. It has to be cared for, cherished, protected.'

'Right.'

'So, sods like Scray and Rice will get what's coming to them, and it won't be bouquets, though it *will* vary in seriousness, one graver than the other. Graver, yes.'

'Right.'

Emily had returned with more tea, and they discussed halberds and their versatility in battle, as part spear and part long-handled axe. They could jab but also splinter helmets and skulls. Tom had feared that, in her womanly way, she'd want to know about his background and home life. He had a narrative ready, though he could see some weaknesses in it. But she hadn't asked. They might be the kind of details Leo said she'd learned not to intrude on. Scray and Rice were not mentioned, either. They would be other incidentals Leo didn't want her disturbed and even upset by, in his attentive way.

Through the AND A now, Tom saw Rice emerge from the apartment block pulling his wheeled suitcase. It looked fatter, heavier, or was that Tom imagining matters as he thought they should be? If someone took an empty case to a rendezvous it ought to be not empty on the return, or why bother to take it empty in the first place? Rice made for the Lexus. Tom moved expertly from the AND A to the LAWN A to watch him as far as the car. Rice didn't seem to give the van any attention this time. Perhaps he'd just handled a very satisfactory deal and felt more relaxed. He loaded the case carefully into the boot and drove off. Tom stayed for fifteen minutes in case Rice's seeming lack of concern just now had been a bluff. He might come back to see whether the van had gone, because he and the Lexus had. Deduction? The van had been on the peep. But Rice's car didn't reappear.

Tom reckoned this whole episode at the apartment block had been so brief that he could possibly slip home for a swift visit on the quiet. After all, the surveillance stint might have gone on for hours more, made feasible by the commode and flasks. It was Steve's birthday today. The detour would add an extra 100 miles or so to Tom's journeys, but he'd learned a long time ago in a car dealer case how to adjust the mileage clock. He'd sent a card, and he would stop off and get Steve a present: an electronic item, small enough to go into Tom's pocket: a super-modern mobile phone, or an iPod, maybe. He would explain it was a 'holding present' only. Months ago he had promised Steve a mountain bike. That wouldn't be possible today. Perhaps for Christmas instead. Not now, anyway. He couldn't accommodate a bike.

The van would take it easily, of course, but Tom didn't intend doing the full distance in it. There'd be too many questions from the kids if he rolled up with that: the main one, naturally, being why had he joined a gardening firm? Neighbours might wonder the same. Iris wouldn't ask. She'd have an idea what it was all about, and it would worry her, scare her. Steve and Laura would demand a look inside the van. The commode would give them a giggle. They might also spot the eight A windows and ask what they were for.

So, Tom would put the van into a multi-storey and do the last few miles by taxi. He'd say he was in the town with a colleague, who had things to see to nearby. This pal had used his car and done the driving, and Tom had to call another taxi and meet him near the city hall for the return hop.

He had a token pee in the commode. It seemed the considerate thing to do because Leo had displayed such evident pride in this fitment, and it would be a kind of rebuff to ignore it; might make Tom look ungrateful, uptight and possibly aloof. He thought of that famous, strange mental state known as the 'Stockholm syndrome' – noticed first, apparently, during a Swedish police operation – where an undercover officer or hostage came to admire the people he was spying on or imprisoned by and went over to their way of thinking and behaving.

Tom did feel that taking a leak in the van showed he had some regard for Leo and wouldn't want to disappoint him, at least as to the commode. This piss spoke of comradeship, fellowship, camaraderie, important undercover assets. Leo looked after his subordinates. The commode figured under the *noblesse oblige* ticket. Tom zipped up, closed the lid, let himself out of the back of the vehicle, then went to the front cabin and drove away. The move out through the rear and around to the driver's door on foot was very visible to anybody in the street, or looking from a window in one of the buildings: an inevitable van weakness because a solid partition divided its two parts. It ought to have been possible to get from the back to the front and vice versa without having to leave the vehicle. But any activity in the back must be blocked off from people outside looking in through the windscreen. Maybe one-way vision, darkened glass could have been installed, but why should a gardening firm or savoury pie business need that? It would have made the vehicle conspicuous.

Tom watched the mirror in case the Lexus showed, but still negative. He heard a bit of a swish and gurgle from behind when he made some ninety degree turns, but knew things would be all right there because the bowl was deep, the hefty wooden lid down, and the whole thing securely fixed to the van wall. Leo was someone who would obviously hate skimping – such as providing only a bucket or bottle.

SIXTEEN

AFTER

In the Home Office cinema now, the screen temporarily blank, Maud held up a sheaf of papers and waved them gently at Harpur and Iles. 'We should talk about this report. You have a copy each. It's among the stuff I gave you to look over in the lunch break. The item's titled—' she bent her head to read – *'"Debrief of outsourced officer T5 by H7, February 3 2011, 1800 hours to 1901 hours, Location, Trombone."* What did you make of it? Were you OK with the coding? But that sounds condescending. Sorry! Of course you saw through the coding. Are you dim, for heaven's sake?' She chuckled.

Harpur wanted to assume this was one of those questions that had its answer built-in – a big 'no', so big that the preposterousness of the question brought on her warm chuckle.

Just the same, though, Maud went on to explain. Maybe she thought most people *were* dim compared to herself. That cordial, beckoning wave with the documents might mean:

159

'These things in my hand are papers. OK? Got that? You have? Splendid! Now, next step: there is writing on the papers. OK? Got that? Sensational! Finally: I should like to discuss these papers and the writing on them with you. OK? Got that? Splendid! Truly splendid!' It reminded Harpur of one of the earliest, uncomplicated French lessons in school, when the teacher held up a pencil for all the class to see and said, *'Un crayon.'*

'T5 is Tom, plus a five letter surname, Parry,' Maud explained. 'H7 is Howard, the handler, with a seven letter follow-up, Lambert. Trombone is to be translated as The Field pub car park, two hours for a quid. Another location they used sometimes was disguise-labelled Viola. Neither had any obvious link to music, but H7 might have been feeling orchestral when he picked the ciphers. "Outsourced", of course, means undercover: he's *out* there secretly in gangland so as to provide a *source* of information about Leo Young's firm. And, *because* he's *out* there secretly in gangland, he's away from any *source* of police help.' Maud gave each of the emphasized words a really terrific whack, so that even the thickest thicko would cotton on.

Iles went sniffily through his handful of papers and found a copy of the one needed. He skipped the heading but began to read aloud the opening sentences, in a mock-prim, mock-clipped, mock-bureaucratic voice: '"T5 arrived on time (eighteen hundred hours) at Trombone and

160

observed all the established procedures for this type of sensitive meet-up. That is, parking some distance from my vehicle, waiting for a short while before walking to it, continuing briskly past my vehicle as if uninterested in it when two other people came out into the car park, then returning when the two had left. He had a carrier bag in one hand containing various food purchases, as if he had been shopping. His manner throughout our conversation was confident and positive." Oh, great,' the ACC said, resuming the normal Iles half-snarl.

'What?' Maud asked.

'He knows how to disguise himself with fruit and veg,' the ACC said. 'I can imagine him shouting words full of mad gladness at being such a nobody: "Look at me, folk. I'm just a healthy eater."' Iles went for a booming, vacuous intonation now. 'Or, rather, *"Don't* look at me, because all I am is just an ordinary healthy eater. I have measured out my life with carrier bags."'

'That's brilliant,' Harpur said.

'What?' Iles replied.

'The last bit,' Harpur said.

'Which last bit?' Iles asked.

'"Measured out my life with carrier bags,"' Harpur said. 'That seems to go beyond just the case of T5. It sounds like a comment on a wider scene, a universal scene, sort of poetic. Is the phrase original, sir?'

'Carrier bags have been around for a long

161

while and are subject to comment by some, Col,' Iles replied.

'Well, yes,' Harpur said.

'It's a recognised ploy in undercover,' Maud said.

'What is?' Iles asked.

'For an officer to kit himself out with something very innocent and run-of-the-mill,' Maud said. 'It helps him or her look as though he or she has some purpose – some purpose other than the clandestine get-together, that is. To sort of prepare a face to meet the faces that he or she will meet. A social background.'

'A couple of cabbages and four Jaffas give him or her a social background?' Iles asked.

'Undercover needs its methodology, Desmond,' Maud said.

'Its methodology couldn't keep him alive,' Iles said. 'The methodology is a farce, a placebo, a pretence that the danger can be countered and seen off.'

Maud lowered her papers for a moment, like dipping a flag in sympathy and respect. 'I think you must have had a tough experience with undercover at some time,' she said. 'It's gone deep.'

Iles slumped a degree or two in his seat and suddenly lost all aggression and jokiness. He shrank. His skin seemed too big for him, like a handed down overcoat. 'Yes, a tough experience,' he replied. 'You could call it that.'

Harpur said: 'A while ago the ACC agreed for

a detective to infiltrate a gang on our territory. The officer was rumbled and killed. Mr Iles has been immovably opposed to undercover ever since.'

'Touching,' she said.

Iles nodded. So his muscular system must still be all right.

'But absurd,' Maud said, as though she'd spotted a weakness in Iles and instinctively grabbed the chance to put the boot in while he was down. 'Yes, absurd, surely?' she said. 'Sentimentalizing one past event, allowing it to control the present and the future. Irrational, half-baked, death-obsessed.'

Iles didn't answer. He disliked talking about this episode. It was one topic – maybe one of only two or three – that he couldn't treat with his usual brassy disdain and steely detachment. His wife's relationship with Harpur was another, naturally.

Iles reread aloud H7's appraisal of T5's manner at their meeting. '"He was confident and positive."' The Assistant Chief recovered and gave that a big, clanging, sneering delivery. 'Grand words for his gravestone. He's going to be killed as a spy only a few months after this wonderfully confident and positive start.'

'H7 writes as it struck him then,' Maud replied. 'It has honesty.'

'Perhaps,' Iles said. 'Harpur can be as hard as gunmetal, but when we read the documents together in the other room even he was shaken by the daft hope and underestimate of danger.'

This was about two-thirds true. Sometimes, when Iles had got himself into a high-level, flim-flam argument about theory, he would call on Harpur to back him up, because he thought of Harpur as wonderfully sane, frank, clear-sighted and extremely limited. If Harpur supported him, it would be in convincing, unsubtle, anti-intellectual, concrete style. Iles considered Harpur could deal competently – formidably – with the basics of a situation, but was not too good on any larger stuff about themes and abstractions: what Harpur would regard as wool. And Harpur knew Iles wasn't completely wrong. For instance, Harpur would avoid getting pulled into a debate about the merits or not of undercover: the kind of wide, airy-fairy, policy dispute Maud and Iles were on the edge of now, with words like 'placebo', for fuck's sake. It could become not much more than an ego clash. She might want to squash him because of his rank, gender and general snottiness. He might want to diminish her because she was young, female, not turned on by him sexually, and a thing of the Home Office.

And so, nitty-grittying, Harpur said: 'Look, forget the drool, what are we trying to get at here?'

'Well, yes,' Maud said.

'Exactly,' Iles said.

'We want to know, don't we, when suspicion about T5's real identity began.'

'Well, yes,' Maud said.

'Exactly,' Iles said.

Harpur looked at his collection of papers. 'H7 says that, at their interview, T5 made three or four major points. T5 told him he had some grounds for believing he might have now been accepted in the designated firm and was trusted. H7 stressed that T5 said "some grounds" and was careful not to overstate this apparent progress. Obviously, we're going to have difficulty swallowing the accuracy of T5's opinion – tentative or not – in view of what happened to him eventually. But, as Maud points out, this is to apply knowledge to the state of things then which could not be available at the time.'

'You wouldn't expect Harpur to come on with this kind of forcefulness, would you, Maud?'

Harpur resumed his summarizing: 'One of the so-called "grounds" was that the head of the firm congratulated himself on being a gifted judge of potential recruits and thought his choice of T5 showed inspiration. Which could be an act – something to dupe him, put him off guard,' Harpur said.

'Certainly,' Maud said.

Harpur referred to his papers again. 'T5 tells H7 the head of the firm had invited him – only him – to his farmhouse to get familiar with the "sinews" and "ligaments" of the firm. This includes an educational visit to Leo's prized Acme van and mention of immediate and possibly future assignments, with or without it. This could reasonably be interpreted as insider privilege, yes? And Young gives him details of the tripartite division of the firm's turf and the alleged abuse of their position in Arabella by J5 and C4. As to the territorial divisions and Young's mother, this might be information already known. It could be something, it could be nothing. The debriefing account doesn't help us with that. It's a standard bit of trickery to seem to dish out secrets as a way of fooling someone and building their confidence, though the secrets are not secrets at all.'

'Certainly,' Maud said. 'Was Tom on guard against such a gambit? We can't tell.'

Harpur said: 'He's instructed to take the observation van to do surveillance, via the A-tops, of a wholesaler who might be supplying J5. In fact, at the handler meeting, T5 tells H7 that it was C4 who turned up and apparently left with a commodity load. H7 recorded the name and address of the wholesaler.' Harpur paused to measure how these facts – supposed facts – looked when taken all together. Then he went on: 'I consider T5 could be excused for thinking he's accepted as OK in the firm. He has apparently been handed a stack of confidential insights and given an important mission. Yes, it might all be show and bullshit. It might not. And if not, it would mean that a mistake by Tom, or mistakes, later than this made Young or others in the firm see through his cover.'

'Well, yes,' Maud said.

'Don't despise Harpur's way of simplifying a problem, Maud,' Iles said. 'It has definitely been known to work now and then. Yes, now and then. I don't think that's an exaggeration. Think of Churchill, who insisted on having problems described on one half sheet of notepaper. That's Col's style. He'll piss on nuances. It's noted in his Personnel Assessment papers at headquarters: "Pisses on nuances."'

SEVENTEEN

BEFORE

Tom ditched his plan to put the surveillance van in a multi-storey and do the rest of the trip by taxi. The idea came to seem cowardly – cowardly and an insult to Iris and the children. A sudden thought had jumped him as he drove: fuck the multi-storey. It was *only* a thought at first, but clear and definite. Then, after another couple of miles, he said it aloud to himself, his tone matter-of-fact, brisk yet conversational, inviting a mildly argumentative response, if there'd been anyone with him to respond. The cab windows were closed and the statement resounded well: that great, comradely rhyme between the Us in 'Fuck' and 'multi'. He reckoned this was how a man *ought* to talk, and especially a man who now and then lately had almost lost track of his genuine self. His genuine self was the one who'd think 'fuck the multi-storey', wasn't it? Wasn't it?

When Tom upgraded from thought to speech he stuck a defiant additional word in front: 'Yes! Fuck the multi-storey.' The, 'Yes!' seemed to him necessary. It showed he wasn't going to back off from that earlier inner blurt: 'Fuck the multi-storey.' Instead, he confirmed it. He might have turned cautious: surely it would be wiser to hide the van away and arrive in his street without the pray-look-at-me-do ACME LAWN AND GARDEN SERVICES display; wiser because who knew how far gossip might reach? He negatived this good sense, though, and relabelled it cowardice. He hated the notion of such furtiveness, particularly when it would be mainly to do with hoodwinking Iris and the kids.

He recognized this as an almost totally dickhead attitude. After all, hadn't he volunteered for a job where furtiveness was not just OK but the very guts of it? You couldn't be undercover and not furtive. At Hilston they'd decided he would be brilliantly suitable – that 'fluidity of persona', as it was sweetly jargonized, meaning a set of characteristics here today and also *gone* today, if the situation needed it. He'd admit, 'furtive' might be the wrong word – too creepy and base. How about 'deceptive' or 'stealthy'? But whatever it was called, he didn't want this grossly unwholesome two-timing practised on his family. With them, he would like his identity to stand solid and true, four-square and honest, as a husband and dad.

This aim he knew to be insane, too. There must always be concealment. The children would regard the van as a disguised police vehicle, and therefore quaint and jokey but

169

essentially good. He couldn't explain that it was in fact a van lovingly devised by an inspired, eminent drugs baron for various company duties, such as keeping a secret, *furtive*, eye on other greedy, maverick and disloyal drugs dealers, sometimes for very long stretches, commode and flasks facilitated. If they heard this, they'd understand then that he must be playing at villainy himself. How else could he be in charge of the van? This might worry Steve and Laura. They'd see the hazards. There'd be questions after questions, youngsters' questions, which meant plain and ruthlessly to the point. And Iris? She would most likely guess at once the van's significance. He had to gamble that when she saw the supposed greenery name on it and heard about the top A observation holes and the commode she'd come to regard Tom's new work as slightly comical and footling. And woman-free.

He stopped at a bank hole-in-the-wall and drew some funds. En route a bit later, he found a cycle shop and paid cash for a Viking Valhalla twenty-four-speed Shimano Altus mountain bike for Steve. This struck him as the kind of thing dads did, with delivery on exactly the right day worth an extra merit mark. Steve might think it weird that dad should turn up with the Valhalla in a strange, bogus van, but he'd agree this didn't take anything away from the terrific pressie, and the van must be how detectives had to behave sometimes to surprise and catch crooks. Steve would be correct about this: his father *was* a policeman in what looked like a non-police van. That failed hopelessly as a full account of things, though, and Tom had to make sure this failure lasted.

But, in any case, he had to ask: should he care what Iris and – or – the kids might think? Hilston would disown him, despise him for this domestic tremor. How come he'd suddenly lost that glorious ability to move so slickly in and out of different life roles? Only momentarily lost, he hoped. Could you be a natural under-cover prospect and yet so feebly and danger-ously scared of some of the game's basic cons? He doubted it. Naturally, he doubted it. And, because he did, he had to comfort himself, buttress himself, with that noisy, hollow yell: 'Yes! Fuck the multi-storey.' After driving an-other four or five miles he shouted even more heartily, 'Yes! Yes! Yes! Fuck the multi-storey.' Anyone glancing in through a van window and seeing his mouth contortions and general facial excitement would think him duetting with some crap rap CD on the audio player.

He still kept a steady watch on the rear-view mirror. He felt he'd been sloppy to look only for the Lexus. Norman Rice had inspected the street thoroughly before entering the apartment build-ing and might have alerted Mr Wholesaler: 'We've got some eyes outside. You've heard of a triple-A to do with credit rating, have you? Well, this is a quadruple-A, probably twice, and to do with something else, such as hideaway nosing. When I leave I'll act nonchalant, as if the van's invisible or is just a van. Maybe you should get on his tail for a charting trip when he leaves. No good me doing it. He'd spot the Lexus.'

So, it could be any model or marque tracking Tom, if there was someone at all. Although he concentrated non-stop, he couldn't pick out constant slipstream company. For a while he wondered about a dark blue Astra which seemed to be in the mirror too often. But he knew himself to be on edge and perhaps over-wary.

Luckily, a couple of coils of spare rope hung on the walls in the back of the van and he'd been able to secure the bike to the commode with one of them. He bound the machine by its crossbar to an arm of the commode chair so that the hinged wooden seat at the front could still be lifted and the bowl used, unaffected by the rope and three half hitches. The tethered Viking Valhalla would be close alongside, whether you were standing or sitting there, but without obstructing.

After the stop at the bike shop he no longer saw the Astra. Quite possibly, Rice wouldn't have risked mentioning the van back there, in case this wholesaler decided Norm and his trade associates had brought potentially hostile attention on him and his vocation. That might anger Cochrane, the wholesaler. And, of course, Norm and his associates *had b*rought hostile attention.

Tom was it, Tom leading back to L.P. Young. Cochrane was selling to a firm within a firm. The firm he was selling to was the Justin Scray rogue firm. And the other firm – not the one he was dealing with, but the one the firm he was dealing with was within – this firm did not care for the firm he was dealing with very much at all and feared that the Scray firm, which, for the moment, was within the other firm, would eventually grow to a point where it nabbed the position of the firm it was now within and become the container firm itself, or even the *only* firm on this patch. Leo Young greatly respected Justin Scray's abilities and regarded him as his Number Three. Tom would be taking Leo the hard evidence – already much rumoured – that those abilities were only part devoted to the concerns of his firm, but functioned also, and perhaps mainly, for another firm, where Scray would be Number One. He had deputed his assistant, Claud Norman Rice, to pick up a load of commodities for their own separate, satellite, hole-in-the-corner, very selective, undoubtedly thriving trade. Leo would detest Cochrane, this rival supplier, for helping Scray smash the *status quo*. Leo cherished the *status quo* because he got his grand status from it, plus Midhurst, the horses, the swimming bath and a wife who could chair a museum committee and knew about halberds, as well as retrieving coins from the deep end.

Tom had found it a good experience opening

the van's rear doors and lifting the bike in. He liked its metal geometry. The bike was aluminium and not heavy but would have fine toughness in its frame. He could imagine this Valhalla getting up mountain tracks with total ease, its range of gears conquering near-sheer slopes. Bikes he regarded as strange but satisfying objects. They weren't like cars or vans which would stand solid on their wheels whether moving or parked. When not being ridden, a bike was simply a collection of tubes, wheels, brake-blocks and other bits and would fall down if not propped or tied like this one, say to a completely stable commode's arm. Someone on the saddle changed all that. An arse of either gender and without age limit turned the bike into a vehicle, able to stay upright for as long as it kept going forward.

Not long ago, he'd read an old Cold War espionage story, *The Spy Who Came In From The Cold*, lately reprinted. In it, an agent is trying to get out of East Berlin and into the West on a bike, pedalling fast. And while he *was* pedalling fast the bike seemed a brilliant, basic escape machine. But then an East German sentry takes aim and shoots the agent. He and the cycle, of course, clatter to the ground and lie there, a spent heap. That word from the book – 'clatter' – had got itself fixed in Tom's memory. It was so right for a bike.

To think Steve would work his magic on the Valhalla and get it performing well delighted

Tom. It seemed to him a very fatherly thing to empower a son in that way, while also reminding him how those who did not move ahead might disastrously topple, like the German agent. There weren't any actual mountains near where they lived, but some hills and hillocks. Steve and the bike must show these could be beaten. Tom wouldn't spell all the symbolism out to him or he'd think his dad had picked up a bad dose of teacher's gab. But perhaps Steve would hear the overtones without any prompting, especially from a bike called Valhalla, with its famed heroic links to the major god, Odin. Tom did feel intermittently that in some ways it was off-key to lash such a noble bike to a recently used, unemptied, commode, although this would be only for a while. However, he *had* to make sure that on the rest of the trip the gift didn't bang about loose inside the van and get dented and scratched, or Steve might think it second-hand. That could take away some of its splendour, obviously.

EIGHTEEN

AFTER

Maud screened three stills of Tom Mallen dead on the building site, Tom Mallen known as Tom Parry for this job. They were obviously night pictures, unnaturally vivid from the flashlight. Harpur assumed they'd been taken soon after discovery of the body. Tom was on his side, knees bent, as if *cwtched* down for sleep. Maud said: 'He seems to have crawled a few yards, then collapsed like that. There was a blood trail, a couple of inches wide at some points.'

She pressed the control button to produce again those white circles on the screen and ringed the leakage. It was on unmade-up, muddy soil at the front of the incomplete house. Harpur could make out the extra wetness, though. That was the thing about flashlight: it might be glaringly bright and unmodulated, but it did make everything clear. The luridness seemed to scream: 'This is what life is like, and death. A typical moment has been flash-frozen, just for you. Get it? Have a good gaze before you drift back to your dopey smugness and sick evasions.'

Maud said: 'Why he crawled towards the house I don't understand. He wouldn't find cover. There *was* no cover. No porch. The front door in place and shut. It explains the choice of this spot for the topping, I imagine. A marksman firing down had him in sight non-stop. If he'd wanted to shoot again, Tom made it easier for him by cutting the distance. But, maybe, when you've been hit on one bit of ground, anywhere else could seem better. What was that phrase from Vietnam – "the killing fields"? So, get into some other field.'

'Or perhaps he thought, "If I can just shift myself even a fraction I'll know I'm still alive, either as Tom Mallen or Tom Parry,"' Iles replied. 'That choice wouldn't have seemed important any longer, would it? Identity a folderol now. Tom or, alternatively, Tom. The bullets had his name on them. Which name? Did it matter? What counted was being able to move. A father of two. He'd feel a duty not to get wasted, particularly not to get wasted with no dignity on some crummy suburban construction project paralysed by funds failure. You can hear him muttering as he dragged his body across the muck, breathing in fragments of himself, wondering how much of his face was left, "God, but what a fucking idiot to come this way." Some of the best conversations are with one's self. It's true, whether you're Mallen or Parry or both. The repartee can be dazzling.'

'Two hits,' Maud said, 'one to the left side of his nose, one in the chest. That order we think, the bulk of the blood from his chest wound.'

'How chests are,' Iles said.

'We believe the two shots must have been more or less together. They're both front-of-body wounds, and it looks as though they came from the same sniper station upstairs in the half-done house,' Maud said. 'It's not a case of knocking him over with the first and then coming down to make sure with another shot. So, cheek for openers, and as he's falling his chest broken into. Either could have killed him. His trousers, socks and shoes were blood-drenched and muddy. In one sense he did well to crawl at all.'

'Which sense would that be?' Iles said.

'This is very high-class shooting,' Maud replied. 'Two pops, two strikes. It's true the range was short, but there's maximum coolness and system.' She put the second photo on to the screen. For this one, the camera had gone down to head and shoulders level. Tom was thin-bodied and thin-faced. To Harpur, the wound looked neat: not much flesh for the bullet to dig out and spatter. The bone of his lower left eye socket and left side of his nose bridge was visible where the tight skin had been split and furled minimally back by the impact. The sight of these flimsy, sample snippets of skeleton seemed to hint that Tom's whole physical structure might be dodgy. His mouth hung ajar, maybe to pull more air into his lungs, damaged by the smack in the chest; maybe to cry out at the pain; maybe to yell a curse at the gunman or a more general curse at Fate for letting him ever get into this whole doomed, shitty, act-a-part carry-on.

Maud said: 'I wondered whether the face shot was meant for an eye and just missed it – an I spy eye; an I *am* a spy eye. Possible. A good moon at the time, I gather, for accuracy. Punishment made-to-measure. A deterrent to others thinking about undercover.'

'It's something nobody should think about,' Iles said. 'These are thoughts leading to muckup and regret. But, look, they're *not* thoughts. They're spasms. That's the message here. It's always the message.'

The third picture came from an even lower angle and showed a big bloodstain on the front of the white 'I love Torremolinos' T-shirt he'd been wearing under an unbuttoned denim jacket, 'love' not given as a word but represented by a red heart, with stubs of artery and/or vein sticking out, ready to get circulation going, as well as love. The heart was of a slightly darker red than the general red around it now, and therefore its shape still possible to make out. The jacket had kept mud off his T-shirt.

Maud said: 'As you'll have seen in the notes, the bullets were from a Smith and Wesson SW99, a very choice piece and well-liked here and overseas. Torremolinos and its package tour naffness were part of the faked Parry persona. We don't believe Tom Mallen ever went there. You'll remember *Prick Up Your Ears*, the playwright Joe Orton's autobiography. He tells one of his working-class pick-ups that his tan comes from sunbathing at Torremolinos. It doesn't, but Orton thinks it's the kind of flashy Spanish resort where his companion for the night might himself have holidayed. Same sort of prole role play from Tom.'

'I adore Torremolinos,' Iles said. 'Oh, but that San Miguel fiesta in September! Even an inveterate Prot like me can share the spiritual zing. I *am* rather a fiesta person, you know – arcing the wine into one's mouth without too much disaster from a flask held high above in that fine old Iberian tradition. You'll hardly ever see a Spaniard drink from a glass. Deemed chichi and wimpish. One follows a country's customs. My mother used to cry out gleefully to me, even as a child, "Desmond, you're *such* an internationalist!" And then there's the bullfighting, of course. How else to commemorate old St Mig but with beast torture?'

Harpur thought Iles had probably never been near Torremolinos, either, but he'd want to wrong-foot Maud whenever possible, because she was the Home Office: make her feel snooty and insular and heathen, disrespectfully out of touch with the saints'-day calendar, and ignorant of wine straight on to the back teeth from a raised-arm altitude.

Maud said: 'He had a shoulder-holstered Browning automatic, as you'll have seen in the reports. It's a nine mm item, like the SW that killed him. His Browning hadn't been fired, or even drawn. Although he thought he would be part of a hunt for Scray, he had a few hundred yards to go before meeting the others and getting to full readiness. We know now, don't we, that he *was* part of a hunt, but as the quarry, not one of the hounds.'

'And did *he* know it, in those last minutes, the crawling, half-nose minutes?' Iles asked.

Harpur picked at the question. Had Tom realized he was stupid to have come this way? Iles could be remarkably intuitive. Although his mind sometimes lurched and plummeted or blanked itself off, it would turn astonishingly perceptive now and then. Yes, it would. But probably not about undercover work. He hated these operations so passionately that he'd bring to any discussion of them only hostility, doubt, darkness, thoroughgoing bias. He would never have admitted there was *any* route for Tom to take that might have been less foolish. In the ACC's view the foolishness began with accepting an undercover role at all. He'd argue that because the whole project started from a catastrophic error of intent, every decision afterwards was inevitably wrong – diseased attempts to justify the unjustifiable. No, not argue. Iles didn't argue. He announced. Occasionally, he had to be ignored. Occasionally, his announcements had

181

to be switched off.

Harpur tried to get at what Tom's thinking might have been, once he'd received the call to join Abidan and the others. Tom would know he mustn't seem dubious or reluctant about the operation against Scray – the supposed operation, that is; Tom couldn't be aware of its real purpose: *he* was its real purpose. He had to seem obedient, responsive, committed, eager to protect Leo's firm from Scray's sly programme of comradely fraud. Anything less could make Abidan and the rest start sniffing. If Tom seemed to delay, he might appear scared to be in on a killing. Of course, he *was* scared to be in on a killing. That should be concealed, though. And so, he needed the quickest path from the mall to the square where Abidan waited for the rest of the killing party to clock in. Or *should* have waited for the rest of the killing party to clock in. The quickest path meant the building site. No question, that was the shortest, the recommended route, the obligatory route. As he set out on it, progressed some way on it, did he have doubts about his safety? Did he suspect, half suspect, that he might have been allocated the mall to scour *because* the swiftest way from there to the square was via the building site? 'God, but what a fucking idiot to come this way,' as Iles had imagined Tom slagging himself off. Did Tom wonder whether he'd given any cause for them to doubt he was what he said he was? The photos didn't show his fingers crossed for luck.

Harpur wanted to visualize the sequence of things. Every detective did that whatever the case. Suppose Maud were wrong and Iles right. That is, suppose Maud's theory of the two shots coming virtually on top of each other were not correct. And suppose Iles's hunch that Tom would have done almost anything to prove himself alive were right. Longing to show – show himself – his body still functioned OK, might Tom have managed to get to his feet somehow after the face bullet? Could he have walked, stumbled, a few paces towards the house and towards the gunman? The T-shirt and its heart would have looked totally clean and intact for a moment: would have looked like an invitation to fire again, the white garment perilously luminous in the dark. And that pictured heart offered guidance towards the real, fleshly one behind: did it seem to call for a follow-up nine mm round, a *coup de grâce* nine mm round? The illustrated heart had not been hit direct, in fact, but close. Then Tom could have staggered on again briefly, blood cascading over his muddied trousers, socks, shoes and the ground, until he went down and remained down on his side, as in the photos. The message: 'I (heart sketch) Torremolinos, but won't be going there any more, if, in fact, I ever went there before.'

And there might be other possible accounts of how the murder took place. So? Did they matter much? Tom had been killed. Was it necessary to know anything more than this? Well, yes, perhaps. Well, yes, of course. Police existed to know more, and continued to exist *by* knowing more, and scheming to know more still. Harpur thought his version of what happened could tell something about the executioner. Against Maud's theory of two almost simultaneous SW shots, Harpur set the possibility of a delay – perhaps a minute or two or even three or four – between. During that gap, the gunman stayed cool, didn't he? He hadn't scarpered fast, afraid the noise when he first fired would bring an audience; would bring potential witnesses. He didn't panic as the flattened, face-fucked victim somehow got on to his knees in the muck, then winched and scrabbled himself on to his feet and possibly seemed to come after the sniper – apparently meaning to fight back, even though his legs must have been nearly goners.

The attacker had stayed calm enough to decide that because a mug shot failed to do the terminal trick he'd go for the heart now, that anatomical, rather crucial heart, under the nicely visible shirt and its useful artwork. This steadiness could suggest the gunman had some experience of small arms and their effective use; had perhaps gone through training in small arms and their effective use; had been taught that a small-arms hit didn't always mean a small-arms death: you hung about, checking. And, if necessary, you offered a subsequent, tidying-up shot or volley.

Police training with small arms was very thorough and always provided a Plan B and even Plans C, D, E and F.

Incidentally, Harpur realized that all of them – he, Maud and Iles – spoke and thought as if the marksman were certain to be a marks*man*. But quite a lot of female police got that thorough small-arms training. Some female police would be cool and tactical and appreciative of a white shirt, plus vivid ticker pic, to focus their sights on in the poor light. They'd be capable of finding their way into an unoccupied property and creating a sharpshooter's nest. This was an equal opportunities career. Any cop could be a self-saving cop, gender regardless, if a nice, established racket seemed in danger of getting blown. Women as well as men knew how to look after their investments.

The screen now showed a couple of photographs of the house used by the gunman (gunwoman). There were front and back views. Maud said: 'Entrance and exit by a rear door. No evidence of forced break-in, so we assume a bit of magic on the lock. That might mean more than one person – a burglary expert, a handguns and deaths expert. Nothing meaningful found in the sniper's selected bedroom we're told. The rear yard – not yet a garden – gives on to a broad service lane, no CCTV. A car might have been waiting there. The house and the houses next to it were boarded up after this episode. Gorgeously late foresight!'

The papers Harpur and Iles had been given to read during the lunch break were official inquiry documents. But Maud also had slides giving reports from the local Press and all the nationals. The murder of a police detective in these unexplainable, no-man's-land circumstances had been a major media story. Harpur could remember coverage in the *Daily Mail* and on television news. That was a good while before he came to have this personal connection with the case, of course. Maud said: 'One can tell they sensed something very clandestine and veiled behind the killing. Naturally, they all refer to him by his real name, Detective Sergeant Thomas Rodney Mallen.'

She had one of the national's account of things on the screen now and ringed a sentence: *'He is believed to have been on secondment from another force with undisclosed duties, but possibly connected to drugs trafficking.'*

Maud did a summarizing session from other cuttings: 'Various terms,' she said. 'Some call it "secondment", others "attachment". One national wrote he had been "drafted in with a special remit outside the normal command structure". She switched slides to the front-page piece in a local and singled out sentences near the top. *'The police investigation continues, its priority to discover why he was on the partially completed Elms private housing estate of four-and five-bedroomed executive style properties at the time of his murder. The site is used as a short-cut, despite prominent "Keep Out" warning notices.'*

Maud said: 'And as we all know from recorded interviews and so on, Tom's body was found by a couple coming back from evening shopping at the Rinton mall, the man qualified in first aid. You'll remember he tries some on Tom, including kiss of life, but no response. Meanwhile the woman mobiles nine nine nine. The man must have got in a bit of a mess through contact. These were good people. One of the police interviews makes it clear, doesn't it, that when tending to Tom and getting him into position for the kiss of life they find the shoulder holster and Browning pistol under his jacket and on the jolly but sopping Torremolinos T-shirt? It must have told the pair they were into something serious and possibly very rough – if they didn't already realize it. That didn't stop them doing what they could for him, though. Yes, good people.'

The tale had continued to run, and cuttings from newspapers later in the week showed journalists had found Tom's home and family. There was speculation in these reports about why a detective should have been sent from one police force to work in another – and to die in another. The guesswork didn't get very far. A Police Press Office statement quoted said: *'Exchanges of personnel between various forces is not unusual. Such arrangements can be very beneficial both for the destination force, which may profit from skills developed in a different context, and beneficial also for the officer or officers concerned in that their experience of the police service is widened. It is not the practice of police forces to comment upon the special skills or circumstances of an officer, particularly when, as in Detective Sergeant Mallen's case, the exchange procedure resulted in this very regrettable tragedy. Normally, the exchanges are positive and useful.'*

Iles said: 'Oh, yea? Not a very satisfactory way to widen an officer's experience of the service, was it?'

Reporters had gone to the Mallen home. Tom's wife must have been too distressed to talk, but neighbours were quoted as saying what Harpur would have expected them to say – that they felt 'devastated' by the killing, and that the family were very pleasant and helpful. It was the TV News grief formula. One paper carried a couple of photographs supplied by somebody living in the street. The first featured a group of young lads with bicycles, apparently about to set off for a ride together. Maud put a circle around one boy. 'This is Tom's son, Steve,' she said. 'The photograph comes from the dad of another of the kids, a Mr Richard Coombs.' Steve Mallen looked about twelve or thirteen years old, fair-haired, thin, with a big, cheerful grin. Maud indicated part of the accompanying interview. *'"Steve had a Viking Valhalla mountain bike for his recent birthday," Mr Coombs said. "He's very proud of it.'"*

Richard Coombs had supplied another flash picture which appeared on the screen alongside the snap of the boys and must have been taken earlier. It showed a white van with the words ACME LAWN AND GARDEN SERVICES in red on the side to camera. Mr Coombs apparently told the reporter: *'"Tom Mallen rolled up in this van one day and parked it outside his house. I thought it was so odd and funny that I took the photograph of it – I mean, he was a police officer! What was he doing in something like that? Without the photo, people wouldn't have believed it when I told them. Now, of course, we're all wondering if the van had some special role. It might be to do with his move to that other force. It could be a sort of incognito van.'"*

'Yes, it could. Good for you, Dicky Coombs,' Iles said. 'One can see the observation holes. Can we enlarge the pic? It's a really brilliant construction. Well done, Leo.'

Harpur said: 'Wouldn't Tom be mad to go home in that kind of vehicle?'

'He was a family man, Harpur,' Iles said. 'For some folk that bond is prime. His son's birthday? Wouldn't the van enable him to arrive with the Valhalla for the celebrations?' The last few words of this statement came out as a burgeoning screech. Iles went on: 'But you're probably not one to understand all this – the prioritizing of family – given that you casually debauch other men's wives, show contempt for their family ties.' Authentic, lively froth began to form on Iles's upper lip. Harpur had already noticed how the ACC's voice proved the acoustics of this little cinema room excellent.

Maud said: 'So, Tom observed Claud Norm Rice from the van.'

'He'd be regarded as a traitor or backslider or potential rival,' Harpur said. 'They might want to get a case together against him, or her. Many of these firms have their fair-play rules. If they're going to kill someone there has to be a bit of a reason. It looks as though Tom had achieved absolute acceptance in the gang and could be trusted with very sensitive and vital work harvesting evidence.'

'Exactly,' Iles said, his tone suddenly sweet and sane and instructive. 'You see, Maud, Col has quite a grasp of essentials despite his disregard for basic moral standards. Ability is not necessarily linked to wholesomeness, cock control and decency. You'll find this difficult to comprehend, but it is so. In some aspects Col's invaluable. In others, Harpur's a consummate shit. But which is the main, the preponderant aspect? That's the conundrum, isn't it?' He smiled ungenially and did not revert to the high-pitched disgust mode. Instead, he began to howl or bay his agonized words, the sound seeming to come from somewhere much deeper in him than the mere larynx. 'This was a man – Harpur I mean – who owed me and my rank and the service generally full and long-lasting fealty and yet in many a cheap and frowsty venue he frequently dipped his—'

'You'd suggest they've deliberately picked the name of a firm with plenty of As in it, would you, Desmond – ACME LAWN AND GARDEN SERVICES – so as to get a full array and spread of peep facilities?' Maud replied. 'Even the conjunction, AND, supplies one. Clever.'

'I'm always glad to see As pulling their weight,' Iles said. 'They have a duty to live up to their position as first in the alphabet.'

NINETEEN

BEFORE

'So, what's with the van outside, Mr Mallen?'
'I needed it to bring the bike.'
'Yes, but lawns and gardens. I mean, what's lawns and gardens? I mean, what's it to do with you – the lawns and gardens? What's the, well, link?' He could be unflinching, this lad, a friend of Steve's. He had given himself a mission to kick the life out of half-truths, the young avenging twerp, and son of twerps. He'd trample a lawn and a garden.
'A friend lent it to me,' Tom replied.
'You're still a cop, though, are you? Like plain clothes, but still a cop, a detective?'
'Oh, sure.'
'Is this for some duty with the other force, such as, like, disguise – saying in red, like, it's to do with lawns and gardens, but really a police vehicle?'
'It's a friend's. He knew I wanted to get back for Steve's birthday, and with the present.'
'You've made some good friends there, have you? I mean, for someone to lend you a van,

even if they don't know you very well, that's really kind. What did he say? Did he say, like, "It's obvious you need to be there for the celebration, so I got this van not in immediate use, as to lawns and gardens, and I'd be really pleased if you'd take that," even though he got no real notion of Steve, never met him or even heard of him till now, most probably?'

'Yes, along those lines.'

'Because you haven't been there, I mean, away, for very long, but he will still lend you a van, regardless?'

'Yes.'

'Do they know you're dodging out of it for a while, coming back here, which is not usually where it gets around to the lawns and gardens, not its home ground – not its home lawn and garden?'

'Who? Do who know?'

'The chiefs.'

'Didn't I tell you this was a loan from a friend? People can be very understanding about some family occasions, for example, a birthday.'

'Which people?'

'If they can help, they will, and providing a van they don't need for the moment is a striking glimpse of this generosity. You're so right, Luke.'

There, soak up the compliment and get lost.

'But you've got to get it back on time?' Luke said.

'Oh, yes.'

'They trust you to do that?'

'Oh, yes.'

'Who, exactly?'

'Clearly, the owner of the van.'

'That's not "clearly". Who?'

'There's not going to be a lawns and gardens need at night, is there? This is putting the van on to twenty-four-hour use – maximizing, like extra shifts at a munitions factory, because of a war.'

'What factory? How does a factory come into it? What war?'

Tom had this van tale ready: he knew there'd be interrogation from Steve and his mates. It might work. Kids weren't always easy to fool. Kids could be plodding and dogged. Yes, they went for the simple, big, awkward questions, like these from Steve's pal, Luke Coombs, now. Luke was a sharp boy, with Community Watch parents. That is, fucking nosy, intrusive parents, poking about, 'to help the community', so they said. Often. They lived opposite. Steve plus friends had been for a swim and jacuzzi outing at the Leisure Club pool as a sort of birthday party, entry paid for by Iris. Could any of them successfully surface dive for a coin in the deep end? Now, they'd come back to the house to eat a pizza supper, pre-ordered to suit their individual tastes and doorstep delivered, paid for by Iris. On birthday treats there was an iron duty to reciprocate at a decent standard. It's what communities were about. The boys had grown too old for a bouncy castle.

Tom would make up the outlay to her – make both amounts up to her. He'd never given Iris any of the supposed expenses cash he collected from Howard Lambert at that introductory meeting with Rockmain and him in the service station: the handler's handout among the crockery. Tom had meant to pass all of it to Iris, but then suffered his powerful attack of conscience about involving the family in a possibly smoke and mirrors transaction; perhaps the first in a series of smoke and mirrors transactions. He jibbed. Instead, he'd treated the amount as ordinary income, *his* ordinary income, and spent it in the normal way. Now, though, he'd give Iris the cash for the Leisure Centre outing and pizzas and Cokes from what he had in his pocket and wallet. It would be, sort of, *here's some uncontaminated loot, darling, to meet outgoings on a uniquely grand day.*

But he realized that the money in his pockets and wallet now might not have been the same if he hadn't spent the lump from Howie Lambert on personal running costs – how things were with money. What you had at present depended on what you had then, no matter how long ago, and what he had then included the lavish doleout from Lambert. So, the family was getting indirectly touched by the taint, if there was one. He could give Iris clean loot largely because he'd been using possibly dirty loot from Howie. This grey area was *so* damn grey and chewy, so complex, that he gave up nagging himself about it. He'd fork out, no matter how the money came to be available. In the kind of work he'd taken on he knew there'd be plenty of knotty, dark moral dilemmas, and he'd better get used to resolving them fast, with the needs of the job always put first. Undercover had its own foggy and compulsive ethics, its own very practical, very adjustable, theology: 'I believe in undercover and will try everything to make it work and save my skin, this skin having a false name and fictionalized background for the occasion, amen.'

There were six boys. Steve's sister Laura hadn't gone to the pool with them: strictly a lads' outing. She'd been at a friend's house but returned now for the scoff. Two extra pizzas had been ordered by Iris, one for Laura, one for herself. Laura was puzzled by the van, too. 'I saw it outside the house on my way back from Cheryl's and wondered what it was for. And Luke's dad was taking pictures with his mobile and having a chortle. He told me a woman had asked him about it, too. He said: "Is your father moonlighting in lawns and gardens, then, Laura?"'

The prick would. Which woman?

'He does a story of the street like in a big scrap album, with photos and drawings,' Luke said. 'It's a sort of diary. Or a kind of log. That van – unusual. He'll put it into the album. It's an event, like, an *unusual* event. He'll write a

196

remark under the photo, such as: "Why such a van next to their VW?"'

'We haven't got a lawn, only paved over and a patio, so I couldn't understand why lawns,' Laura said.

Iris offered her the bike yarn, speaking with plenty of what might sound like true sincerity. Tom was grateful. It shifted attention to the Viking Valhalla, thank God. The machine stood propped against the sideboard with a birthday tag they'd given him in the shop tied on to the saddle stalk: 'HAPPY, HAPPY BIRTHDAY, STEVE. LOVE FROM MUM AND DAD.' The bike looked lean and hungry for mountains. Tom wondered whether the double HAPPY overdid things. But he reasoned: one each from Iris and him. 'Yes, great,' Laura said. 'And adult size?'

'Definitely,' Steve said. 'I'm thirteen now.' He'd probably be the youngest of the boys. Teendom was taking over.

'We're going to have a big ride-out together on Saturday, all of us,' Paul Harker said. 'I've got a Gary Fisher bike.'

'Terrific,' Tom said.

'I've got a Rockrider,' Greg Mills said.

'Also terrific,' Tom said. Maybe these were classier, dearer models than the Valhalla. Tom knew he'd better sound impressed.

Luke said: 'Mine's a Dawes Saratoga Comfort, front suspension.'

'Terrific,' Tom said. 'Adult?'

197

'Of course,' Steve said.

'My dad will do photos of us starting off,' Luke said. 'More for the album. "The mountain bike gang." That's how he'll describe it, I expect.'

Tom thought they might not be satisfied with this sort of juvenile, mummy-run party next year. He felt damn glad he'd made the effort to get here for an important day, pleased he'd ignored the risk. It was a farewell to childhood: twenty-six-inch wheels on their bikes. That was about as big as they came, unless you wanted a penny-farthing.

Iris had been alone in the house when Tom arrived, the boys still at the pool, Laura with her chum, Cheryl. Iris and Tom kept discussion of the van short. When he mobiled to say he was on his way, she'd told him: 'We might have half an hour alone if you're quick, Tom. And I'll get another pizza.'

'Anchovies and mushroom,' he said. He had put his foot down. The back and forth swishing sound in the commode grew stronger as he cornered at speed. Tom realized it wasn't a very noble thought, but the sound recalled for him that *From Here To Eternity* scene on the film channel when Burt Lancaster and Deborah Kerr are getting close to it in the grand Hawaiian rollers around Pearl Harbour time. The mind and memory went their own way, didn't they, no guaranteed suitable tone?

Iris must have been watching for him at a

window and she'd opened the front door before he reached it. She'd held out her arms to take him and hold him to her. They kissed in the doorway, a long, strong kiss, the kind of kiss that should be natural to people who'd lived together for fifteen years, assuming the fifteen years had been fairly tolerable. Fifteen years was quite a while. Then she said: 'How come?'

'What?'

'The transport.'

'Reconnaissance.'

'Of what?'

'Tell you later.'

'You're right. What does it matter?'

He realized he would like to take Iris out to the van and have her on its metal floor. This wouldn't be totally the same as Lancaster and Kerr in the waves, but similarly unconventional and significant. He needed something beyond Norm Rice and the substances trolley to make this vehicle memorable. He'd say: 'So come and have a look at the interior, if you're interested, Iris. It's quite a remarkable piece of equipment, with intriguing facilities.' He'd pulled into a lay-by a few miles back and emptied the commode basin under a hedge, so there'd be no unpleasantness about the fitments. Once inside, he'd close the doors and she'd guess the real intent. There was a light in the van and he'd leave that on, at least until they'd undressed and picked the right spot to lie down. The plan would excite and please her. She'd like the deviousness, as if this were their first time and needed to be set up by seduction trickery. Tom thought love-making in the van might help bring the five sides of his life together: husband; dad; cop; cop masquerading as Leo Young's man; cop masquerading as Leo Young's man masquerading as a lawns and gardens man. And it should show which were prime: husband and dad, weren't they? Husband/dad, yes. Oh, yes. He wanted to believe this. To have it off in the van would part prove that, because they'd be interested in none of the accessories, such as Thermos flasks and folding chairs, just their own bodies and feelings. No need for the eight A observation windows: they wouldn't care about things outside, only their closed-off, clothes-off, private area, private areas, secluded and symbolic – symbolic of human passion ready to give it a go wherever, unbothered about discomfort.

For a time, their only thought would be: what else is a van for except to make love in? He'd put his folded jacket under Iris for comfort against the steel. This wouldn't be a soft, sandy beach to cup her buttocks. He didn't want her bruised and recriminating. Very pale skinned women like Iris marked easily as they went into their later thirties. Iris was tall, but, obviously, not too tall to fit across the width of the van. She had on jeans and a roll-neck blue sweater. That was all right. They weren't fiddly to get off – only the one jeans-waist button. He could make a pillow from her clothes, so as to keep her hair out of any muck on the van floor. She wouldn't mind this kind of unusualness. Although Iris liked system, it meant the occasional break from the customary startled and delighted her. If her hair did get dirtied it wouldn't matter because she shampooed every day, sometimes twice. 'Apple and Almond' or 'Lupin and Lavender' – that sort of alliteration.

He'd junked the van-sex idea, though. To open it and climb into the back with Iris might be too blatant. Tom had realized from the beginning that Neighbourhood Watch was sure to eye the baffling vehicle. Tom did open the van's rear doors but only to unlash the Viking Valhalla from the commode, bring the bike in and place it for the big showpiece effect when Steve and the rest returned. Then he followed Iris upstairs. She'd be ready for him. Perhaps he was the one getting seduced: the lawns and gardens man invited in and made use of; a bit of horticultural rough. He didn't feel in a resisting mood. He fancied homecoming contact with well-cared-for breasts. But in bed at first he'd sensed she was guarded – not cold or hesitant, though per-haps wondering whether despite that fine endur-ing kiss from an enduring marriage everything was all right between them still. By 'all right' she'd mean there'd been nobody else while he was away, and maybe subjected to all those famous sexual pressures which could get at undercover police: 'credibility coitus', as it was known. But she'd know that to ask about this would kill all the possible sweetness of these grabbed, lucky minutes.

And, gradually, as the pleasures of their togetherness took over, Iris seemed to put all uncertainties aside. Her responses had grown as committed and urgent as his own, her arms locked across his back like hawsers: escape me never – another film title. They were not a couple of kids. They *had* a couple of kids, one of them a mountain-biking grown-up. She and Tom knew how to be tender with each other when it counted, and how to be violent with each other when it counted. OK, so her skin might get bruised. That wasn't life-threatening.

They got dressed quickly afterwards. Now they did act like kids, hurrying in case it became obvious what they'd been at. He wouldn't have worried if it *were* obvious. What should these boys and Laura expect, after Tom's absence? He sensed Iris would have been embarrassed, though. She might not like Steve's pals to know he had a hot-arsed, seize-the-day-or-night mother. And Steve might not care for it, either. Downstairs, Iris had gone to the front-room window again and looked at the van. 'What you call reconnaissance is surveillance, is it, Tom? Do I see peep holes at the tops of the As? Who was it said, "Hell is other people's peep holes?" Surveillance of whom? Is it a disguised police vehicle?'

'No, not police. I thought, tell the boys and Laura if any of them get curious that I needed it to bring the Viking Valhalla.'

'This doesn't answer the sort of questions they'll ask, does it?'

'I don't know. It should beat them off.'

'They'll want to know why lawns and gardens.'

'Because it's a lawns and gardens van.'

'Is that an answer?' She turned from the window. 'How long can you stay?'

'A couple of hours.'

'Oh.'

'I'm supposed to be working.'

'At what?'

'Reconnaissance, I told you.'

'Snooping? Surveillance. You get in the back and observe through the peep holes, is that it?'

Yes, that's entirely and absolutely it. I've got a vital commission from the head of the firm, Leo Percival Young. It's a very responsible assignment, a possible indication of full acceptance into the tribe, a declaration of: 'In thee, Tom, I put my trust.' He wants to know if one of his people is swindling him by filtering off high-quality customers. Niche work if you can get it. He's someone Leo *doesn't* trust and the contrast is very favourable to me. I'm the one who has to supply the evidence, validate the death warrant. Leo likes all the formalities properly attended to, especially when it's a slaughter item.

This thought scampered through his head, as that recollection of Burt Lancaster and Deborah Kerr in the breakers had. They remained as thoughts only, though, and unexpressed. 'I needed the van to bring the bike,' he replied.

'OK, OK, you're not talking.'

'There's a fixed feature in there that I could tie the Viking Valhalla to so it didn't get thrown about and damaged.'

'OK, OK, you're not talking.'

The pizza delivery had arrived then, just before Laura, and the boys turned up not long afterwards, radiantly clean and sleek from the swimming, diving and jacuzzi, fascinated by the parked van.

Luke started his quizzing. Others joined in.

Paul Harker said: 'It says lawns and gardens but could it of been about anything, anything at all, Mr Mallen, such as "Loft Conversions" or "Car Infirmary For All Your Dents And Scratches", or "Patio And Driveway Solutions"? There's a lot of vans saying "Solutions". The important thing is it don't say who you really are because it's for creeping up on villains without them knowing you're creeping up and then bursting out on them and shouting, "Armed Police!" not, "Lawns and Gardens!" or, "Loft Conversions!" There's observation holes in the As, aren't there, so they'd know when to burst out?'

Greg Mills said: 'God, Paul's grammar, Mr Mallen! He can be understood, though, if you concentrate. Anyway, you could have plenty of support in the back of the van sitting on benches around the vehicle walls, like paratroopers in a plane waiting to jump. But this support would be other officers, maybe wearing navy blue baseball caps with "Police" on them in white as a surprise, and rounding up all sorts.'

Harry Nelmes said: 'You in the front, driving, you'd have to be wearing dungarees, or something like that, so you'd look like you were used to working in gardens and getting the dandelions and other weeds out of lawns, so a lawn could *be* a lawn, not just grass with weeds. It would be a giveaway if you had on a suit and collar and tie. These would be plain clothes, yes, but the wrong plain clothes. You haven't got dungarees on now, Mr Mallen, but that's probably because you're off duty.'

Greg Mills said: 'Or most of the time he could be watching from in the back of the van. He would not be seen, although he'd be seeing, so it wouldn't matter about his clothes.'

'Grub up!' Tom replied.

Iris and he handed out the pizzas and ate their own. After that, there was a vampire DVD for the lads and Laura. Tom helped clear the room of plates, glasses and cutlery. In the kitchen, Iris said: 'Do you know what I'd like, Tom?' She answered before he could. But he would have guessed right. 'A ride in the van,' she said.

'Yes?'

'Possible?'

'Of course.'

'I'll tell the gang, then. Just a quick spin.'

'Fine,' he said.

He drove, with Iris in the passenger seat. He took the road he'd arrived by earlier.

'I want to get fucked in this vehicle,' she said.

'Yes, I know.'

'The back's not full of those support cops Greg mentioned, is it?'

'Don't believe so.'

'It will be like putting an imprint on this van, on this bit of your life.'

'Yes. I did something the same with the Viking Valhalla.'

'Despite all the shadiness, when it comes down to essentials ... Well, when it comes down to essentials, I'm one of those essentials.'

'The most essential essential, Iris.'

'This van is not outside my sphere. I can commandeer it, utilize it.'

'True.'

'Do I sound desperate, as if I'm trying to convince myself, Tom?'

Yes, some of that. But he said: 'All of it's spot on.'

'Sad?'

Yes, like that. A flavour of finality. But he said: 'Joyous. Positive.'

'There's a lay-by a couple of miles away on this road, isn't there?' she said.

'I think so.'

'On the other side.'

'Yes.'

'Here,' she said, in a few minutes.

'Yes.' He pulled over and stopped there again.

They climbed into the back and closed the doors.

'We can make a pillow with your clothes,' he said, 'so you don't get your hair mucked up from the floor. And I'll put my coat under you.'

'These admin details,' she said. 'Unimportant. The fuck's what's important. It takes possession of this horrible vehicle, tames it, colonizes it, incorporates it into something sweet and deep, makes it just a handy love venue.'

Temporarily. But he said: 'Oh, yes, yes. Lie across. The van's wide, luckily. It can cope with tallness.'

'Yours, too. I'll be on top. I'm in that kind of mood – imperious, controlling. Here's the pillow, and, yes, fold your jacket for a fender under your arse.'

'Ah, *that's* what you meant by wanting a ride in the van.' On the way back to the house he bought some petrol.

TWENTY

BEFORE

Tom put the van odometer back to what it should be, cutting the mileage record by the distance for the round trip home, plus the there-and-back jaunt to that all-purpose lay-by with Iris, this being only nine miles, but he wanted everything exact. Undercover, even a minor failure to tally could start suspicion. Meticulousness – that's what he aimed for, meaning care over detail. Meticulousness – that's what his masquerade and his life depended on, like the lives of all snoops. Meticulousness wasn't a word he'd normally come out with, but they'd recommended it very forcefully and very often at Hilston Manor. A tutor there said 'meticulous' used to mean fearful of consequences, from the Latin, and that a degree of fear was right for undercover people: fear of getting rumbled. If the words of the national anthem had been composed at Hilston, they'd have made it 'send her meticulous', not the bloodthirsty 'send her victorious'.

But the drive back had been in the dark, so it

wasn't possible to be meticulous about watching for tails: one set of headlights looked like another in the mirror. Anyway, he felt pretty certain his worries about the Astra had been unnecessary. It certainly hadn't stuck with him. He'd written notes of the van's mileage readings during his extra travels, so it was easy to do the sums and adjustments before returning the vehicle to Leo Young at Midhurst. In some ways it hurt Tom to wipe out any trace of that journey he'd made with Iris. It seemed to mean that all the brave things she'd said about taking over the van, turning it into part of their love life, were cancelled – or had never amounted to anything but a wish, a hope. The van had become the job again, and only the job, not a happy humping site, with some of her warm clothes as a pillow and his folded jacket saving his behind.

Of course, she'd hinted that behind the show of boldness and conquest, she knew what the reality was: and so she'd asked him whether her efforts at optimism sounded desperate, sad. Silently, he'd decided they did. For her the van signified separation, distance, secrecy, career-mongering, complicated dangers. Yes. And the van was intended chiefly for taking an A-hole interest in what happened outside itself from eight possible angles, not for mature aged, farewell, marital fucking inside.

Tom texted Young from a petrol station near home to give a summary report on the Norm Rice shopping visit. It was after midnight. The text would suggest he'd been outside Emblem Court continuously until now. 'Deputy collected materials as per sched using luggage trolley, TP.'

There was a reply from Leo: 'Nice work. Leave van in grounds. Your car is checked OK and ready with keys near the stables. Sleep. Meeting here eleven a.m.'

Tom added what he estimated to be the right amount of fuel to cover the journey back to Iris and the children and so on.

When he drew up at Midhurst next day just before eleven a.m. in the BMW, Leo came out from the house with Martin Abidan to greet him. Leo's wife, Emily, waved to Tom from an upstairs window, a genial, comradely wave. Leo and Abidan walked over to the stables and Leo opened the doors. Tom got out of the BMW, went to the van, drove it into the stables, and parked near the black Mercedes. At the petrol station twenty-four-hour shop in the night he had bought beakers of tea, coffee and soup and filled all the Thermos flasks. He wouldn't let on at once, though, now. He thought he'd keep this as a good surprise for some point deep into the meeting. He knew it would delight Leo. The Thermos lids acted as cups, but, because there might be more than three at the meeting, he had washed out the beakers and brought them in his pocket, plus some sweeteners, dried milk in an envelope, and a teaspoon.

Ivor Wolsey arrived and joined them. Leo

unlocked the back of the van and they all climbed aboard. Abidan unfolded three picnic chairs. Leo himself sat on the hinged cover of the closed commode. The others formed a semi-circle around him. Compared to the commode, their chairs looked flimsy and unserious. The commode's solid wood and its thick arm rests gave Leo a kind of unique dignity, like a guru with grouped disciples eager to feed on his dicta. Also, the commode put him slightly higher than Tom, Abidan and Wolsey. Anyone glancing into the van would realize Leo's position proclaimed leadership, despite his absurd pin-headedness. Although he was short-legged, his feet reached the floor all right, never mind the commode's extra bit of height. He wore excellent, unscuffed black lace-ups, size seven or possibly seven and a half.

Leo said: 'Emily being at home, it's more ... well ... more private to talk here. The van's our conference chamber for today. And she wouldn't want us clogging up one of the rooms, would she? Anyway, I love this vehicle. Such a grand piece of planning.'

'Absolutely,' Abidan said. 'I've never seen it before.'

'Not many have,' Leo Young said. 'It's fairly new. Tom's been on a little excursion for me in her, utilizing the A junction point observation windows. And she was all right, was she, Tom? Behaved herself fine? Made your task so much easier?'

'Fine,' Tom said. 'A doddle.'

'How long did it take – the wait?' Leo asked.

'Nine hours, about,' Tom said.

'So the supplies and the commode were convenient?' Leo said. He pointed out the rack of Thermos flasks to Abidan and Wolsey.

'True,' Tom said. 'Indispensable.'

'Three flasks – tea, coffee, soup,' Leo said. 'You filled up in advance, did you, Tom? A good variety of hot standbys. These build and sustain morale. Logistics.'

'Right,' Tom said.

'This van makes you independent, that's the beauty of it,' Leo said.

'Right,' Tom said. He thought a time must come when Leo referred to the van as 'iconic'.

'What sort of excursion?' Wolsey said. 'I didn't know work of that type was planned. Has it come up in previous discussion? Not that I remember.'

Leo gave a kind of smile. Tom regarded it as unquestionably a smile, Leo's lips drawn quite a way back over his cared-for teeth. His miniature face gleamed, radiating lavish intolerance. On a bigger spread of complexion this might have seemed less concentrated, but Leo could offer only a quite skimpy area, so his expression had a burning, very focused intensity. Maybe Leo felt ratty with Wolsey for arriving late. 'Think around a mo for fuck's sake, would you, Ivor, before spouting please?' Leo replied.

'Excuse me, Leo, but think around in which

respect?' Wolsey said.

Leo sat right back. He stretched out his arms along each of the rests and gripped the curled ends. Yes, 'dignity' was the word, or even 'grandeur'. Now he reminded Tom of a monarch in one of those TV costume plays, growing regal and severe with followers. 'In respect of priorities,' Leo said.

'Well, yes, but there's quite a number of *them*,' Wolsey said. 'I'm not clear which you have in mind, Leo.'

'Is that so?' Leo said. 'Is that so? You're "not clear". A pity.' The smile had gone, but he spoke with perfect, false gentleness. 'You heard of Justin-fucking-Scray at all, Ivor? Or fucking Claud Norman Rice? This was an executive decision. I didn't need a company vote. A firm can't be run proper if the head of it got to consult at every stage.'

'Tom's been handling a project on those two?' Wolsey asked. He sounded shocked, maybe amazed to hear that someone new to the firm drew such a key assignment; shocked, amazed and bypassed.

'Why shouldn't he?' Leo said.

Ivor thought about that and then obviously took account of Leo's dark temper and wanted to back down. He raised both his hands for a moment, like *kamarade*. 'No reason, absolutely no reason,' he replied. 'Just a surprise, Leo. As I said, I didn't know any operations were under way, that's all.'

'What – you thought I'd just let them two, Scray, Rice, suck the business dry in their brazen way, did you, Ivor? I'm supposed to lie back and enjoy getting shafted, am I? You in favour of them two, then? You got a sweet salary linkage there, perhaps?'

Most likely, Leo saw betrayal everywhere. At Hilston, course members had been warned top dogs of a firm could get like that: 'the Robespierre syndrome', as it was called after the French revolutionary politician who ran what was known as 'the Reign of Terror' but who eventually got head-chopped himself. This, rather than Ivor's lateness, might explain Leo's sudden, wild rage. But, no, Leo didn't see betrayal *everywhere*, did he? For example, not betrayal by Tom Parry. The reverse. Apparently the reverse. Tom got trusted to carry out crucial, delicate reconnaissance solo in Leo's adored van. Yet this was Tom Mallen, though for the time being, Tom Parry, whose designated and only objective was in fact to betray and nail Leo. Naturally, that wasn't how it would be officially described by those running him. They'd say 'to gather possible evidence against Leo Percival Young by certain approved, confidential, continuously supervised procedures'.

Leo didn't speak again for a while. The van's back doors remained open. The horses moved about in their stalls, whinnying occasionally and snorting. These were the only sounds in the stables building. Tom felt there wouldn't have been many business meetings around Britain held in such conditions – a van as boardroom with background animals. He thought Leo might be waiting for his anger to fade. Maybe he realized the outburst against Ivor, and the accusation of paid-for treachery, had been hysterical.

Then, Leo leaned forward, as though to make sure the message came across OK, but stayed securely with just the four of them. 'What we got, via the van and Tom, is a picture of Norm Rice rolling up in his proud, red Lexus at a known wholesaler's property and taking away definite freight for subsequent undisclosed dealing with punters who should of been ours, should of been the firm's. *This* fucking firm's. Not some splinter outfit's.' Passionately, he struck the right arm of the commode with two blows from the side of his fist. They obviously signified rage, but perhaps also, resolve.

He said: 'Tom watched Rice as errand boy for Scray, pushing a case on castors for the bulk. What we have here is a kind of massive theft. They're stealing our best customers, that is, who *would* of been our best customers, but who got intercepted, who got hijacked, by that gifted turd, Scray. It's a prime disgrace.'

Tom reckoned indignation seemed to suit extremely well someone in such excellent three-piece, dark worsted tailoring, and the fine black lace-ups. Tom had noticed before that fury from a man in a buttoned-up waistcoat had exceptional edge, even someone short.

'Nine hours!' Abidan said. 'That's some tour of duty!'

'This is the beauty of the van,' Leo said, a smile back, but more or less authentic now. 'It can stand there, like, in total innocence, its harmless identity, or *alleged* identity, present in pretty lettering for all to read – its connection with healthy, familiar settings, such as back gardens, obvious. And, inside, the operative is utterly comfortable, nourished, untroubled by lower bodily pressures, and capable of multi-scrutinizing via the A-windows.'

'Great,' Abidan said.

And Tom could more or less hear their minds whirring – Abidan's and Wolsey's – asking themselves, could a van wait there that long, unbothered by wardens or the police; unnoticed from his window by someone super-alert and nervous because he's about to do an illegal, highly murky deal with a courier who's perilously deep into a conspiracy against that baron of barons, Leo Percival Young? And they might think, too, that the courier himself would be very aware of risk and looking out for suspect vehicles doing crafty surveillance. The pretty lettering *was* pretty and very professionally done, but that didn't mean it got swallowed.

Leo said: 'This kind of meeting – a planning meeting – well, obviously I'd usually invite Justin Scray. But you won't be surprised by his absence. Although he's number three in our company and, in some ways, a valued high-flier with several undoubted flairs, it's impossible for him to be one of us today in this unusual van venue. Why? Because he's the very object of this meeting, isn't he? He is our topic. If he was here, he wouldn't be present to discuss but to be discussed, and not in a friendly style, either. All right, this time it was Norm who actually done the transacting re new supplies of the commodities, but who's behind Norm? Who *sent* dear, two-timing Norm? I've already give you the answer to that one, though I'm sure you could of seen it for yourselves. This kind of filthy behaviour by Scray is not so very new news, is it? We've all known about it. Or, we all had an idea it was happening. The accounts showed something rotten going on. But proof? That we was short of, until this brill expedition by Tom and the van. I don't act without proof.'

'You're well known for such carefulness, Leo, for such thoroughness. Ivor will confirm that, I'm sure,' Abidan said. He was giving him a chance to get back into harmony with Leo. Empathy Abidan liked relationships to be peaceful and healthy. He could have been a Foreign Office diplomat, even an ambassador, if his career hadn't happened to turn in this different direction owing to an acute, businesslike interest in the substances.

Ivor rushed to accept the help. 'Definitely,' he said. 'Talking to people from other outfits, I often hear them say how strict and uncompromising Leo is about the need for good evidence before, say, a full removal or punishment slapping. It's not always like that in their own firms, and they feel some shame.'

'Which people from other outfits do you talk to?' Leo said. 'What you talking to them *for*, Ivor? What you discussing me for? I don't think I want the company's name or my name discussed by all sorts.'

'Not all sorts, Leo,' Ivor said. 'One or two.'

'Even so,' Leo replied.

'Ivor would be very discreet, I'm sure of that,' Abidan said.

'What do *you* think, Tom?' Leo said.

'It's the kind of informal, possibly useful contact that needs a lot of caution,' Tom said. 'Things can be learned from such conversations, quite possibly valuable insights into other firms, but there's also the danger of revealing too much about *our* firm.' He gave the *'our* firm' hefty emphasis, so as to stress his membership and constancy.

'Exactly,' Leo said. 'Caution. What I'd like to know is how my name came into things at all.'

'It was in a very favourable way,' Ivor replied. 'Positive, absolutely.'

'In commerce, this kind of commerce, there isn't no favourable way of talking about another firm's chief. No positive way. If his name is mentioned it's because some sod is thinking: how do I push, kick and elbow that one off of his top spot and grab his rich domain?'

'Favourable and positive because they admire how you get a true case together before someone is made the subject of extreme treatment,' Ivor said. 'It's considered sort of rare and therefore refreshing.'

'There's no admiring, either, in this trade. They're feeding you them little bits of praise to smooth and lull, so you'll go on talking about me and the firm, and they'll be listening for things you won't even know you're saying, but they'll be filleting your words for info, quite often words you'd imagine were totally OK and even dull, but they'll sniff at them, for their own reasons. It's how questioning works – known as interrogation, of course. They'll let you chatter away, like a woman on a bus, and they'll fix on some tiny point you might not of noticed at all speaking, but they will tie it to other tiny points and this will help them get the entire picture. And you'll be wondering how they done it, even though it was you who gave them the stuff.'

'I know Ivor will be more cautious from now on,' Empathy said.

'"Cautious" – that's Tom's word, and it's a good one,' Leo replied. 'There's a saying about "throwing caution to the wind". At school, I remember we had to read a story where "he threw caution to the wind" on account of an adventure. Well, the wind don't need that caution, so it shouldn't be thrown to it. I'd like you both to discuss with Tom later the many aspects of cautiousness that might be required.

He'll show you how these work, how to get the best out of them.'

Ivor Wolsey said: 'It will be a privilege to accept advice from—'

'You'll notice there's someone else, beside Justin Scray, not present at this conference, who would normally be here,' Leo replied. 'No, I don't mean Norm Rice. He's always only been a dogsbody, a lackey. He don't come in on policy discussions. Policy decisions tell him what he got to do. That's his only connection with policy. So, not Norm Rice, but Jamie Meldon-Luce. Nobody could call Jamie a dogsbody or a lackey. Skills. Ample skills, a bucketful. He supplies them, e.g., he sees what's what in an accounts sheet; second e.g., he has sources who bring quality insights; and third e.g., he's a wonderful Wheels, delicate in his touch, yet also familiar with the flat-on-the-floor-almost-through-to-the-road accelerator. And it's in that respect, the Wheels respect, that he would usually of been at a meeting such as this, because, obviously, something's got to be done about Norm Rice and Scray, which will need high-grade driving. The place where this action is to happen I haven't completely decided yet, but it's definitely going to require proper transport to carry the scold team and bring them away, possibly stained or even injured.

'However, the point about Jamie is at present he's got a daughter doing Mary Magdalene in a church play and he's going to be there to see it, got to be there to see it. Naturally. She's eight. This is support for her from Dad and Mum. What are people going to think of them if they don't turn up to watch and join in the final clapping, if clapping is allowed in a church? For reasons I might explain later, the correction we have in mind for, say, Claud Norman Rice, first, the poxy louse, has to be done on a certain, specific day – the day of the church play with Carol Jane Letitia doing Mary Magdalene, as a matter of fact. But even if that was not so, I wouldn't want Jamie driving on this one. Forgive me, but I wouldn't. Maybe it's a weakness. How I see it is, I couldn't really ask someone whose daughter's going to be, or has been, taking a top level role in a church play – no, I can't ask him to carry out an operation where someone is going to get beaten half to death, at least half, owing to foul behaviour in a business context.

'All right, what we'll be at is absolutely deserved by Norm in the court of natural justice, and it's all backed up with facts supplied to us by Tom and the van, what could be referred to with total accuracies as an indictment. I could still not feel right about it, though. In them circumstances – a religious event via Jamie's daughter – it wouldn't seem appropriate to ask him to do this necessary ferrying at a date so close to the church event. Finger irons might be in use and other metal. Do you see what I mean when I say inappropriate? This is a taste matter.

It would be wrong. It would be crude. It would be disrespecting a family occasion – his family, and also a holy occasion. I would not feel correct if I demanded Jamie get this Wheels job done, regardless of his little girl acting a whore who gives it up when inspired. And this being so, I'm going to ask Tom here to take that role.'

Leo had another smile. It contained wryness. Tom had noticed a while ago that Leo possessed several types of smile and certainly knew when to use each of them. It amounted to an outright flair with him, a sort of RADA – trained aptitude. He said: 'That sounds as if I'm asking Tom to take the Mary Magdalene role. No.'

Tom had a chuckle at this, and after a moment Empathy and Ivor did, too.

'But do the *Wheels* role for me, Tom, would you?' Leo said. 'This has a certain tidiness about it, because, of course, it's on account of your terrific work in this very van that we are on to Rice and Scray in a confirmed and clear way, though work at a different location, obviously – watching the dealer's property, noting the arrival and departure of Norm.'

'Iconic,' Ivor said, sucking up late, but possibly not *too* late.

'What? Leo said.

'The van,' Ivor said.

'Well, yes, it could be referred to with such a word, I suppose,' Leo replied. 'It's not for me to describe it like that, because I had a part in the design.'

'Definitely iconic,' Ivor said.

Tom considered that a shag within the marriage bonds, although unusually situated, in no way damaged the vehicle's iconic status.

Leo said: 'When this meeting's over, I'll take you to have a look at Norm's place, Tom, so you'll be familiar with the route and the surroundings, and especially the best leave-the-scene roads.'

'Fine,' Tom said. 'But perhaps now is the occasion for a little van-based refreshment – to clinch the all round impression we have of its magnificent character – yes, its pure, iconic nature?' He stood and stepped towards the flask rack.

'The Thermoses?' Leo said in an excited whisper, vivid anticipation aglow in his economical face.

'What else?' Tom replied.

'This is wonderful,' Leo said.

Tom took the flasks down and set them on the van floor, more or less where he'd lain when getting interim on-topped by Iris. He set one of the extra beakers alongside them as well as the teaspoon and sweeteners. 'So, what will it be?' he asked them.

'Brilliant,' Leo said. 'This gives a striking glimpse of the van's capabilities.'

'I think you should have first choice, Leo, as host,' Abidan said.

'The soup is oxtail,' Tom said.

'Soup, then,' Leo replied.

Tom put some into a spare beaker for him.

'Tea for me,' Empathy said. 'One sweetener.'

Tom poured, stirred and handed him the cup-lid. There was a community character to the occasion now, and Tom felt pleased to seem part of it.

'If there's soup left I'll have that, please,' Ivor said. This would be another move to restore good vibes with Leo – the shared taste for oxtail, possibly showing a genes similarity.

Tom poured again and gave him the soup. Tom himself took coffee with two sweeteners.

'This is ideal,' Leo said. 'It's hardly like work at all, more a happy, relaxed, social get-to-gether.'

'Yes, indeed,' Tom replied.

Leo said: 'There *is* work, of course – arrang-ing plans for possible removal of that shite, Scray, and, in any case, for smashing some badly delayed regret into Norm. But the joy of the situation and circumstances takes away the drudgery of it.' A kind of intimate cosiness existed inside the van and phrases like 'poxy louse', 'that shite, Scray', and 'smashing some badly delayed regret into Norm' seemed to float for several moments around them, affectionately cosseting Tom's ears, and, presumably, the ears of the others.

He said: 'If anyone wants to switch for a refill, there's the other spare beaker.'

'This soup will be enough for me,' Leo said.

'Ditto,' Ivor said.

Leo said: 'I like to think of Tom, secure and patient in the van, constantly checking the outer scene via the A-holes, possibly sipping a soup or coffee, even while deep into vigilance. And then, suddenly, after nine hours, to his grand satisfaction, here comes that fucking swindler, Norm Rice, pulling or pushing a case trolley, like someone at the airport off to Ibiza. Tom's wait has been *so* justified. I'd like you to recall what I said in my second e.g. about Jamie – if he gets a tip it's going to be a tip you can bet your castle on. Jamie gave us the dealer's particulars, name, address, specialities. And so Tom, in the van, can place himself at the right point, un-observed but observing. Did you ever think during this trip to and from that you might have a tail, Tom?'

There'd been the Astra. But that was on a route Tom shouldn't have been using at all – the road home: to remain unmentioned. And, in any case, it definitely disappeared after the stop at the bike shop. The Astra had gone its own way, unconcerned with the van, only on the same road for a while by fluke. 'Nothing, Leo,' Tom said.

'You were keeping an eye?' Leo replied.

'Constantly,' Tom said.

'I knew you would,' Leo said. 'Basic. Elemen-tary. This van has a wonderful ordinariness about it, and yet it isn't ordinary at all.'

'Right,' Tom said.

'Maybe Norman's case on wheels held cash

funds when he went in, to make a purchase; then the materials on the way out,' Empathy said. 'This is an image of how the market functions in a free society. A paradigm. Money to begin with. This money handed over. And in exchange come goods.'

'You must of been doing an Open University Master's degree in Business Studies on the quiet,' Leo replied. 'What I'm after now is a tableau.'

'Certainly,' Ivor said.

'I think the case might have been empty on the way in,' Tom said. 'Not that it's material, I suppose.' It was material in helping prove Tom had truly been there and observant.

'A tableau in the sense of considering the whole stack and spread of possibilities,' Leo said.

'This has ever been your style, Leo,' Ivor said. 'Overarching.'

'The personnel in this tableau being Scray, Norm and us,' Leo said.

'Exactly,' Ivor said.

'Why the fuck do you answer, "Exactly"? How do you know what I'm going to say?' Leo asked.

'I meant "exactly" in general, Leo,' Ivor said. 'Sort of globally.'

'I'm what's referred to as "pragmatic",' Leo replied.

'No gainsaying that,' Ivor said.

'Scray: a high-grade operator with a collection

of customers that I – we – want and intend getting,' Leo said. 'Now, maybe them customers got faith in Justin Scray as to quality of the product, price and security. Important factors. This is a valuable supplier-client relationship.'

'Very,' Ivor said.

'Therefore, we don't necessarily want Justin killed, regardless of how much the fucker has earned it.'

'Which he undoubtedly has,' Ivor said.

'We want him *with* us, not wiped out and with nobody. If he's with us he brings that crowd of devoted, disposable-incomed punters with him. They've got not just a habit but a habit of dealing with Scray. OK, the false bastard is as false as false will ever be, but it's only us who think he's a false bastard, *know* he's a false and stealthy bastard, because it's to us that he's the false bastard. His customers don't see it the same. *They* regard him as a true, reliable, honest gent who comes up regular with a packet of their delights every week or so. They long to stick with him. He's their beloved, safe, accommodating Mr Snort, or the Marquis of Mainline.'

'I love it,' Ivor said, giggling. '"Mr Snort!" "The Marquis of Mainline!" Maybe "The High-Commissioner of H".'

'We need him,' Leo said. 'What we don't need is daft rage, a stupid search for vengeance.'

'Yes, we need the bastard,' Ivor said.

'This is why I spoke of a tableau,' Leo said.

'Of course,' Ivor said.

227

'In this tableau we get to Norm Rice as openers.'

'The poxy louse!' Ivor declared.

'We gives him some pain and possible breakages, but not on an absolutely immense scale which might lead to medical and police poking about. Norm wouldn't want that; it would be like an intrusion on his privacy. *We* wouldn't want it, either, obviously. I'd like it so he can manage, say, the splints and poultices by himself, or through dear ones – no hospitalization and all the snags that could bring for the firm, such as questions re how he got in that state, whatever it might be. People outside the trade are not going to understand that Justin and Norm were asking for it by their obnoxious behaviour.

'Norm's not our main objective, clearly. His injuries will be sort of messengers, and they are aimed at his master and scabby honcho, Justin Scray. And what do these messengers tell him, then? They tell him, first, we know what the fuckers are up to, owing to our own confidential methods, the chief of them methods being a tastefully customized van. Two, we don't like it. Three, we're not going to put up with it. Four, this is what a churl in their private outfit gets after he's been fully observed doing a deal to feed this secret string of punters; and if a nobody in his organization gets this, Scray better start thinking what might come to him, such as not just a bit of rough-house but something that

228

suits his higher rank, for instance, a volley in the tit region.

'My reckoning is he'll want to talk terms with us then, the terms being he stops fucking about with a select list but brings them to where the people on that list ought to be, that is, with us. Then, he can come back to his position in this firm and use his talents as they ought to be used, not for a firm within the firm, but for the firm.'

'Right,' Ivor said.

'This is why I said a tableau,' Leo replied.

'And that's what it is, a tableau,' Ivor said.

'This is why I said "pragmatic",' Leo replied. 'I look at the situation and, despite hatred and contempt for what they're doing, I put all that aside and ask myself: what's best for the firm? I ask it in a cool, constructive way. And what's best for the firm is Scray, unslaughtered at this stage – yes, at this stage – Justin Scray working with us, and his special battalion of big-spend customers added to our own and given a very hearty welcome.'

'Right,' Ivor said. 'That's definitely pragmatic.'

'I ask myself, what's business about?' Leo said.

'This is the question,' Ivor said.

'Business is about accruing,' Leo replied.

'Ah,' Ivor said.

'Accruing – i.e., building up – income and capital, and, as one of the ways to this, accruing customers. Justin would bring a nice sheaf of them with him, customers who should of been ours, anyway, in the first place, the unscrupulous prick. But you probably think, Ivor – how can this sod get brought back fully into the firm at number three, going ahead of such as yourself, even though he been behaving in that dirty fashion?' Leo said.

'No, no, not at all,' Ivor said.

'Like, as if Scray advises himself as part of his career plan, "Go and betray the management and get promoted for it, Justin,"' Leo said.

'You're the one who has to make decisions and policy about personnel, Leo. Everyone accepts that,' Ivor replied.

'Don't be so fucking understanding and feeble,' Leo said. 'It's why you get walked over.' Leo stood, opened the commode lid and produced a blue covered ring binder from the basin. He re-closed the commode and sat down again. He opened the ring binder. It contained what looked like a few lined sheets of paper. 'Jamie has done some research and come up with a list of people using Justin Scray and Norm as their suppliers,' he said. 'Jamie don't claim this to be complete, but he offers it as a guide to the kind of customers intercepted by them two. The names don't matter. It's the probable wage level, the earnings status that's important, you'll agree. We got to act, no question.'

He looked down at the top sheet in the binder and began to nod as he counted: 'One, two, three four, five Chamber of Commerce people; two airline pilots; three RAF pilots, including a woman; two head teachers; three regular soldiers above the rank of major; likewise, two naval officers above the rank of lieutenant commander.' He turned the page. 'Seven university lecturers and professors; two medical consultants and five doctors; four boardroom industrialists; two newspaper executives; four master plumbers; three software and IT specialists; three beauty parlour owners; two mastiff breeders; one high sheriff; two boutique proprietors; one stand-up comedian who gets on TV.' He closed the binder. 'This will give you some notion of the scale of greed and disloyalty we're up against.'

'Appalling,' Ivor said. 'This is conspiracy – no other word will do.'

'We've been dozy and careless,' Leo replied.

'You shouldn't sink into self-blame,' Ivor said.

'I blame all of us,' Leo said. 'There's a holy duty to put things right. That's why it's so necessary to give Norm a bit of heavy bruising and so on at this junction.'

'Absolutely,' Ivor said. 'Oh, absolutely.'

TWENTY-ONE

BEFORE

The ring binder's page three and four contained pencilled plans of Norm Rice's home inside and out. Tom kept the binder open on his lap now. He had the black Merc passenger seat. Leo drove. 'Marvellous detail,' Tom said. 'Even the furniture layout shown.'

'Furniture is often a tactical factor in this kind of unforgiving mission,' Leo said. 'Vital to know its location. Furniture is capable of turning the tables – tables being themselves furniture, of course.'

'Who mapped it?'

'Jamie. Furniture items can be an obstruction, a hide-behind shield or rampart for its owner,' Leo said. 'And furniture can also be an attack weapon. Think of a straight-backed, tall-backed, strut-backed, Rennie Mackintosh style chair of true timber swung in an arc to mince someone. I don't want any of my people on the end of that – getting hit by both beautifully shaped rear chair legs at the same time, one on the skull, the other cracking the shoulder, worse even than the "old one-two" in boxing. Unlikely Norm will go into a cower and collapse when our party arrives. Most probably the bastard can get brave. Oh, he's skinny, yes, but that don't mean he won't fight. Even someone so underweight believes he got an entitlement to live how he wants to live. This, obviously, is a mistake. It's arrogance. It's selfishness. He has to be flattened, Tom. He'll be resisting the will of the firm, which I call a sort of massive, insulting treachery, and the fact he's only twenty-seven don't excuse. He ought to be able to understand the needs and rules of a community, such as our long-established, happy, comradely organization.

'Originally I thought, given nice weather, take him out to some decent country spot and hammer him there, pleasantly secluded by the greenery and grand tree trunks, some many decades old, or even more than a century, very much part of our noble English heritage, not to be matched, most probably, in any of them fucking euro-zone countries, with their fucking Black Forest, that kind of thing. These are the type of surroundings where delivery of a reproach for disloyalty would seem appropriate. But real problems might result. Can you see that? It's another example of what's known in the military as "logistics", Tom. The chief question arising would be: do we leave him there afterwards – secluded, yes, but not totally off the tracks? Does he die on account of a beating *plus* exposure? Wrong objective. It would be going too far. He's not Justin Scray.

'Although Norm's got no right to live how he wants to live, he *has* got a right to some kind of life, the kind we say is OK, so far. If you join a firm, the firm's thinking's got to be *your* thinking. For example, Tom, consider a nun signing up to one of them holy orders where they stay in the convent, maybe silent. It wouldn't fit if she went out on the quiet and got herself a job as, say, a sub-postmistress or assistant manager at a squash club. Those are absolutely OK posts for someone else, but they don't fit what this nun promised when she went behind the wall voluntary. It's the same with Norm. If he was just starting in the business, starting solo, he could deal with who he likes. But this is not the case with him, is it? He's part of a firm, and that firm's got its requirements, namely exclusivity – I don't know if you ever came across that term, Tom.

'Maybe somebody out walking the dog finds Norm, possibly unconscious, maybe disabled, perhaps with enough strength left to call out now and then, hoping for help. They'll mobile for an ambulance, won't they? This is plainly a total inconvenience for us, drawing that sort of attention we don't want, but, according to normal standards, they'd be doing the proper thing. In fact, they'd feel they didn't have no choice. This is "Good Samaritan" baloney: find a wounded human being, so respond like a human being. Very nice. They would say they couldn't pass by on the other side of one of them grand old trees.

'It sounds simple and logical, but, of course, it's got a deep fucking fault. When it's a matter of seeing to a sod who's been robbing us of customers and therefore earned income in a totally uncaring, even flippant fashion, the normal standards are not the ones we're in favour of, are they? We'd have our own, very personal, very natural, ideas about the situation, and these are not mainly to do with Norm's health. If he was discovered like that and put in an ambulance, ask yourself what comes next, Tom, in the sequence. What comes next is the police get told. That's the sequence. Routine. Maybe the media. Someone would be sure to know he works for us. I don't want all the fuss and inquiries. Such as, "Is he one of your associates, Mr Young? Have you got any thoughts on how he got to be very seriously damaged up among forestry, this not being his usual area at all?" There's a business to be nursed along, and I got no taste for questions about someone pole-axed to this side of death in a dell, which he deserved.

'Also, if we don't leave him there to be found but take Norm home in the car following this encounter, there's the possibility people passing or at their window see him getting assisted with lovely tenderness from the vehicle at his address in Delbert Avenue, maybe a leg obviously useless for a while at least, or his jaw swinging askew, like an open door in a storm on only one hinge. Then, too, there's the possible mess in the car. Did you ever see *Pulp Fiction*, Tom, a film? Someone gets accidentally shot on the back seat and blood flies in a very embarrassing, coverall fashion throughout the interior. It wouldn't be as bad as that with Norm, because there'd be no explosion to give his blood and bone fragments wings and jet power, but bad, all the same.

'In his house for the beating, it will be much more a neatly contained incident with a fair degree of precious domestic privacy. This is fine. You'll have heard the saying "an Englishman's home is his castle", which still has some meaning even though the bloody government pokes about everywhere these days, so if you can get entrance to that castle you got him in extremely promising conditions: the team are protected by his property, although he himself isn't, because you're inside there with him cosy, uneyeballed by neighbours, and determined to make a memorable, very definite impression on him. Norm Rice got a partner, Cornelius Something, but he's locked up now for menaces, so we should be able to get Norm alone and probably not gun-armed in his honest little dwelling. You've met that other popular phrase "he, or she, was a very private person", I'm sure. It's the sort of thing they get householders to say on TV News when someone living in the street has been discovered as a mass murderer who chopped up the bodies and posted pieces to various charities anon. Well, of course anon. Who's going to sign a gift tag on a toe? But, anyway, this is the kind of existence Norm likes as far as the social side goes. He don't seek a lot of company, only Cornelius, when he's not doing time. Of course, Norm will go and meet others if it's part of the job, such as some secret, major merchant who'll fill his castor case for him and take the payment. That's a different situation, isn't it?

'The main features to notice in the plan is where there are walls shared with the next door properties, Tom.' Leo glanced down for a moment, took a hand from the Mercedes wheel, and pointed to some lines on the sketch. 'Those've got to be avoided or neighbours might hear the carry-on, could even feel a bit of a tremor to their villa if someone's flung against the wall, although Norm's body weight is low, admitted. In fact, that might mean he's easier to fling, such as someone could throw a cricket ball further than a football, owing to size. And it's not just the blows and falling about, but possible shout-screams. This is not fair on other citizens in Delbert – they want a peaceful life, and why not? – and, in any case, it would be bad to get their curiosity started up.

'Therefore, only certain areas of the accommodation should be used: possibly a central room where there's a telly, so the sound can be turned up, masking most of the action. Put it on to where there's big music, or an old war film, such as *Wake Island*, with Brian Donlevy, plenty of din, not someone poncing about at a flower show, voice down in case of disturbing the bees and causing sour honey. I don't mean TV turned up to a daft level, because that would make it sound like something must be wrong, as much as the banging, yelling and tumbling would. You'll notice the TV is marked in very clear on the drawing. A TV is furniture, so you'll see that's one reason why it must be included in any illustration.

'Running a firm of this calibre, Tom, I got to have all-round vision, I need to think continuous of eventualities. Planning the perfect expedition is all very well, but you got to realize the unexpected could suddenly smack everything off course, like Scott of the Antarctic where the temperature went down so much lower than usual. I got to stress, it would be important not to let the target male fall against the TV, because this could bring it down with a noisy crash to the floor, noticeable in one of the next doors, and, beside that, do enough damage to the set to stop it working, so it can't conceal other sounds. I think of this scheduled episode with Norm as very like ballet – much activity of an extreme physical nature but *governed* activity, *precise* activity, Tom, not frantic and chaotic. Here we are. The white front door, number twenty-seven.'

It was a street of terraced houses opening

straight on to the pavement, obviously built for workmen's families to rent late in the nineteenth or early twentieth century. Most would be owned now, not rented. Many had been re-roofed in imitation slate and the wooden window frames replaced with PVC. Something similar had happened to the front doors, no longer of solid wood. Mock brass knockers aimed for a period touch. So did coach lamps here and there. The red-brick frontages of several houses had been painted over in pastel shades – light blue, ochre, turquoise – quite a prettifying disaster. Just the same, these cottages would probably last at least another hundred years. Leo parked around the corner, and they went on foot to reconnoitre a lengthy back lane running behind the Delbert odds. A stone and mortar wall about three metres high separated the rear gardens from the lane. Each house had a wooden door in the wall, originally so residents could put out rubbish and ashes for collection. 'Clearly, operational decisions must be left to the attack unit on the day, in line with prevailing conditions, but my own method would be: enter by the front door, withdraw via the garden and lane door,' Leo said.

'The first stages needn't be violent at all. It would look simply like a friendly visit. Of course, Norm will probably realize at once it isn't that. Maybe he wondered about the van the other day. Anyway, he'll guess he's been rumbled. But neighbours wouldn't see anything brutal about the call, or even unusual. These could be colleagues looking in on Norm, perhaps for entirely social reasons, say to console about the clink absence of Cornelius; or to discuss some aspect of business, the neighbours not knowing what that business is, I hope.

'Exiting might be different. Maybe it should be more out of sight. As I've said, Tom, I got to consider all eventualities such as damage or staining to one or more of our punishment troupe, which is how I think of them. I mean, for instance, blood on clothing, and, or face, and, or in somebody's hair. Blood in the hair, matting it and seeping down to the forehead and neck, is very noticeable in a quiet, respectable district. People won't want their children to view something frightening like that. Also the possibility of bone injury, limping, and/or torn garments, and/or ear rips. Even if none of that is so – and God grant it's not – there will be a ruffled, possibly breathless state for these lads. After all, they'll have taken part in something quite strenuous immediately before this withdrawal. This is why I referred to ballet, Tom. Dancers in, for instance, *Swan Lake*, will look wonderfully fit and elegant while they're actually performing and pissing about with the swan, but when they reach the dressing room I bet they do some mighty gasping and mutter, "Thought I'd never fucking get through the lifting tonight, such a tug on the crotch."

'I don't say park in this lane, Tom, while things are taking place, although that would cut the distance for our people leaving. The point is, if things go wrong somehow – which they definitely should not – but if they did, locals, such as more damn Good Samaritans, thinking trouble in Norm's place, could block both ends of the lane with vehicles. And so no matter how good a Wheels you might be, Tom, you and the other boys would be snookered. All right, you'd all be carrying something and the interfering sods wouldn't – they'd be just Delbert proles. But we don't really want that kind of blast off situation. Something like this might have very various results, results no bugger can't properly forecast.

'And another point is that the law might have armed response cars around the area, and they'd arrive with enough weaponry to take on the Foreign Legion. I'd recommend: park where we are tonight, which gives you two possible routes out of the district. People returning to the vehicle after the meeting with Norm should, if possible, walk to it, in a relaxed and very ordinary way, acting affable chat, like some good, chummy session has just took place, with possibly extremely constructive office talk.

'You'll say, people will wonder why the group hadn't parked right outside the house, if the call was so straightforward and harmless. Tom, there's always going to be a snag or snags in any scheme. Think of famine relief with half the money going to the crooked fuckers supposed to be using it on meals for the starving. The art is to find the prospect that's got the fewest snags and go for that, go for it with max confidence, max determination. Them's the qualities that made Britain great in a previous era, such as Trafalgar, such as Waterloo, qualities not, unfortunately, very plentiful now, maybe due to all them wind farms or the destruction of grammar schools. I expect Norm's been smuggling in gear to Cornelius on visiting days, and it might be difficult to make the journeys for a while. In any case, he'd hate to be seen by his lover scarred and/or disjointed. I'll try to fix some interimmed way for Cornelius to get his stuff. I don't want to seem uncaring, and we got no animosity for Cornelius: his menaces didn't come our way. Tom, you might think it's all a bit severe on Norm when, really, the chief thing is to get a warning to his mate, Justin. But Norm had a choice – to go with him or not go with him in this crafty abuse of the firm. Norm went with him. Norm's taking his slice of the gains. He's got to answer for it, or where is trade morality, where is order? I have to be a custodian of them high matters. It's part of leadership.'

They walked out of the lane and back to the Mercedes. Leo said: 'Two obvious points got to be considered, haven't they, Tom?'

'One, he has to be at home when the call's made. Two, he must let the lads in via the front door and without any signs of resistance,' Tom said.

'Absolutely right, Tom. You got aptitude. I

seen it from the very beginning. Also known as intuition.'

'Thanks, Leo.'

'I think we can timetable him pretty well. Jamie's done a survey of his work pattern and it's regular. In fact, it *has* to be regular because he's dealing with repeat customers who turn up at set times and want him to be there. Many are professional personnel and look for the kind of reliability they demand from their staffs, for instance hospital surgeons who'd expect the nurse to be ready with a jar for the gallstones. And the ride over in the Lexus to their private supplier is also regular for time and day of the week. So, we ought to be able to arrive when Norman's definitely at number twenty-seven. Next – what if he won't open, or opens and then tries to fight the lads off, struggling to keep them out? If he won't open, and we're sure he's inside, it will be a matter of someone, or maybe more than one, going around the back, climbing the wall if the lane door's bolted, and breaking in through a window or the kitchen door on to the backyard. Obviously, there'll be a chance that this kind of entry – the wall and possible kicking in of the kitchen door – will be noticed from other houses. That's a risk that's got to be took, though. Jamie has been in the property – Norm being at the time, as it seemed, a kind of mate – and says the kitchen door is of a very flimsy ply nature, easily boot- or shoe-shattered.

'Likewise, if there's resistance on the front

doorstep we got to be ready for it – finger irons, for instance, or a pistol butt – and Norm must be bundled back into the house, while the one doing this bundling is hidden from the street by another lad or lads standing behind and concealing these swiftly-over, necessary measures. If Norm's still conscious as the party leaves I'd like somebody to inform him that I certainly have Cornelius in mind, and there should be no very long break in his jail-aid – we having plenty of experience of getting such products through to any of our people inside who forward a request. It would be best that whoever gives him this comfort should get up very close because his hearing might of been affected.'

TWENTY-TWO

AFTER

Maud said she was going to bring a colleague in to run the closing session of the afternoon. There'd be a half hour's break before she arrived. Maud suggested that Harpur and Iles should return to the lunch room. A waitress would bring tea and biscuits. They could refresh themselves and perhaps discuss in private how things were going. Maud wouldn't join them there. She had to familiarize the colleague with the projector controls in the cinema.

When the waitress had gone, Iles said in a terrifyingly humane, even tender, tone: 'I would hate you to think I'd be an encumbrance, Col.'

'You, sir, an encumbrance? In which respect?'

'This is a woman searching, hoping, indeed, questing.'

'Maud?'

'I'd like you to think of her in this fashion.' He blanked his face for a moment to suggest he wished to order his ideas very sensitively. Iles could get sensitivity into his face occasionally, but it required willpower. He had plenty of this on call. It took time, though. 'She's surrounded here by people like herself, Col. That is, ultra-sharp, polished intellectuals who've come into the civil service – Home Office in this case and at the very select Administrative grade – eager to find the golden road to the summit, or near it. Oh, you'll say the young Edward Heath came top in admin-level entrance exams, so it can't have been much tougher than the old eleven-plus. That's a political slur, Harpur, I fear. Maud and the rest of them could have picked careers in academe, the media, the church, salon hair-dressing, politics or the City. They all chose functionary-dom, however. And now, what we have to consider, Harpur, is whether such same-ness, such rampant parity, is what she looks for in life. Does she want her man to be of that kind – a sort of image of herself, a simulacrum, with gender adjustments, which clearly you possess? I have to reply that this is not my notion of the essential Maud. I cannot see her as a stick in the mud.'

'Right, sir. Your own view of the Home Office might well suggest it must be regarded as the mud side of that saying, but it would be alto-gether another kettle of fish, as it were, to imagine Maud as a stick in it. Yes, a stick would definitely be quite another kettle of fish.'

'Col, this is a woman who looks at me, listens to me, respects me fully, and comes to feel that I am like those colleagues I've just spoken of, though in a different profession. She sees in me the same plentiful elite characteristics and the same quality of intellect, at least matching her own. Oh, yes, at least. The same quickness of mind, the same easy, comprehensive mental scope. This is, in my view, a woman who wants to venture, to range. She will not allow herself to be limited to her male equivalents, possibly her male superior. Oh, yes, quite possibly her superior. And so, as a dalliance prospect, I am passed over, to be frank, rejected, and she turns to you, Col. It can be detected at every moment in that other room. The delightful, tangy odour of blatant sex juice manufacture.' He closed his eyes, put his head back and breathed with ostentatious depth and thoroughness through his nose, rerunning how he had savoured the air in the film room, though without the actual odour itself available now, of course, or until Maud's return, unless she had cooled down and possibly swabbed herself.

'I do not resent this focus upon you, Col. You might question that, but I plead with you to accept it as wholly true. She is tired of braini-ness, except as a work tool, a workaday tool. She has no taste for the brilliantly educated, because she has been brilliantly educated her-self. She turns to someone like you, Col – some-one who has done quite reasonably well, given your substantial natural drawbacks and incoher-ent, crippled schooling, a schooling that achiev-ed its glittering zenith with long-division and naming Paris as capital of France. She wants to get fucked, Harpur, of course she wants to get fucked, of course, of course, but not by someone possessing similar gilded attributes to her own. This would be only half a step away from a wank. She requires someone radiating rough-house strangeness and the primitive. I've looked her up, as you'd expect, Col – starred First from Cambridge, pleas from her dons there to stay on and enjoy a research fellowship and who knew what thereafter? This bidding for her was prob-ably very largely on account of her grey matter and scholarship, not the cordial tits and fine, unbluestockinged, openable legs, though these might put her a little ahead in a competitive interview, other things being equal. She de-clined the invitations. Why? These reasons are not set down anywhere. One can speculate, though. One can infer. That enclosed world she regarded as not her natural world. She desired the new, the unfamiliar, the spectacularly under-refined, or absolutely unrefined if possible.

'But, blow me, in a manner of speaking, she joins the civil service and finds herself in pretty much the same sort of grouping as if she'd stay-ed at Cambridge. Confusion. Frustration. And then you and I arrive. Or, rather, *you* arrive. I? I am discarded from the outset as too suave, too acute, too learned, too much like herself and her grossly gifted associates here. To Maud, you represent escape, Col. You, Col, are that fuck from another crude, quaint, yet tolerable milieu, from a region of no social or intellectual standing, yet not to be entirely written off, not to be shunned, but, on the contrary, to be welcomed into her affections with cries of: "Yes, yes, at last, the uncultured pearl!"

'My proposal, Col, is that we are expected to-night or tomorrow to start our inquiries up there in that suspect outfit. I will go ahead, alone. You can have a couple more days and nights in London, with all that should entail. This arrangement will require a bit of faking, but nothing too difficult. It will prove that, properly managed, even the Home Office can produce a boon. She'll have a flat somewhere, so you won't have to fork out on a hotel. Something very lovely, blessed and lasting can develop from this. I wish to help it along.'

Naturally, Harpur wondered about the motivation for all this. Iles wouldn't normally use the word "encumbrance" about himself, even to deny he'd be one. He saw others as encumbrances. Did the ACC fear that Harpur and Iles's wife, Sarah, might restart something, and hope a Harpur–Maud relationship would prevent this? Or did Iles want to prove to Sarah that Harpur was simply a shagger-around and his spell with her lacked any meaning, had been just an episode, a game? *Yes, Sarah, I travelled solo to start the investigation. Harpur wanted to loiter in London because he thought he could knock off one of the Home Office pieces. I could have overruled that, of course, but I knew he'd have been no use as an assistant. If he thinks he's missed a bang he's incapacitated by annoyance and regret. Best indulge his drab but compulsive tendencies.* The ACC would be able to hint that his and Sarah's relationship was so much more solid and lasting than anything Harpur had offered, or could offer in the future.

'I'd cover for you, Col,' Iles said. 'I'd start on the preliminaries and then we could really get going when you arrived, rejuvenated, strengthened and enlivened by sweet experiences with Maud. I see you as doubly entitled to her treats: you're a single man, and you have this extremely underprivileged, indeed, non-privileged, background. Who knows whether that connection with Denise, the beautiful and very popular, undergrad will continue? She'll want to look about, won't she, Col? It's natural in someone of her age and abilities.'

Harpur had thought about Maud, certainly. As Iles said, anyone could have picked up the signals from her to him. She had actually described her feelings. And, if it wasn't for Iles's gracious spiel just now, Harpur might have given her more thought. As Iles had also said, the link with Denise was a little on-off, a little fragile. She was a student, lived a good part of her time among students, and would have friends among other students, some male. For students away from home, friendships could get very close.

But, in his devious, unfathomable way, Iles had made anything with Maud impossible for

Harpur. He drew back from giving Iles the power to demean Sarah by telling her she'd been something on the side for Harpur, among several somethings on the side. He couldn't allow that cruelty. He would avoid sounding pious, though. 'It's kind of you, sir, and so much in character, if I may say, but I don't find Maud attractive in that way.'

'You what?'

'No. And I'm extremely keen to be in on the inquiry from the very start.'

'You're what? We're talking here, Harpur, of an extremely well-made, youngish woman, beautiful, bright, who is eager to put out for you.'

'These days I go for young, not youngish, ones, sir. It's probably a failing, but I have to put up with it.'

'A woman, Col, whose salary probably already matches yours, and with a fine pension in the offing, despite the fucking Coalition.'

'I'm very much in favour of equality of pay and conditions in the public service, sir.' Harpur thought: kick this conversation into the worthy, safe realm of political theory, batter Iles with smarmy OKness. It slightly pissed Harpur off, though, that the ACC should have clumsily made any response to Maud's hints, and more than hints, out of the question. At approaching forty, Harpur fretted about lost chances, but this one was definitely lost. Damned decency and regard for Sarah Iles had struck him a dirty rabbit punch. Those words from Iles to Sarah that Harpur had imagined about his disabling rage at missing an opportunity had a quota of truth.

Iles said: 'Here we have a woman searching for something other than glamour, charm, wit in a man. You're not going to meet many with such modest demands, combined with pale green hungering eyes, non-tombstone teeth, ready thighs.'

'I'm proud that our country was probably one of the first to insist on proper conditions for women in State jobs, and perhaps private companies are now catching up, though not fast enough, most impartial commentators would agree,' Harpur replied.

'Fuck me, I'm tuned into Radio Four's *Woman's Hour*,' Iles stated.

TWENTY-THREE

AFTER

In the film room, Maud introduced her colleague Belinda Pitman, from the Customs end of Her Majesty's Inland Revenue And Customs. Maud said: 'Because Customs handled this part of the case independently, the material they have is separate from our own and you won't have copies of it.'

'We like to sit on our doings, so to speak,' Belinda said. Harpur thought she'd be about Maud's age, dumpy, cheerful looking, mixed race, blue-trimmed white training shoes, jeans, oatmeal coloured sweater, deadpan tone.

'Belinda heads their "Identification, Tracking And Retrieval" section,' Maud said. 'ITAR's work will often run parallel to police operations and sometimes intersect, usually to the advantage of both.'

Belinda had the control pad and put on to the screen a picture of what seemed to Harpur a block of flats, a block of non-council, very pricey flats. She said: 'In line with our identification and tracking roles we've been watching for a while a substantial importer/wholesaler of the commodities, Robert Hillcrest Cochrane, aged thirty-three, also known as Rudy Griffith Laidlaw Spence. He lives here at sixteen Emblem Court, a first floor flat with his wife, Fern, also thirty-three. The flat has four bedrooms, three bathrooms, two receptions. The front door's equipped with double mortise locks, a Yale, judas hole and chain. Furniture: John Lewis superior. Rent: three thousand nine hundred and fifty pounds a month on a year's lease paid by direct debit from the Cochrane joint current account, which is fed from a Cochrane reserve fund to keep the current balance at never less than ten thousand pounds. This is Fern's second marriage. No kids from either. We identified Robert/Rudy two months ago and have watched him continuously since.'

She fiddled with the controls. 'We'll go over to film now, your actual moving pictures.' And they moved. Belinda said: 'We're now looking at the rear of the building and Fern emerging from Emblem Court's private underground car park.' She's in a Land Rover.' The clip was too distant and too brief to get much idea of her looks, except that she wore thin-framed glasses, at least for driving, and had her mousy-to-blonde hair to shoulder length. Belinda said: 'We think a shopping expedition. We're not really interested in that.'

No, but she wanted to boast of ITAR's thoroughness and concealed camera expertise.

Was that it? Not exactly. Another piece of film followed, this time at the front of the block again. A red Lexus drew up not far from the entrance and the driver put a prepaid card into the pavement meter. He was about twenty-seven, slightly built, his dark hair close-cut. He might have been a jockey on his day off. He took a trolleyed suitcase from the car and pushed it ahead of him towards the entrance of the apartment block. Belinda said: 'At this stage, of course, we didn't know who he was or whether he had arrived to trade with Cochrane/Spence and would go to number sixteen. But we thought it might be significant that he showed very shortly after Fern had gone. Timetabled? Get her out of the flat while a deal was done? Actually, there had been a mobile phone call to say OK to come now, but this was something else we didn't know at the time.'

Now, another still shot, once more the front of the building, but taking in a more extensive area of the road. A white van with a company name and a phone number on the side to camera stood next to another meter: ACME LAWN AND GARDEN SERVICES. Near it were a Twingo and a Focus. Belinda said: 'We were watching front and back from hired office rooms opposite. Not a totally desirable method because of possible leaks. But continuous surveillance from a vehicle could become noticeable, even if the vehicles were constantly swapped. Hogging a meter will get on someone's radar. We routinely called in for a check on anything that parked within fifty metres of the front entrance and stayed more than half an hour. On this day we got names, addresses and occupations for a curtain-maker and fitter as owner of the Twingo, and a maths coach as owner of the Focus. We took these to be genuine and OK.

'The Lexus registration gave us Claud Norman Rice of twenty-seven Delbert Avenue, businessman. The van registration did not exist, apparently, nor the phone number. This seemed interesting, though we still had no proven link between the Lexus, the van and sixteen Emblem Court and Rob/Rudy. It occurred to me, of course, that the van might be a disguised police surveillance job. Perhaps we weren't the only people who'd targeted Cochrane/Spence.

'We asked for a voters' list confirmation on the Rice name and address and got a positive. We had two cars on standby, an Astra and a Citroën. I needed to decide whether to concentrate on the Lexus or the van or both. I picked the van only. Sure, if it turned out to be a police unit, I'd look a thicko – an interfering thicko, possibly messing up an operation by allies, nominal allies. But I think I sensed somehow that it probably wasn't a police vehicle. The registration would have been given a proper, concocted, fake, official record at the Driver and Vehicle Licensing Agency in Swansea if so, and a woman officer with an attractive voice would have answered to the phone number as Acme

Lawn and Garden Services. These would be routine parts of the deception.

'Anyway, I settled in my head that if the van moved off very soon after the departure of the Lexus this would, in fact, establish a link and I'd commit both standbys to following it – relay tactics. There appeared to be no need to shadow the Lexus because we knew where it would probably be going and could fix a peep duty there without any of-the-moment urgency. The Astra could take the first stint behind the van, with the Citroën lying further back, well out of mirror reach, ready to change positions with the Astra at some point to be agreed by the drivers on mobiles, hands-free mobiles, need I say?'

More film. The visitor came out from the apartment block with his wheeled luggage, glanced about, then went to the Lexus, lifted the trolley in to the rear, got behind the wheel and drove away. The screen blanked. 'Now, we're at a minute or so later,' Belinda said, and the film began again, the camera on the white van. A man of about thirty-five to forty came from the back of the vehicle and took the driving seat. He started the engine. Harpur recognized him from the Maud material. 'Sergeant Tom Mallen,' Belinda said, 'also sometimes Parry.'

'Dead whichever, now,' Iles said.

The van left, but not in the direction Rice and the Lexus had taken. A blue Astra followed the van, and not long afterwards a Citroën followed the Astra.

Iles said: 'So, no, the van was not a police gambit? Tom had been pulled into a power fight in one of the firms, hadn't he? This is how it always is in undercover. The seemingly simple process of putting a man or woman into spy is catastrophically affected, catastrophically shoved sideways, by some totally uncatered for, uncaterable for, factor. He should have been pulled out as soon as this fucking van had been identified for what it was.'

'But I say again, we didn't know at first what exactly it was, except falsely registered,' Belinda replied. 'And we didn't know, either, that an undercover officer had been placed in one of the firms. None of us could have recognized Tom Mallen, alias Parry, outside Emblem Court.'

'Of course you didn't know,' Iles said, 'of course you didn't recognize him. The two parties, police and Customs, worked separately, kept secrets from each other. And this separateness did for Tom eventually, or quicker than eventually, yes?'

Harpur could see that Iles was beginning to irritate Belinda. She kept her cheerfulness, but her voice, already very level, almost throwaway, became cold and super-rational. 'I'm not a police officer, but I can visualize certain types of crime where only an undercover operation could crack it,' she said.

'Visualize away,' Iles said.

'Is it possible that at your high rank, Mr Iles, you've forgotten some of the basic very formidable, very basic, problems that might confront your detectives?' she said.

'No,' Iles said. 'I forget nothing. I don't know how to forget.'

She became more aggressively reasonable. Perhaps earlier in her life she'd had to find a way of dealing with racist bullies and did it by intellect, or tried to. Iles was not, was never, racist. But he could bully well enough. Belinda said: 'I wonder if Mr Harpur – possibly more used to the everyday demands of policing, the, as it were, realities – I wonder if he sees the undercover debate differently.' She paused, obviously waiting for Harpur to say his two-pennyworth.

Maud cut in, though. It was as if she wanted to protect Harpur from a dangerous disagreement with the ACC – dangerous for Harpur and his career and general comfort under Iles. Yes, it was obvious she had developed those feelings for him, so forcefully spoken of earlier by Iles. Harpur couldn't respond, though. Perhaps in a way this was his own method of dealing with pressure, almost bullying, by Iles. Harpur would use it to keep himself sort of chaste, the opposite to what Iles intended. 'Maud said: 'Tell us about the road trek on the tail of the van, Belinda. I've heard some of it,' she explained, turning to Harpur and Iles. 'It's fascinating.'

'Maybe you're easily fascinated,' the Assistant Chief said.

'Not by you,' she replied.

259

Belinda gave a little, amused moue. 'You two been squabbling? Or is this only banter? I love banter. Remember the butler in *The Remains of the Day*, who says he'll have to learn how to banter, so as to keep up with his new boss?' She sounded patient, commanding, bookish, like an elder sister coping with two ill-behaved younger kids. Perhaps the head of ITAR outranked Maud and even Iles and felt entitled to patronize. Or perhaps this was another learned technique for dealing with stroppy people: treat them as harmless, confine them to the jolly old banter department. She got on now with what mattered. 'I won't do a full reading of the debriefing logs from the Astra and Citroën drivers, just what seem to be the significant bits – or what we can hindsight view as the significant bits. They spoke into recorders. I have transcripts:

'Astra: "Van pulls in at large cycle store and driver appears to buy a mountain bike. Puts this into van. Rear doors open for minutes and I see him roping bike to possible commode chair fixed to right wall of van. Call V.L.J. in Citroën and suggest this good moment for position change. Top-up fuel."

'Citroën: "Van pulls in to lay-by. Purpose unknown. I have to drive on. Can't stop in lay-by for fear of suspicion as tail. Drive mile to next lay-by ahead and wait for van to pass. Resume position."

'Astra: "Mobile message from V.L.J. saying, 'Van in lay-by.' Drop speed to give van time to

260

clear lay-by. Seems OK."

'Citroën: "Van gets local attention parked outside house at Wilton Road (eleven). Driver takes mountain bike into house. A light goes on upstairs and is then extinguished. Neighbour photographs van. Girl, about twelve, arrives at house then group of boys, young teenage. Pizza delivery. Youngsters' party? Astra takes over surveillance while I bring fuel up to full."

'Astra: "Van stays two hours then driver and woman about his age get into cabin and drive to lay-by used previously. Purpose unknown. Have to drive on. Roundabout. Return. Van has left lay-by. Is parked at eleven Wilton venue again. It leaves. Tail for forty miles, when Citroën takes over."

'Citroën: "Van stops for fuel. I watch from far pump. He puts in minor amount, as if adjusting. Buys three beakers of drinks from twenty-four-hour shop and takes them into rear of van. Doors open. Distant, but appears to pour them into other containers. Texts. Resumes journey and drives to known country house property of Leo Percival Young, Midhurst. House stands apart, so am exposed if watching. Withdraw therefore. Mission concluded. Possible saloon car left property soon after my withdrawal but it would have put security of operation at risk, so unchecked."'

TWENTY-FOUR

AFTER

'"As if adjusting,"' Belinda said, in almost that same deadpan tone, but Harpur thought he could detect some special warmth and even excitement there, sort of leadership-speak. 'This we now believe was an astonishingly sharp interpretation. Indeed, the culmination of an astonishingly fruitful operation.'

'Yes?' Iles said. 'The damehood is on its way.'

'Naturally, we went back to Wilton Road next day and did some inquiries to determine the significance of number eleven,' she said.

'"Determine the significance?"' Iles said.

'Well, yes,' Belinda replied. She spoke this with what sounded to Harpur a kind of saintly, forgiving patience, as if even the dullest prick should expect ITAR to go back and systematically try to develop and add to what they'd discovered the day and night before, more or less by chance.

'What kind of inquiries?' Iles asked.

'Basics,' Belinda said.

'Which?' Iles replied.

'The obvious,' Belinda said. 'We had the Mallen name, names, from the voting register, of course, and the net, but nothing beyond.'

'And how did you and yours get *beyond*?' Iles said. 'Did you knock at number eleven and say, "Good morning, Mrs Mallen, but who are you and your man *beyond* that mere name? And who were all those kids?"'

'No, not eleven. Even before we'd discovered he was a cop, we knew something pretty complex must be under way and tact would be needed,' Belinda replied. 'By tailing the van on the return we'd established a link between the driver and Leo Young at Midhurst. And checks had shown the van and Acme horticultural specialists were phoneys. I went with the unit myself to make sure our people were careful.'

'So how did you get your information?' Iles said.

'In the normal way for these kinds of delicate inquiries,' Belinda said.

'Which normal ways?' Iles replied.

'Oblique rather than head-to-head,' Belinda said.

'"Oblique" meaning?' Iles said.

'Not head-to-head,' Belinda said.

'"Oblique" meaning you asked around,' Iles replied. 'Neighbours, the local shop, if there is one. The man who did the photographs.'

These were statements, not questions, but Belinda treated them as though they were. 'Yes,' she said. 'How else?'

'And when you were being oblique, how did you explain why you wanted to know about eleven, why you were stalking a police officer? Whom did you say you were?' Iles asked.

'Admittedly tricky,' Belinda said.

'Tricky and perilous,' Iles said.

'Unavoidable,' Belinda said.

'Oh God, a reproach,' Iles replied.

'We were TV researchers for a coming programme on neighbourliness. So, for instance, what do you at number seven know about the people at, say, choosing entirely randomly, eleven?'

'God,' Iles said.

'It worked,' Belinda replied. 'TV is a magic term. People thought they might get on the screen.'

'How do you mean, "It worked"?' Iles said.

'We got some useful stuff. Very useful,' Belinda said.

'You think everyone swallowed the TV tale?' Iles said.

'It doesn't matter, does it, if some didn't?' Belinda said.

'Yes, it matters,' Iles said.

Belinda said: 'But it's not as if Sergeant Mallen were operating as undercover in that area, was it? He was working a long way from eleven Wilton Road.'

Iles raised both hands in the air and kept them there for half a minute. He might have been trying to get God's attention, to ask Him how much longer he, Iles, had to put up with this crapaloo from Belinda. Iles didn't seem to get an answer, though. He lowered his hands. 'Scenario,' he said. 'Someone who doesn't believe the TV yarn – and the list would run into millions – gets on the phone to the local constabulary and reports that a crew of flagrantly bogus buggers have been around the houses asking questions about a police detective who's a neighbour. He adds that the day before, the detective, Tom Mallen, was home, driving a van the joke of the road, with a company name ACME LAWN AND GARDEN SERVICES on it and a phone number which, in his public-spirited way, he has tried but which is unobtainable.

'The message is passed up the line and reaches a lad or lass in the nick who knows Mallen has been sent *sub rosa* to another area and another police force to do undercover. He or she rings the other force and asks what Mallen is doing back home in a crazy van. Isn't he supposed to be quietly embedded in one of their major drugs firms? Should he be here? Is this a collapse of security – the undercover man joining up with the family man? Has he been rumbled and followed and are these doorsteppers after him?

'Now, as I understand things from Maud, the suspicion is that Tom Mallen lost his cover somehow and was shot by a renegade police officer or officers in that other force who has, have, a lot to hide, such as an established, lucrative commercial treaty with Leo Percival Young, ensuring clandestine police aid to him and his firm. Lucrative to both sides. Suppose this officer, or one of these officers, takes the call about Mallen from the local force here? As a matter of urgency, the officer tells Leo he's just heard that there's a spy cop in one of the firms, the spy's duties lately to involve driving a white van advertising Acme Lawn And Garden Services with a phone number that doesn't exist, but which has been tried by our sceptical neighbour.'

Belinda said: 'A bit far-fetched?'

'Which bit?' Iles said.

'Tortuous,' she replied.

'Things always get tortuous in undercover. And sometimes just torture,' Iles said. 'You go clumping and obliquing about there, spouting questions, quickening people's curiosity, more or less fingering him. Are you surprised he's dead?' he said.

'With subtlety,' Belinda said. 'We did our inquiries with subtlety.'

'I'm sure that would be so,' Maud said.

'Oh, it must be OK, then,' Iles said.

'In a way, I admire you for your concern, Mr Iles,' Belinda said.

'In *which* way?' Iles said.

'Yes, it's admirable that you behave as if you're the only one who would know how to conduct a sensitive trawl for information,' Belinda said. 'It shows confidence. It shows, well, yes, a sensitivity to match the sensitivity of the task'.

'The task shouldn't exist,' Iles replied. 'Undercover is shit. No amount of sensitivity or any other ivity can put that right.'

Belinda didn't pause, but went on chattily: 'Well, anyway, we found that the husband/father in the Mallen family was a sergeant detective officer, Tom Mallen, and that he'd been away from home for a while, and was away again by the time we returned. We were told there'd been a birthday party for the young son, Steve, and that his father had made a special trip home for the occasion. There was a general feeling among neighbours that his duties elsewhere involved secrecy, which would account for the strange, seemingly non-police van. Of course, as soon as I heard from our people that the man was police, I assumed an undercover project and ordered exceptional care in the way questioning was conducted from then on by the ITAR unit.'

'With sensitivity, I expect,' Iles said. 'That was the word, wasn't it? But by then most of the fucking damage had been done.'

'At this point, I felt I could see some of the picture,' Belinda replied. 'It's why I spoke of Vincent Jackman's – V.L.J.'s – guess in the Citroën about the fuel "adjustment" as being so spot-on. It seemed to me that, as we can all see now, the van had been sent to watch Emblem Court by Leo Percival Young, possibly to check on private, off-limits dealing done by the man we'd identified from the Lexus reg as Claud Norman Rice. Handling such an important task for Young would seem to prove that Tom had become a trusted operative.'

'A trusted operative who had become *so* trusted that he had to be shot pretty soon afterwards,' Iles said. 'What had intervened?'

'The assignment at Emblem Court might have finished very quickly,' Belinda replied. 'Tom Mallen, acting as if for Young with the Acme van, decides then that he can get home for the boy's birthday and back again without compromising his undercover identity. He wants to assert temporarily something of his real self – the father/husband self. I imagine many undercover people feel this kind of urge occasionally. It helps them ring-fence their real personality, and their sanity. He buys the mountain bike as a present. These items don't come cheap – usually hundreds at least – but he's determined to make a strong, clear message for the boy. The bike says, *"Here I am, home with you, your father doing fatherly things, and I've arrived in time because it's vital a dad should be with you on the right day to celebrate the occasion. It's a priority."* Most probably, Tom needs this reassurance, this statement of his category and solid status in an ordinary family, more than the boy does. Later, Tom drives to a lay-by with his wife, Iris, and we assume this was for love-making to mark his return, and which might have been difficult in a house full of kids – their own

268

and the party guests. He had arrived before any of the children assembled for the pizzas, so there might have been earlier bonking in the house. We've heard of a bedroom light switched on. Possibly, his wife wanted the second session as a means to bring this outlandish, possibly sinister, van within her, as it were, range, her control. It's Mrs Mallen's attempt to reclaim Tom from something so flagrantly part of the job. Maybe we can all understand that. And he, in fact, might have anticipated this reaction from her and had already cased the lay-by on his way to Wilton Road. This sojourn in that lay-by is the equivalent to the mountain bike.'

'It is?' Iles said.

'He's saying in this fashion, *"Iris Mallen, I am Tom Mallen, Mallen, Mallen, your husband. It's why we're here, darling."* He'd regard this as crucial, to counter those troublesome Press stories about undercover men forming relationships within the target group or firm so as to prove their genuineness. This van-shag has overtones, has inspirational symbolism. Then, he ships his wife back home to Wilton Road, says goodbye to all, and starts his journey to Midhurst. In a service station not far from there he takes a moderate amount of petrol aboard. He has probably already refuelled when not under surveillance, most likely after the lay-by lay. He now puts enough in the tank to make it seem he's only been as far as Emblem Court. He behaves "as if adjusting". Aren't I right, and this was brilliant decoding of a situation by V.L.J.? The van goes on to Midhurst, and is possibly left there. Vince finds himself in more or less open country near the house and exposed. Wisely, he departs, but, as he does so, sees the headlights of what appears to be a saloon car leaving Midhurst, though he's too far off to get a proper view. This we now assume was Tom on his way home in a different vehicle.'

Maud said: 'Perhaps Leo's wife, Emily, was in for a busy time at the museum next day and Leo wouldn't want Tom disturbing their kip.'

TWENTY-FIVE

AFTER

Harpur said: 'Let's sum up what you'd discovered from the van episode, then, Belinda, shall we? Sort of tabulate.'

'Harpur's like that,' Iles said. 'For Col, itemizing is a fetish, a passion, a true and powerful passion. Give Harpur a handful of numbers and he'll soon find paragraphs and sub-paragraphs to cement on to them. It's his comparatively minor equivalent to building the pyramids.' The ACC's voice began to boom and slither depending on which way he pointed his mouth, taking in Belinda, Maud and Harpur. The film room's marvellous acoustics seemed to fix on different prime qualities in his tone and emphasize one or the other according to the angle it came at them from. It made Harpur think of what he'd read about Cinemascope in the 1950s and 60s, when sound effects for the extra-wide picture used to attack the audience from surprising directions, and at all kinds of pitch. 'Mind you, it's not Harpur's only fucking passion, of course, oh no,' Iles said, 'fucking is another of his fucking passions, particularly if he can wangle sly, cajoling closeness to, say, the wife of—'

'As I see it, Belinda,' Harpur said, 'what you knew after this excursion can be listed as one: your importer/wholesaler target, Cochrane/ Spence, did deals with Norman Rice. Two: via Tom, the police might also get to know this eventually, or sooner. Three: Leo Percival Young suspected—'

'Wangle sly, cajoling closeness to, say, the wife of a higher-placed colleague, much higher-placed – an accredited member of the Association of Chief Police Officers, often shortened to ACPO, as you'll be aware—' Iles continued, 'who used to trust him, and who was willing to tolerate his oddities, clothing and minimal education, and even to regard him—'

'Three: Leo Percival Young suspected this dealing went on and had sent Tom in the van to check,' Harpur said. 'Here we have careful, fair-minded leadership. 'Four: this suggested that Norman Rice—'

'Even to regard him, in certain limited respects, obviously, as a friend,' Iles stated. 'Thank you, thank you, thank you, Col. Ingratitude comes instinctively and as of right to you, the way bullshit does to Archbishops. I see a special—'

'This suggested that Claud Norman Rice was nominally part of Leo's outfit, but in Emblem Court had been acting privately, underhandedly, treacherously,' Harpur said. 'Five: once you discovered Tom was a police officer you would deduce that he—'

'See a special vindictiveness in his behaviour,' Iles said.

'Deduce,' Harpur replied, 'that he had achieved a considerable degree of acceptance.'

'As though to give me appalling emotional pain – cause it to *me*, personally and uniquely – had become an essential element in his disgusting pleasures,' Iles said. 'He was choosy. It had—'

'A considerable degree of acceptance within the firm,' Harpur said. 'He had been entrusted with—'

'—to be my wife,' Iles replied. 'This has become clear, because, although Maud here – quite a passable looking piece, no moustache, of good career and financial standing, commendable arse, able not only to manage the screen controls herself, but to coach you, Belinda, in this skill – yes, although Maud has these qualities and is more or less chucking herself at him, her breath flagrantly fondling his dewlap at one stage, he refuses to be pulled, despite his present single status and untethered girlfriend, plus a generously colluding offer from me for him to neglect his duties in that other region temporarily, so as to have a lovely, unhurried bang session, unhurried bang sessions, with—'

'And now, Belinda, to list what you did *not* know, even after your ITAR foray and discoveries,' Harpur said: 'One: was Rice acting on his

273

own behalf or as an agent, fetcher-and-carrier, cat's-paw, for another or other interest/interests? Two: if so, which? Three: what was Mallen's cover name in the firm – because, of course, nobody in the Wilton Road area would know it, including—?'

'A lovely, unhurried bang session, unhurried bang sessions, with Maud,' Iles said, 'she employing many intriguing, intimate techniques, probably already familiar to Harpur from years of unscrupulous research, but not to be undervalued on that account, for instance, Maud gleefully yet respectfully taking Col's—'

'Including his family at number eleven,' Harpur said. 'Another unknown. Four: what was Leo Percival Young's reaction now it had been established by Tom that a firm within his firm did function as had been rumoured and was hijacking very desirable trade?'

'Belinda, I'd like you to think about that woman,' Iles said, his voice-timbre suddenly back from its obsessive whine or howl to mere contempt.

'Which woman? Maud? Your wife?' she said.

'Mrs Mallen,' Iles said. 'She and Tom tellingly re-ratified their love in that lay-by ceremonial conjoining, and possibly earlier. Perhaps she took some genuine comfort and reassurance from this. She could accept his departure without quite so much anxiety and angst. Then, whoosh! The next day, you and your cohort arrive and knock doors in a widespread, thoroughgoing swarm style, vigorously trawling for information about eleven and Sergeant Tom Mallen, whose name they'd get from neighbours and/or central address records. You say you didn't go to eleven yourselves. That's something, I suppose. But, of course, householders who'd had a visit would be curious, perhaps worried – including, probably, the one who might have phoned the local police – and several of them were likely to ask Mrs Mallen what it was all about, ask also whether she knew of this sudden disturbing invasion – sinister invasion. Her happiness, maybe already dodgy and frail since Tom had gone back to undercover duties, would instantly crumble.

'She'd be terrified, and so would anyone given such reports. The situation is worse than before his return home.' Iles began to do present tense, for increased impact – like Wolsey did in the long interview. 'She has guessed the kind of work Tom is at elsewhere. She'll realize he perilously imagines himself secret and secure. Now she's confronted by the fact that strangers have been around the place hunting him and anything about him in what will look like a very organized and determined pattern, speaking snippets into pocket recorders using unlocal accents to record their findings. She'll want to warn Tom, won't she, and fast? But she doesn't know where he is and has no phone number for him. These are standard, basic, undercover precautions. Families and lovers must not have the power to initiate contact. Calls might come at awkward times, and lead to dangerous nosiness among members of the firm. They'd speculate that these calls are not from the background he has spun them. Communication can be only single direction – from Tom to her when he thinks he's got some secluded, unbugged minutes, not her to him. She has to wait for a bell. She'd probably have sensed that the phone number on the van was a fiction. She might not even have made a note of it. And, if she had, and dialled, she'd find it to be what she expected, a dud, a nothing, a mask, confirmation of a *cul de sac*. Meanwhile, she knows Tom's got big jeopardy and might not be conscious of this.'

'Text? Voicemail?' Belinda said.

'Both regarded as totally insecure for undercover,' Iles said.

'It's alarmist speculation,' Belinda said. 'Your analysis is full of what-ifs – "possibly", "perhaps", "probably", "likely", "might", "maybe".'

'There are no certainties in undercover,' Iles replied. 'We have to deal with the possiblies, the perhapses, the probablies, the likelies, the mights, the maybes. It's known as foresight. It's known as preparedness. It's labelled "worst case scenario". Hardly anything's secure in undercover. It relies on good luck, and good luck's no twenty-four/seven ally. Even when it seems to be going OK, undercover is always only a metre ahead of peril.'

'You're saying I helped bring the peril nearer

in Tom's case by following up the van lead?' she asked.

'No, it was you who said that,' Iles replied.

'I found myself driven by a logical imperative,' Belinda replied.

'You did, did you?' Iles said.

'The operation at Wilton Road left some questions, as Mr Harpur has said. How, then, to deal with these? I decided we must put Claud Norman Rice under continuous watch. This would help us discover whether he had been acting on his own behalf at Emblem Court or in concert with someone else. As far as ITAR and Customs generally were concerned this would be crucial data. If a someone else existed, the surveillance would probably reveal who. These are the chief uncertainties listed by Mr Harpur. Of course, we know the answers now, but at the time we still had plenty to learn.

'Because our case remained very incomplete, I felt ITAR should proceed alone for a spell, without looking for police help in our activities. I wanted a fully documented report on the circs before I made that move, particularly the names of associates, and super-particularly the identity of who might be overlording this satellite firm. To invite earlier participation by the police would have been sloppy, in my view.'

'Yes?' Iles replied. 'You wanted the glory, the collar.'

'In any case, I realized Tom would probably report to his handler about Rice at Emblem

Court, but that meeting might not happen for a while. We would concentrate on Rice, at least until then.'

'And, as you pointed out, we know the result now,' Iles said.

'I did not feel I had a choice,' Belinda said.

'You'd created conditions where you didn't, in the best traditions of the Light Brigade at Balaclava, now spelt with a c not a k,' Iles replied. But he spoke almost sympathetically. That didn't faze Harpur. He had seen and heard Iles become almost kindly once or twice before within the last few years. Quite possibly twice.

TWENTY-SIX

BEFORE

They had a singalong while driving towards Claud Norman Rice's place at twenty-seven Delbert Avenue to bring him some censure on behalf of Leo, following that A-hole-observed Emblem Court commerce. Mainly, the intention was fists and boots/shoes only, though Ivor Wolsey had a short piece of rubber-coated lead piping in his right sock. Leo had stressed he'd like Norm to survive, not necessarily unmarked but breathing independently. The object was merely to offer a sort of serious reproof, which could be interpreted by Justin Scray for what it was – a last oblique but plain warning. Leo had got hold of the word 'proportionality' from somewhere. He wanted Norm's punishment to be in proportion to his fairly measly status and the degree of offence.

Empathy Abidan liked German lieder, especially some by Robert Schumann and by Anton Webern. Obviously, he had to do these more or less totally solo because the others in the car didn't really know the pieces, although they might have heard Abidan giving them a belt elsewhere previously, perhaps more than once. At the wheel, Tom did try to hum a few passages as accompaniment, but he felt that, though lieder certainly had definite traces of a tune to them here and there, they were not the sort of tunes that stayed in your head, unless you were Empathy, and most probably even he'd had to work at it. You never knew which way the compositions would go, again unless you were Empathy. He did trill each number with terrific confidence, daft energy and enthusiasm, as if there could not be any doubt at all about what came next as to the notes. The words were German, but this didn't give Empathy trouble. He must have decided that if you fancied lieder you had to make an effort and learn some of the lingo: Empathy liked to be reasonable and positive, although he could sometimes get nonreasonable, anti-reasonable, funk-led.

There was a procedure for the music. Abidan would never just start crooning one of the lyrics without an introduction. He'd told Tom he wanted to establish a context and always spoke the title first, usually translated, and mentioned the composer – Schumann, Webern, sometimes Mahler. He had the right kind of voice for lieder: tenor, his tone melancholic and deeply inconsolable when a lover's rejection was the theme; but bustling and pert if about silvery fish in limpid Alpine streams. Most folk could stomach Empathy's sodding hullabaloo as long as it didn't go over, say, the ten-minute mark. A knack for snuffing out encores was to have something else poised ready as Empathy brought one of his blares to an end, speed essential. Today, Tom got in with 'Clementine' and Hugh Fortune with 'Yellow Submarine'. No matter if not everyone had the words verbatim: la-la-la-ing these old numbers was easy because the melodies had such strength and simplicity.

And, to Martin Abidan's credit, he joined in. Tom thought this willingness to adapt would be one of the reasons he was called Empathy – he valued comradely, two-way mental contact with others. With *some* others. He wouldn't seek it with Norm Rice who'd shown arrant disregard for loyalty to Leo. There'd be a different kind of contact for Norman. Now, alongside Tom in the firm's Audi, Mart used full, soaring volume on 'Clementine' and got harmonious, good-natured amusement into the lines about her feet size.

It had been Empathy's suggestion to Leo that Hugh Fortune should take the fourth place in the car and help with the Norm setback. Tom hadn't met Fortune before this trip. Apparently, he'd had some training as a boxer when young and knew where to put a punch that would bring pain but not do dangerous damage. He had never unarguably caused a death. One of his most brilliant assets was radiant calmness, regardless of disturbances and threatening out-breaks around him. Leo had been pleased with Abidan's recommendation. 'Despite possible rush and some urgency at the end, Hugh's the type who'll remember to inform Norm somehow that, if he's put out of things for a while through injury, I'll look after Cornelius, his partner, at least until he's released and can set about organizing himself again,' Leo said. 'I don't want either of them – Cornelius or Norman – fretting about Cornelius's well-being. The attack on Norm is simply a matter of business hygiene. It is confined to him – and, of course, by percolation, to Justin Scray. Most companies have to correct wayward tendencies in their staff now and then. It can be unpleasant but is crucial.' Because Abidan himself would occasionally get a bit overheated and wild, he might have deliberately gone for someone like Hugh as a standby counter-influence.

Leo was away in Wales. Empathy said these days Leo never went on this kind of thump outing. He'd outgrown such operations, outranked them, now. He and Emily loved Pembrokeshire. Gaunt, abandoned old industrial workings on the coast at Porthgain 'always gave Emily a thrill', Leo had told Tom, 'the past being very much her chosen area, and, of course, the past is extensive'. Empathy said that on this kind of jaunt, they'd book in at a hotel and possibly buy a watercolour or two from a gallery in St David's, dithering about which ones so Leo could get himself remembered and alibied, just in case Norm did slip under during the visit, despite moderation. The local drugs squad would be aware that Norm worked for Leo, and this connection might bring difficulties. Empathy said Leo didn't know much about watercolours but he did know about alibis.

His absentee arrangement required exact coordination, and so the call at Delbert Avenue had to be on a particular Thursday; the Thursday, as it happened, when Jamie Meldon-Luce's daughter was Mary Magdalene in the church play. As a result, and because, also, Leo saw a decorum objection to using Jamie for this brand of unholy crusade near the Magdalene date, Tom was asked to do the driving. 'Emily's appointments diary is so crowded that there are few weekdays when she can be absent from the museum,' Leo had said.

And Tom knew Norm might not be home on a Saturday or Sunday. That apparently depended on when he visited Cornelius at Long Lartin, often staying over in a B&B near the jail. Leo ruled out dealing with him up there partly out of civilized, almost sentimental, respect for Norm's and Cornelius's affections; also because to get at Rice effectively in such a place would be tough. 'Other guests and staff around,' Leo said. 'I worry about the party walls in Delbert Avenue carrying sound, but in some of those boarding houses it could be worse. Rooms have been split up to make more accommodation, and it's only plastered breeze block dividing.' Leo considered that sort of risk unnecessary as Norm could be quite effectively done at home, given accurate timetabling and suitable locations in the property. These were very clearly shown on the ring-binder plans.

Of course. Tom wondered whether all these special timing conditions were a sham, concocted so Jamie wouldn't be available as Wheels and Tom could be drafted as replacement. It might be Leo's polite way of getting new boy Tom gradually involved in the rough end of the firm's work. Leo did believe in careful, subtle management. That was why he wanted Norm only gravely knocked about, not killed. In the same sort of way, Leo might intend to bring Tom by nicely graded stages into violence situations. A Wheels did not leave the vehicle during an operation. On the reconnoitre with Leo they had discussed parking for the Norm project, not the details of what would happen inside the house.

If there'd been a manual for Wheels it would state the driver should bring the personnel to the right spot – a house, a bank, a building society – and then wait for them to return. The front line people would probably aim to quit the scene very fast. It could complicate things if one of them had to get into the front, start the vehicle and cope with traffic. Injuries might make that difficult or even impossible, anyway. But a Wheels would be there already, prepared and eager behind the wheel – that's one reason he or she was called Wheels, after all! – three doors possibly open for quick access, most likely with the engine running from the moment he first glimpsed one of the attack party coming back. Or perhaps the Wheels had, in fact, kept the engine idling from the moment he put the action group down. That was definitely how some Wheels operated, scared the ignition might pick a crisis moment to fail. Answer? Make ignition – re-ignition – unnecessary.

Tom wouldn't be at the actual meeting with Norman, but, of course, he realized he could be regarded as an accessory to what went on – an accessory before the events as well as after. If any of it ever came to court, he knew the judge would not think much of an undercover operation where a police sergeant assisted a grievous bodily harm assault, or worse, because he had to maintain his disguise as a fully committed member of the gang. Judges saw crook gangs as the enemy, and anyone who helped them, even in an allegedly fine and ultimately non-criminal cause, was also an enemy, and might get a bollocking in the summing up, his evidence ruled inadmissible, and told the Bench would be recommending prosecution. Ultimately was too ultimate and too uncertain. Thank you, My Lord. Tom had thought quite a bit about the shady morality of undercover and during these recital minutes as the Audi approached Delbert Avenue the shadiness grew shadier. A quiet couple of seconds occurred. Empathy jumped in smartish with what he announced as an R.M. Rilke poem brilliantly liederized by Webern. So, now, all together in the chorus!

Hugh Fortune spoke over the lilt. 'Don't like it.'

Maybe bluntness came with his flair for calm. 'That's bloody rude,' Ivor Wolsey said.

'Something not right,' Hugh replied.

'With which?' Ivor Wolsey said. 'Rilke or Weber or Mart?'

They had turned into Delbert Avenue.

'The silver Renault Laguna,' Hugh said.

'What's wrong with it?' Ivor said.

'Blacked rear windows,' Hugh said.

'So? Plenty of cars have them,' Ivor said.

'But *they're* not parked near twenty-seven Delbert Avenue,' Hugh replied.

Empathy shut down the Webern. The silver Renault stood pretty well opposite number twenty-seven and would have a fine view of it.

'What did you mean "not right", Hugh?' Empathy asked.

'I thought I saw movement in the rear,' Hugh said.

'So?' Ivor said. 'This is a car with people in the back? Is that important?'

'Keep going, Tom,' Empathy said.

'Who'd watch Norm?' Ivor Wolsey said. 'What for?'

'Police?' Empathy said. 'Customs?'

'But why Norm?' Ivor said. 'He's a next-to-nothing.'

'He can lead to someone who isn't,' Empathy said.

'Justin Scray?' Ivor said.

'Jamie got the supplier's address from some-where, didn't he?' Abidan replied. 'And Tom watched and confirmed Norm's call there, for a purchase, we assume.'

'And you're saying someone else with similar info but from a different source was also out-side the dealer's place, on the watch?' Ivor asked.

'How it seems,' Empathy replied. 'Customs, most likely,' Empathy said. 'You had a squint around this area with Leo, didn't you, Tom? Is there a rear entrance, a rear exit?'

'Yes,' Tom said.

'Let's look,' Empathy said.

They turned out of the Avenue. A man in his thirties, baseball cap, jeans, dark anorak was on his feet beside a parked small Fiat gazing along the full length of the lane. 'And keep going again, Tom,' Empathy said.

He sounded tense, half way to a nerves on-slaught.

'They'll have our reg, dawdling around like this,' Ivor said.

'But we haven't bloody done anything, have we?' Empathy said.

'And we're not going to?' Hugh said.

'Dead right,' Empathy said. 'Am I supposed to get Leo on his mobile, poncing about in some culture shop, or hotel cocktail bar, and say, "Oh, Leo, that little saunter we had planned has run into a bit of a hazard. The place is swarming with law in at least two vehicles. But would you like us to proceed with the thuggery regardless? Always keen to oblige." Keep going as ever, Tom. Home.'

TWENTY-SEVEN

BEFORE

If they decided to kill, you had to go along with it. Pack law. Basic. Anyone who went under-cover knew this. He had a nine mm Browning, not a weapon he would normally have picked. He liked Heckler and Koch products better: was trained on them. But the training had been police training, of course. The police famously loved HK. Too famously.

Weekend. Leo and Emily had gone to Pem-brokeshire again. The alibi factory was back in production. Following the mess-up over Norm, Leo had left orders for Scray to be done direct, Abidan in charge, as previously at Delbert. Leo had considered Empathy's decision to withdraw from there very much then the right one, very much a wise one. It boosted Leo's regard for him, and trust in him. Leo hated unnecessary risk. But he seemed to sense that some in the firm might feel Abidan had overdone the cau-tion, chickened. And it was natural for Leo to respond to that by showing his confidence – his increased confidence – in Empathy by giving him not a mere repeat of the Delbert sortie, but a much greater assignment, the wipe out of Scray.

Norm Rice still had snoops around his place, anyway, so couldn't be got at, in Mart's, and therefore Leo's, view. Possibly, Norm had spotted the surveillance – the Laguna and the Fiat, or whatever alternatives turned up since: he appeared to have been behaving very carefully, most probably making no contact with Scray or with the Emblem Court importer. Leo had decided that if he had to abandon a roundabout way of reaching and frightening Justin Scray, it was best to forget this fiddly obliqueness and finish him. Leo was usually very much a gradualist, a plodder, even, but sometimes he would abruptly decide such little-by-little tactics were not getting anywhere, and he'd make a stark change of pace. So, 'Do Scray.'

Tom did wonder about Empathy. He had seemed too near to breakdown at Delbert. But: *if they decided to kill you had to go along with it*. And if the chief decided Mart should run things, you had to go along with that, too.

Jamie Meldon-Luce was available this time and drove the Volvo. His cardigan intrigued Tom. Because of its chunkiness and plentiful swathes of excellent wool – Shetland through-and-through, most likely – it did hide Meldon-Luce's Browning automatic very well. OK, so the cardigan could be regarded as a piece of equipment, like body armour or knuckle irons, and therefore a plus. But Jamie spoke of it as an attractive, chic part of some general fashion rediscovery of cardigans, and not just for the ancient; no, for smart men of every age, including getaway drivers maybe still in their twenties. What with the cardigan and Mary Magdalene, Jamie had to be regarded as an original.

Above all other plus factors, though, Meldon-Luce had an absolutely glittering reputation as Mr Wheels. That might be vital. Tom didn't want to be done by bullets from a police rapid response vehicle, even if it would be friendly fire for him; not for Jamie, Empathy Abidan and Ivor Wolsey, though, suppose everyone made it back to the Volvo after knocking off Justin Scray. The rapid response crew wouldn't realize the Volvo contained a fellow cop, only in the Volvo at all to convince local villains he was *not* a cop, but one of them. *If they decided to kill, you had to go along with it. Pack law. Basic.* Rapid response marksmen worked to a different pack law, though.

Tom, immediately behind Meldon-Luce as they drove to the Scray territories in Arabella, could examine the top back bit of the cardigan, on M-L's neck. This was a new garment, and a current, strong statement about the desirability of such gear. Jamie's had none of those wispy tendrils that can hang from even the best wool if it has seen wear. The pale greenness bordered on turquoise, and looked very fresh and undandruffed. Its colour didn't really go with the pink of the back of Jamie's neck, but he probably hadn't considered this, and the people who sold him the cardigan wouldn't mention it in case that pissed him off and broke the deal. But a green cardigan probably wouldn't go with the skin on *anyone's* neck.

Alongside Tom in the back of the Volvo, Empathy Adiban seemed uninterested in singing today. He talked football for a while, then brought out a Walther automatic and checked the chamber, just as if this was as natural a thing to do in a Volvo as talk about the art of curling corner-kicks. But Tom had watched him check the Walther already, just before they all took their places in the Volvo. This encore wasn't *sang froid* but a bit of a twitch. Would he be able to hit Scray if they *did* find him? The Walther might be a very accurate piece, but not if the gunman had the shakes. Maybe Mart had been just as jumpy on the way to Norm Rice at Delbert Avenue. Tom hadn't noticed, though. There'd certainly been terminal jumpiness at the sight of the Laguna and Fiat. In any case, the Scray excursion was to do with his death, not merely a duffing up.

Perhaps Empathy would rely on Ivor Wolsey and his brilliant gun-craft to do the actual job. Tom also wanted to rely on Ivor Wolsey and his brilliant gun-craft. Probably even Leo relied on it for this kind of chase, although he'd give Ivor some snarl and contempt now and then. A slump-stricken building site lay on either of the routes Tom must take from the mall to Empathy or Ivor if a summons came, and he thought he might be able to loiter there for a minute or two in the hope that Wolsey would have put effective holes in Scray before Tom arrived. *If they decided to kill, you had to go along with it. (But dodge close involvement if you can.)* He thought a slight delay crossing an unlit building site would be credible. Although vandal kids had flattened or half-flattened security fencing, to negotiate the gaps in the dark would still be tricky.

Wolsey: he just sat there alongside Jamie in the front, staring towards the future, apparently focused utterly on the job. Tom decided there were only two people in the car badly troubled by nerves: Empathy and himself. Abidan's tension showed in his messing about with the Walther, re-messing about. Tom realized the stress might be special for Mart Adiban: he'd been told finally to see off another member of the firm, possibly even a friend until now. He knew the reason, of course, and would accept it, but might also feel regret and some confusion.

Tom reckoned his own jitteriness produced this daft mini-obsession with Jamie's cardigan. For fuck's sake, a cardigan was a cardigan. It did the required jobs: clothed Jamie's top and concealed the Browning pistol in his shoulder holster. After all, nobody was going to ask Tom to do an article for the *Style* supplement of some Sunday paper on the fashion prospects, or nonprospects, of cardies for blokes. He had needed to buttress himself. Admiration for the quality of Meldon-Luce's woolly soothed Tom, made him feel for a moment here and there that things would be OK and helped get his mind off the horror at being on a slaughter jaunt. Whereas Empathy might be upset because he had to organize the killing of a mate, or at least one-time mate, Tom was upset, and more than upset, that he had to be a kind of accomplice to *any* killing.

No jaunt. Tom realized he'd picked the flip-pant word to try to downgrade the gravity of what was happening; what was planned to happen. And the planning had been very precise and detailed – that is, very precise and detailed up till the required moment when one of them found Scray. It couldn't be precise and detailed about that because nobody knew in advance where exactly he'd be, what degree of body-guarding he'd have with him, whether he'd be in a car or on foot, and whether he'd be expecting a cheerio-Justin visit. But *of course* he'd be ex-pecting a cheerio-Justin visit after all the warn-ings about hole-and-corner private trading. Tom had met him two or three times, and Justin wasn't dim. No firm could put up with someone doing very personal deals. He'd know that. He'd be aware he had taken on special risk.

Jamie pulled in on a double-yellowed, reces-sed pavement bus stop, as the schedule ordered. Tom had wondered whether this might make the

Volvo noticeable. Although the car would stay there only long enough for him, Ivor and Empathy to get out and walk up Monthermer Street to their dispersal point, people could get very ratty about seeming defiance of the road regs. They regarded it as symptom of a general growth of lawlessness and of imminent social collapse and chaos. Tom saw a middle-aged woman pedestrian staring at the car with full-scale disgust. If she'd had an AK 47 she'd have used it on them for the sake of civic decency. Abidan gave her an apologetic smile. Another sign of how he got the 'Empathy' nickname. He, Tom and Ivor walked across the road towards Monthermer Street. Jamie took the car out into the traffic again. He'd drive to the Mitre Park area, wait for them to return after the cleansing, and get the three away fast.

Tom had to store all the main facts of the day in his memory. The Hilston Manor course repeatedly declared note-taking disallowed, whether on to paper or a machine. Police were, of course, into the habit of making notes, so, to counter this, the Manor had to keep on about the absolute ban undercover. Because judges went queasy and negative about undercover evidence, Tom knew he might never have to give his stuff in court; but the information he'd bring might still guide and prop a prosecution. Why take the risks of undercover if not?

They walked three-abreast up Monthermer. Tom thought that at moments they might look like the gang in the *Reservoir Dogs* film, setting out on their villainy at the start of the picture, though the Monthermer group were only three and the pack in the movie a lot more. Also, now and then, Abidan exercised his special flair for courtesy and stood deferentially aside to let through people coming from the other direction. The kind of swagger shown by the *Reservoir Dogs* contingent was very absent when Abidan did his gallantry. Tom watched him for any further signs of pressure after that business with the Walther, but Empathy seemed serene and self-controlled now.

At the top of Monthermer they paused for a moment, grunted goodbyes and then took their individual routes. There was no more briefing. Everything had been said and re-said at the planning sessions earlier. No briefing could have taken care of Tom's chief worry and direst problem, anyway: what should he do if he found Scray first, selling, or supervising selling, around the Rinton mall? Tom was supposed to call Ivor and Empathy at once and, when they arrived, start the onslaught.

That is, he must initiate the murder. This would be different from merely being present – and passive – at a killing. He'd have to carry a big slab of the responsibility, of the guilt, in fact. In a way, he'd be the main man of the death squad. What would a judge make of that if there were a trial? Tom an *agent provocateur*? Or worse. He tried to comfort himself with the thought that of the three possible locations for Scray, the Rinton mall seemed least likely. During the weeks leading up to today's hunt, talk in the firm had almost always been about Scray's activities in the arcades or Guild Square. Tom had the idea that because he was still fairly new to the outfit and untested in turf fights here he'd been given Rinton. Leo's gradualism hadn't completely disappeared, perhaps. Thoroughness dictated the area had to be searched, but it would almost certainly prove null. Pray God, yes.

TWENTY-EIGHT

WELL AFTER

Harpur's schoolgirl daughters, Hazel and Jill, liked to bring Denise and him an early morning cup of tea when Denise had slept over. He knew why. They wanted to make the arrangement between Denise and him seem normal, not wrongful, not disreputable – seem like family, in fact – more than only the body side of things. Usually, one of the girls would knock the door and wait for an answer before they came into the bedroom each fluting a hearty, unstinting, 'Good morning, both!' though this was not a totally invariable rule. Probably, they'd decide on some days that to knock on the door suggested Denise and Harpur needed lovers' privacy, needed time to get themselves back into decent positions, adjacent in the bed and not more than that; their breathing level, no gasping, their faces unreddened by passion and activity. This impression of cautiousness they dearly wanted to get rid of. A family should be at ease with itself, the members accustomed to walking in and out on one another with no warning. So, occasionally, they'd just walk in.

He'd talked to them a few times about sex. It seemed the right thing for a single parent to do. But he could tell that while he blathered on with carefully imprecise, generalizing language they were translating it into the specifics between him and Denise. Usually, Hazel would kill off this kind of conversation. 'Yes, yes,' she'd say. 'OK, Dad, we get the essentials.'

Denise wasn't family but an undergraduate at the university up the road, not very much older than Hazel, and very much younger than Harpur. Although she had a student room on campus she often spent the night with him. For some time, since his wife was murdered in the local station car park, he ran this one-parent household. Hazel and Jill obviously felt – earnestly wanted to feel – that the tea and a four-sided chat in the bedroom, before breakfast together downstairs later, part restored things to how they used to be when their mother still lived here.

Denise had helped Harpur's sister look after the girls while he was away with Iles on that investigation for Maud and the Home Office months ago; but he knew his absence had disturbed the girls and made them even more keen now on keeping things strong and settled at home in Arthur Street. He'd be going away again with Iles today but back this evening. Just the same, he could tell his daughters felt tense, vulnerable, anxious.

'Where?' Jill said.

'Hilston Manor,' Harpur said.

'What is it?' Jill said.

'Like a college,' Harpur said.

'Such as Denise goes to,' Jill said, 'learning French poetry about what happened to the snow that was here not long ago?'

'No, it's not the same is it?' Hazel said. 'Denise's type of college doesn't have that kind of name. They're called after the city or county they're in, or "Imperial" or "Such and such Metropolitan". I should think this one Dad's going to is a special police college. They'd like to have a posh, historical name for it – Manor. In the old days there'd be a squire or something like that, for instance a royal courtier, or Admiral of the Fleet, in a manor house. Of course, police refer to their ground as their "manor". It's one of those words that has slumped a bit, the same as "Parliament" and "intercourse". A manor house would have a boot-scraper in the porch for after strolls over turf acres, and I don't know how many bedrooms for guests and servants and views out on to the estate with deer and a maze and a plashy fountain. Now, I should think, all the bedrooms have been turned into rooms for lectures and general police jabber about "the community", and how to knock members of it about with that special long truncheon.'

'Yes, that sort of thing,' Harpur said.

'To do what?' Denise said. She was sitting up alongside Harpur in the bed, nightdress on. She

300

lit a cigarette from the previous one. He had never seen more powerful or more symmetrical nose jets of smoke than Denise's. Obviously, they came from wonderfully deep inside her and had worked up this headlong pace by the time they got to her nostrils and double exit. They always excited Harpur, and he loved the acrid tobacco taste on her lips and teeth, but his daughter were present now, so he had to make do with the damn tea. Hazel and Jill would get on at Denise sometimes about her fags, but she'd deaf-ear them, the way undergraduates of her age could deaf-ear anything they didn't want to hear and concentrate on what they did want to hear – moronic rock music. 'The cost of smokes!' Jill would say.

'The cancer!' Hazel would say.

'Yes, to do what at this Manor, Dad?' Jill said. 'You two going to be teachers there or students?'

'To contribute to a course,' Harpur replied.

'Which course?'

'They have many different courses at Hilston for police from all over the UK,' Harpur said. 'Budgetary, traffic, undercover, public order, home security and so on.'

'Have they got one on how to do verbals?' Hazel said.

'What's verbals?' Jill said.

'Oh, wake up, kid, get real, will you?' Hazel said.

'What's verbals?' Jill said.

301

'Detectives putting words into people's mouths which they didn't say. These words can be written into cop notebooks so whoever is supposed to have used them can be convicted and sent down,' Hazel replied.

'You always have to be anti-police, Haze,' Jill said, 'and spouting ancient gob-juice like "wake up, kid" and "get real".'

'Well, why don't you wake up, kid, and get real,' Hazel said.

'What course, Col?' Denise asked.

'This is one for senior officers on how to investigate possible failings and even corruption in another police force,' Harpur said.

'You and Iles did one of those, didn't you?' Denise said.

'When you helped my sister look after things here, yes,' Harpur said.

'Dad and Ilesy were in the papers,' Jill said.

'Yes, it made the Press and TV, didn't it?' Denise said. 'An undercover guy shot, killed?'

'That's how it started,' Harpur said.

'I've got the newspaper clipping stuck into my scrapbook because you were part of it, Dad,' Hazel said. 'A man called Mallen, but also a sort of code name, Parry.'

'Tom Parry,' Harpur said.

'And because you and Des Iles went poking about on their ground, you got the one who done it – a cop hisself, would you believe?' Jill said.

'Did it,' Harpur said. 'Himself.'

'Yes, he did it, this other cop, himself,' Jill

said.

'We failed,' Harpur replied.

'No!' Jill said. 'He got life, didn't he, the cop who done, did, it?'

'We failed,' Harpur replied.

'I don't see that,' Denise said. 'Are you getting all 'umble, martyring yourself? They wouldn't invite you to this Manor place and lecture other officers on how to do it if you failed. It would be like asking Gordon Brown to give a talk on how to be a great prime minister.'

'We got the right verdict,' Harpur said.

'So, you didn't fail, did you, Dad?' Hazel said. 'That's what police are about – getting the right verdicts, regardless.'

'What's that mean?' Jill said.

'What?' Hazel replied.

'"Regardless",' Jill said.

'It means regardless,' Hazel said. 'The right verdict is the one that gets someone sent to jail, regardless.'

'Regardless of what?' Jill asked.

'Regardless of anything else,' Hazel replied.

'Which anything else?' Jill said.

'Anything,' Hazel said. 'I expect they have a course at this Manor on how to get people sent down, regardless.'

'Are you being nasty again, Haze?' Jill said.

'You're going all metaphysical on us, are you, Col?' Denise said.

'What's that mean?' Jill said.

'This is all a bit beyond you, kid,' Hazel

replied.

'It's a bit, and a good bit, beyond all of us,' Denise said.

Harpur said: 'In a way, Hazel's right.'

'Which way?' Jill said.

'Yes, Col, which?' Denise said.

'About what policing is. You nick those you can, even though you know you might be – are – missing the real, main villains. We nibble at the perimeter. It's called, by some, "zero tolerance". That is, hitting the smaller people, the smaller offences, in the hope this will deter not just the low-levels but the chieftains, the bosses, the barons. Or, that's the published statement of the aims. It's a PR gambit – a device to make it look as if purposeful police effort is under way. And purposeful police effort is. But aimed at nobodies or, at best, middling brass, like in the Parry/Mallen case. The major brass remains unreachable.'

'You sound crushed, Dad,' Jill said.

'He'll get over it,' Hazel said.

TWENTY-NINE

WELL AFTER

Harpur felt Hazel must regret having been so rude and niggly and hard, and, maybe to compensate, she went for her scrap book. She opened it at the page where she'd glued the news-paper cutting about the Tom Mallen/Parry murder trial. Sitting on the end of the bed, she read bits of the report to them. "'A police officer was found guilty yesterday of ambushing and shooting to death another officer who it was feared might expose a network of police corruption. The Home Office had ordered investigations by officers from another force because of delays in solving the murder, thought to be the result of attempts to cover up the crime. Detective Inspector Courtenay Jaminel was sentenced to life imprisonment, for a minimum period of eighteen years.

"'Prosecution evidence during the case said that the Home Office investigating team of Assistant Chief Constable Desmond Iles and Detective Chief Superintendent Colin Harpur suspected that the accused, or an associate of the accused, had received information about the presence of an undercover officer planted in a criminal firm with which Detective Inspector Jaminel, and possibly other officers, had a corrupt financial connection. He had heard from someone in the firm of an opportunity to surprise and kill the undercover officer, Sergeant Thomas Mallen, who was acting under the name Tom Parry. Detective Inspector Jaminel waited hidden in a partly completed house on a building site which it was known that Parry would have to pass through. Jaminel shot him from an upstairs window. Jaminel was gun-trained. The weapon used was not police issue and has never been found."'

Hazel skipped and summarized. 'It says that although the gun was still missing, Jaminel had broken down and confessed under interrogation by the two visiting officers – Dad and Des Iles, who confronted him with evidence they had unearthed. This consisted of arriving at a short list of officers not simply gun trained but also capable of exceptional accuracy, and then working through the shortlist and eliminating those alibied. Jaminel withdrew the confession and pleaded not guilty, but the jury believed the investigating officers. That seems to show a lot of skill and persistence by the two of you, Dad, not failure at all.'

'Ilesy is bound to be great in the witness box,' Jill said. 'The jury wouldn't have the nerve to disagree with him.'

'Col would be damn good, too, in his own different way,' Denise said.

'Oh, of course,' Jill said. 'For definite.'

THIRTY

WELL AFTER

Maud was at the Hilston lecturette and discussion. She wore a navy blue silk suit, tall
heels, a chunky pewter-beaded, Celtic-style
necklace, an imitation dahlia buttonhole, and
unquestionably looked very approachable. No,
not unquestionably. There had to be questions.
Harpur felt deeply glad that the 'family' get-
together with Denise and the kids had taken
place, and taken place only hours earlier in the
bedroom and at breakfast. His recollection of
those binding sessions remained fresh and influential. They armoured him. They helped him
feel that Maud might appear approachable, but
not approachable by him. He had something else
and he'd stick with it, with them. Yes. The way
smoke spurted straight and laser-like from
Denise's nostrils had to be unique and uniquely
thrilling to watch, and perhaps to get speared by,
depending on where his head was.

Iles, in uniform, and switched over for now
to reasonableness, did most of the talking at
Hilston, stressing the need for good preparation

before actually going into another force and starting the hostile, unflinching inquiries. 'For instance, Col here, my valued colleague in the assignment, heard of some activities by Mallen/ Parry with a strange van away from his proper ground – a trip to celebrate his son's birthday. This was an understandable wish by the under-cover officer, but possibly, it has to be said, the cause of his tragic death. Harpur calculated that there might well have been a phone call from one force to the other about the breach. Customs snoops had the van under scrutiny, had followed it, and then began intrusive research among Mallen/Parry neighbours, attempting to dis-cover more about the van and its provenance. We used this inspired piece of imagination by Col as the start of our questioning and general digging. It established our, as it were, tone for the investigation. You will know how it paid off.'

Harpur wondered about amending this. Of course, it had been Iles who did the speculating about a possible inter-force phone call. Iles almost always provided the speculation and imagination, what he would sometimes call 'the gifted, gilded, surmise'. Harpur guessed the ACC still aimed to build him up, give him stature, and prove to Maud that she should go after him hard, so as to make sure Harpur didn't try an affair revival with Sarah Iles. The ACC was crediting him with ownership of a vivid and clever imagination now, on top of basic, nitty-gritty, plod strengths. Iles probably realized that few women would go for basic, nitty-gritty, plod strengths, and the few would not include Maud.

Harpur decided to let the flattery go, though. To give the correct version would look like sucking up to Iles, and Harpur always tried to avoid that, unless he could overdo the smarm so much it became roaring mockery. In any case, it hadn't been the telephone call – the presumed, utterly unverified phone call – that really opened up the inquiry. It had been Claud Norman Rice, a fetch-and-carry twerp in the local drugs commerce.

There were about twenty very senior officers as audience for Iles and Harpur at Hilston, seated in one of those magnificently spacious ex-bedrooms of the Manor that Hazel had mentioned, some plain-clothed, some uniformed. Iles, at a fine, oak lectern, said: 'As far as we can make out, Mallen/Parry did not have at the time of his murder any serious information about the corruption of a police officer, or police officers, so the death is especially meaningless and sad. Such information was there to be had, but he didn't find it. He lacked time. This will almost always be the case in undercover. Virtually everything is against the likelihood of success.'

Harpur had the impression that Iles believed they *had* found the information. He could be right, at least in part, but only a long time after the events; and certainly only in part, in very minor part, Harpur thought. The ACC said:

'You'll have been able to read up on the case details, so I don't need to go over all of them now. I have to tell you, though, that when Harpur and I arrived for our survey in this other domain we had the idea at once that some wrong impressions and assumptions had been made during earlier examinations of the facts.' He paused and grinned a vintage, Iles-type grin – combative, contemptuous, hugely and for ever uncomradely. 'By the way,' he said, 'I think it's very brave of Hilston to ask me to speak here today because my views on undercover are well-known – well-known and negative. I believe the Mallen/Parry disaster helps endorse this judgement.' He did that plain and emotionless, nearly venom-free. Iles always expected his judgements to be endorsed – as routine, as inevitable – so why get triumphalist? That would be a kind of absurd denial of his all-round genius. Victory was standard.

He said: 'Both Harpur and I thought that not enough attention had been given to Claud Norman Rice. Her Majesty's Customs and Inland Revenue put him under continuous watch for a while following an observed courier job to Robert Hillcrest Cochrane, age thirty-three, at Emblem Court, but he'd become aware of that, decided on precautions, and therefore offered no further leads. The surveillance was abandoned. Harpur considered this slack, almost perverse.'

Actually, it had been Iles who considered it *fucking* slack and almost *fucking* perverse', but, again, Harpur let that go.

'Accordingly, we went to see Claud Norman at twenty-seven Delbert Avenue. He lived alone, pending release of his partner from Long Lartin. He was cooperative to a degree. He felt reasonably in the clear.'

Iles had recorded this interview and played the tape now on the lecture room machine. 'Harpur speaks first – as ever,' Iles said. Harpur did, but was soon pushed aside by Iles's genius and relentlessness.

Harpur: 'I'd like to talk to you about your visit to Emblem Court.'

Rice: 'Yes?'

Harpur: 'You arrived in a Lexus and had a trolley case.'

Rice: 'Is either of those an offence?'

Harpur: 'What was in it on your return?'

Rice: 'A private matter. Not socks.'

Iles: 'Excuse me while I have a muted guffaw. Norm, there's nothing we appreciate more than humour from those wishing – as you do – to give us help. I'll get over it shortly. Now then, I have the feeling you knew you were being observed during this Emblem Court visit. The thorough look-around you performed suggested this, some concentration on the van, at least when you arrived.'

Rice: 'Of course. That crazy Acme stuff.'

Iles: 'Yes, such alertness is what one would expect of a veteran professional like you, Norman.'

Rice: 'Professional what?'

Iles: 'You're someone who has through skilled functioning acquired a CT hatchback five-door Lexus, a pleasant property in Delbert Avenue and a long-term partner, Cornelius Maximilian Hughes-Temperley, aged twenty-five. We know we are dealing with someone deft, experienced, discerning. But to move on: I have the feeling, too, that your host, Cochrane /Spence, had spotted the van. He'd be very watchful. This is an almost inescapable deduction. He'd have an eye continually on the road outside.'

'Rice: 'More "of course". It's natural to the trade he's in. He was van-wise even before I rang his bell at sixteen.'

Iles: 'Right. To take this a little further, though: I have to tell you, Norm, that it's my belief – my suspicion – that he asked his wife, Fern, also thirty-three, to tail this van. Harpur and I have seen Home Office film of her leaving from the rear of the Emblem Court building. There was a mobile call from him to you saying when she was in place, so you could make the visit to sixteen, and there'd be the means to check the van's travels afterwards.'

Rice: 'Perhaps.'

Iles: 'The Customs people, in their slipshod style, considered the exit by Fern of no significance – a shopping trip.'

Rice: 'Well, I suppose in one aspect that was true – she was going to shop the van and its driver, wasn't she?'

Iles: 'It's amazing the ease with which you see humour in many a situation, Norm! This helps give you a very rounded personality, much appreciated by Cornelius, I should think, when not banged up. Getting back to Emblem, though: eventually, there was quite a convoy of vehicles on the way to Tom's home ground: the van, two Customs cars – an Astra and a Citroën – and Fern in the Land Rover.'

Rice: 'I don't know all sides of it, but Fern went.'

Iles: 'And my impression is, my intuition is, that she managed to stick with the van on that fifty or so miles until it reached Wilton Road. Very skilled tracking. She didn't get stymied by the mysterious lay-by stop on the way.'

Rice: 'Fern's quite a capable piece.'

Iles: 'She's at Wilton ahead of the increased Customs influx that would arrive next day, does her own bit of door knocking or other inquiring, and finds out who lives at number eleven. Answer – Tom Mallen, a detective sergeant, who hasn't been seen around his home or the area lately.'

Rice: 'Something like that, I expect.'

Iles: 'The information goes from her to Cochrane/Spence, from him to you, obviously, and then, I feel sure, from you to Leo Percival Young, aged forty-two, because you knew you weren't much favoured by him and wanted to win him over: you're asking him to forgive and forget the Scray connection. "Here's the gift of

hot, very confidential insights, Leo, dear."
You'd probably guess that the van had one of his
people in it, one of his people who'd behaved in
a worrying, unexplainable way. You're telling
him about a betrayal of some sort. This good
turn vastly strengthens your position vis-à-vis
L.P. Young.'

Rice: 'Like that, yes. This was extremely vis-
à-vis.'

Iles: 'Leo is staggered, appallingly hurt, because he thought he'd personally picked a great
lad in Tom Parry, a potential heir. This is super-
disloyalty.'

Rice: 'He was terribly upset and enraged. He
said what had happened involved a disgusting
insult to the "living integrity" of the van – "the
fucking acme of insults" was one phrase.'

Iles: 'Result? Leo ordered the killing. He'd be
in touch with his contact, contacts, inside the
local force and tell them of the danger – an
undercover guy who might know ... might know
a barrel-full. Nobody knew *what* he knew.
Actually, it wasn't much, but this they couldn't
tell at the time, of course. Leo advises this contact, these contacts, that he's got a trade hunt for
Scray lined up and it can be the opportunity to
do Tom and conveniently make that appear a
Scray act of battle. He'll inform Empathy Abidan, who must have been hellish nervy on the
car trip – Tom a passenger with him and doomed. Then, of course, the yelling and screaming at
the getaway Volvo. He knows Tom won't be

coming. Ever. Jamie Meldon-Luce doesn't know it and so wants to wait. Abidan takes the car and in a semi-fit does all that pavement damage.'

Rice: 'None of this can I confirm, obviously. You're speculating now, Mr Iles.'

Iles: 'Good speculating?'

Rice: 'Speculating.'

Iles: 'Speculating very credibly?'

Rice: 'Speculating. Leo is free, has never been charged. How could he be? Where's the evidence that would stand any chance in court? It's all make-believe and what-ifery. I'm back full scale with his firm now. So's Justin, of course. He decided it was safer. So it is.'

Iles switched off the machine. 'Meanwhile,' he said, 'as a result of the Customs sweep up near Wilton Road, Harpur imagines this bolshie neighbour ringing the local police to complain about mysterious, allegedly-media people looking for Mallen. And possibly – separately – including Fern Cochrane. She'd have been around asking questions. Someone high there who knows Tom is undercover on the other ground sees the dangers in this and gets in touch with his handler fifty odd miles away. That's Howard Lambert. He would be shocked and furious, and regard the breach of discipline by Tom as irreparable. But possibly there were no arrangements for a meeting with him, or a safe phoning time, for a few days. And, during those few days and nights, the building site offered its facilities. A mess-up of mess-ups – not at all rare in undercover.

'We talked to Lambert, obviously. He wouldn't admit he'd been told about Tom and the van. I have to be careful what I say here. There are libel laws. But let's put it in general terms: if a handler is told his man has been blown, that handler ought to disregard any previous agreements for meetings or calls and get to the undercover officer somehow, anyhow, and tell him to disappear. Delay should be unthinkable.

'Now, I said that the officer from Tom's home force would, in Harpur's scenario, have got in touch with Lambert. We have to ask how he would get in touch. Phone – landline, mobile? Leaks possible?' Iles gave a small, modest, forgive-me-do wave. 'All this last bit is admittedly a guess. Norm dubbed it "what-ifery". Or what I called, when talking to Rice, "intuition" – in this part of the narrative, Harpur-type intuition, but very, very feasible, I'd say. My own dogged imaginings about the discovery by Fern, and Harpur's suggestion of the interchange between the two nicks, are what enabled us to take further Maud's belief that the killer might be a police officer, narrowing down the options. There is still a place in detective work for inspired conjecture, thank God.'

There were questions at the end of Iles's address. Another Assistant Chief, hair receding fast, wizened, rasping said: 'But, excuse me, you were sent there, weren't you, to find out why local inquiries were taking so long – were possibly going to take for ever. The target was not just the detective inspector sniper but someone, or maybe more than one, above the inspector, who had decided to see there was no progress on the Mallen/Parry case because all kinds of disclosures might ensue. Those "let's imagine" games from you and Harpur – are of no real significance, are they? The inference I drew was this: the Home Office considered the corruption went higher than Jaminel and was considerably more ingrained and ranging than could be dealt with by conviction of one middle-rank officer. I heard, didn't I, that the Metropolitan's psychologist, Andrew Rockmain, was brought in early? He's hardly one to be involved in anything of low priority, such as mid-rank corruption. With respect, Iles, would you say you'd caught the sprat but not the mackerel?'

'Of course I'd say it, cliché or not, baldy,' Iles replied. 'It's what the fucking tape tells us, isn't it? Weren't you listening, you shagged-out dolt?'

Harpur said: 'Yes, we couldn't get Jaminel to disclose who had been looking after him, giving him protection – how far up it went, how widespread, what kind of working arrangement with L.P. Young, and which officers were participating. He was more scared of retaliation than of jail. We kept at it, but the confession was as far as he'd go. We failed,' Harpur said.

Iles said: 'In fact, our evidence against Jaminel wasn't all that strong – the shooting accuracy and the false alibi he presented. But Col's remarkably focused, forceful, though fair interrogation destroyed him.'

In fact it had been Iles's ability to outsmart and confuse Jaminel that had done most to destroy him. Once more, though, Harpur let it go. 'We had a little success,' he said. 'On the biggie, we failed.'

'No, no, you're not one to fail, Col,' Maud cried out. 'You're not ... well ... not built to fail.'

'Thanks, Maud,' Harpur said. 'It's good to have you on...' He'd been going to say 'on my side'. He changed it, though, to: 'On our side.'

Perhaps she detected the scurried revamp. Maud gave a small pursing of the lips, a wince, more or less, and turned away in an abrupt move, making her necklace rattle slightly.

'Col sees everything very straight,' Iles said. 'It's a tic of his. This time, he's right.'